PRAISE FOR JOAN HESS AND HER CLAIRE MALLOY MYSTERY SERIES

"LIVELY, SHARP, IRREVERENT."
—*New York Times Book Review*

"A WINNING BLEND of soft-core feminism, trendy subplots and a completely irreverent style that characterizes both the series and the sleuth, all nicely on stage." —*Houston Chronicle*

"WON ME OVER ... AN ASSURED PERFORMANCE THAT WILL HAVE ME HUNTING OUT OTHER CLAIRE MALLOY MYSTERIES." —*Boston Globe*

"AMIABLE ENTERTAINMENT WITH AN EDGE.... Hess's style rarely flags."
—*Kirkus Reviews*

"Joan Hess is one very funny woman."
—Susan Dunlap, author of *High Fall*

"Hess delivers another tartly told mystery."
—*Publishers Weekly*

"A breezy and delightful read ... Malloy is one of the most engaging narrators in mystery."
—*Drood Review*

Other books by Joan Hess

The Maggody Series

MALICE IN MAGGODY
MISCHIEF IN MAGGODY
MUCH ADO IN MAGGODY
MADNESS IN MAGGODY
MORTAL REMAINS IN MAGGODY
MAGGODY IN MANHATTAN
O LITTLE TOWN OF MAGGODY
MARTIANS IN MAGGODY
MIRACLES IN MAGGODY

The Claire Malloy Series

STRANGLED PROSE

MURDER AT THE MURDER AT THE
MIMOSA INN

DEAR MISS DEMEANOR
A REALLY CUTE CORPSE
A DIET TO DIE FOR
ROLL OVER AND PLAY DEAD
DEATH BY THE LIGHT OF THE MOON
POISONED PINS
TICKLED TO DEATH

BUSY BODIES

A CLAIRE MALLOY MYSTERY

Joan Hess

AN ONYX BOOK

ONYX
Published by the Penguin Group
Penguin Books USA Inc., 375 Hudson Street,
New York, New York 10014, U.S.A.
Penguin Books Ltd, 27 Wrights Lane,
London W8 5TZ, England
Penguin Books Australia Ltd, Ringwood,
Victoria, Australia
Penguin Books Canada Ltd, 10 Alcorn Avenue,
Toronto, Ontario, Canada M4V 3B2
Penguin Books (N.Z.) Ltd, 182–190 Wairau Road,
Auckland 10, New Zealand

Penguin Books Ltd, Registered Offices:
Harmondsworth, Middlesex, England

Published by Onyx, an imprint of Dutton Signet,
a division of Penguin Books USA Inc.
Previously published in a Dutton edition.

First Onyx Printing, May, 1996
10 9 8 7 6 5 4 3 2 1

REGISTERED TRADEMARK—MARCA REGISTRADA

Printed in the United States of America

PUBLISHER'S NOTE
This is a work of fiction. Names, characters, places, and incidents either are
the product of the author's imagination or are used fictitiously, and any resemblance to actual persons, living or dead, events, or locales is entirely
coincidental.

For my darling daughter, Becca,
who has never mastered the art of
speaking in capital letters

ONE

I am not an adept liar, which I think speaks well for my character. However, this deficiency has propelled me into sticky situations in the past, and I had a foreboding feeling it was about to do so again.

"Tea, Miss Parchester?" I said into the telephone receiver. "I'd love to, but I—I simply don't see when I could—well, I was planning on organizing my files, and I promised Caron that I'd drive her and Inez to the mall, and—"

Miss Emily Parchester had taught high-school students for forty years before her retirement and therefore was unimpressed with my sputtery excuses. "Oh, do bring the girls with you. I so enjoy their youthful enthusiasm. I'll see all of you at five o'clock."

Groaning, I replaced the receiver. In that my bookstore was bereft of customers, I received no sympathetic, curious, or even incurious glances. The die was cast: Miss Parchester, a mistress of manipulation, was expecting us for tea. In the past, I'd masqueraded as a substitute teacher in order to come to her rescue when she'd been accused of embezzling money from the journalism accounts *and* poisoning the principal. I'd done extraordinary things (among them being charged with three felonies—a personal best) when her basset hounds were kidnapped by an unscrupulous lout. Although the concept of a cup of tea should have sounded innocuous, it didn't.

I picked up the feather duster and attacked the window display. In the fierce August sunshine, pedestrians ambled by the Book Depot without so much as a look of longing at all the worthy literature crammed inside its musty, cramped confines. Business had been poor all summer, as usual, but it would pick up shortly when several thousand earnest students arrived to improve their minds, as well as their chances for lucrative employment, by enrolling at Farber College. Very few of them would do so in the liberal-arts department. Business and accounting textbooks had spilled onto the shelves once reserved for Mr. Faulkner and Miss Austen. I stocked enough slim, yellow study guides to pave the road to the Emerald City.

It occurred to me that I would be forty years old by the time the semester began. I peered at my reflection in the dusty glass, wondering if said anniversary would coincide with an outbreak of gray hair and the awakening pangs of arthritis, rheumatism, bunions, and all the other maladies that accompany old age.

I concluded I was holding up fairly well. My curly hair was predominantly red, and my mostly svelte body had not yet capitulated to gravity. This isn't to say there weren't some fine lines around my eyes and a few gray hairs. All were the result of being the mother of a fifteen-year-old girl with a propensity for melodrama and an enduring ability to keep me speculating about the quality of life at the nearest rest home. The one occasionally favored by Miss Parchester had seemed congenial, although I doubted they served cocktails in the evening. On a more positive note, visiting hours were restricted.

But not at the Book Depot. Caron burst through the door, accompanied by her ever-loyal sidekick, Inez Thornton. Caron shares my physical attributes but not my imperturbable personality—or my lack of proficiency in matters requiring mendacity. For her, right and wrong are nebulous concepts defined solely by her personal objectives at any given moment. She's not so much immoral as she is egocentric. Copernicus would have loved her.

Inez is quite the opposite, which is why I suppose they're steadfast friends. She's a composition in brown and beige, all blurred together like a desertscape done in watercolors. Her eyes are leery behind thick lenses, and her mouth is usually pursed in speculation. She has not yet mastered the art of speaking in capital letters, but she has a talented mentor.

"You said you'd drive us to the mall," Caron began accusingly. "I finished doing my hair an hour ago, and we've been Absolutely Sweltering on the front porch waiting for you. I came within seconds of having a heat stroke. Inez had to help me upstairs so I could get a glass of ice water. My face was bright red, and—"

"I said I'd take you at five o'clock, dear," I said. "I can't close the store in the middle of the afternoon."

She rolled her eyes. "And disappoint all these customers lined up at the cash register? I hate to break it to you, Mother, but you could get rid of the books and start selling auto parts—and no one would notice."

Reminding myself of the legal ramifications of child abandonment, I went behind the counter and perched on the stool. "I'd notice," I said mildly. "I can't read a carburetor in the bathtub. In any case, you, Inez, and I have been invited to have tea with Miss Parchester. I'll take you out to the mall afterward."

Inez drifted out from behind the romance rack. "I thought she eloped while she was on that bus trip to the Southwest. Wouldn't that make her a missus-somebody-else?"

Caron was not interested in anyone else's marital status. "Tea?" she croaked, as horrified as if I had mentioned an invitation for a cup of arsenic. "We can't go to some dumb tea party this afternoon. I need to shop before school starts. Otherwise, I'll have to show up Stark Naked on the first day. Not only will I be expelled, but I'll be the laughingstock of Farberville High School and will have no choice but to kill myself on the steps." Clutching her throat, she staggered out of view to find a book on expediting death in the most gruesome manner within her budget.

I nodded at Inez. "Miss Parchester did indeed elope. She and Mr. Delmaro were married just across the border in Mexico, but he succumbed to a heart attack that very night while they were"—I paused to search for a seemly euphemism, even though the girls had gone through a period of reading every steamy novel in the store and undoubtedly knew more than I—"consummating the marriage. It turned out he already had a wife who'd purchased his-and-her cemetery plots, so Miss Parchester sent the remains to her and resumed her maiden name when she returned to Farberville."

"They had sex?" whispered Inez "Miss Parchester's got to be as old as my grandmother, or maybe older. I don't think my grandmother . . ."

"That's disgusting," Caron called from the vicinity of the self-help books. "Sexuality is a function of youth. Old people should devote their energy to gardening or playing cribbage." Her head popped up long enough for her to glower at me. "Or drinking tea."

Inez was edging backward as if she expected her best friend's maniacal mother to come out from behind the counter with an ax. "My grandmother plays duplicate bridge three times a week. She says it's really a lot of fun, especially the tournaments."

"I'd like to think I have a few good years left before

I need to find a hobby," I said. From behind the racks came the sound of someone humming "Happy Birthday." This did nothing to brighten my mood. I picked up the feather duster and was preparing to stalk the miscreant when the bell above the door jangled.

Peter Rosen hesitated in the doorway, possibly bemused by the ferocity of my expression and the disembodied humming. He has dark hair, a beakish nose, a perpetual tan, and white, vulpine teeth. He dresses like a very successful Wall Street mogul, from his silk tie right down to the tips of his Italian shoes. When he chooses, he can be charming. His mellow brown eyes twinkle playfully and, at more intimate times, downright provocatively.

There are other times, alas, when his eyes turn icy and his bite is quite as bad as his bark. These worst of times coincide with my civic-minded attempts to help the Farberville CID solve crimes. Peter Rosen is my lover; Lieutenant Rosen is my nemesis. Frankly, lectures and accusations of meddling do not make for a harmonious relationship.

"Are you under siege by mellifluous hornets?" he asked.

"I wish I were," I said, reluctantly lowering my weapon. I told Caron and Inez to return at five and shooed them out of the store. I then lured Peter into my office, where there was such little space that we had no choice but to press our bodies together. Certain events of the previous weekend were discussed in endearing murmurs, and when we finally returned to the front room, my face was as red as Caron's allegedly had been earlier.

Peter peered behind the racks to make sure the girls hadn't crept back inside the store. "What's the current crisis?"

"We're having tea with Miss Parchester. This ghastly scenario means they won't get to the mall until six o'clock and Caron will be forced to commit suicide in front of the entire student body."

He gave me an odd look before picking up a paperback and pretending to study its cover. "Miss Parchester lives on Willow Street, doesn't she?"

"You should know, Sherlock. You and Farberville's finest staked out her house for three solid days. It's a good thing I found her and convinced her to turn herself in before she was tackled by an overly zealous rookie." I paused in case he wanted to engage in a bit of repartee, and then added, "I'll give you a ten percent discount if you want to buy that book. I haven't read it myself, but according to the catalog, it's the best of the alien slime time-travel fantasies."

He hastily replaced it and took out a handkerchief to wipe his fingers. "So Miss Parchester invited you for a cozy tea party? Did she say anything about the purpose of it?"

"The purpose of a cozy tea party is to drink tea while balancing a plate of cookies on one's knee and making genteel conversation about the weather."

"We've had a lot of complaints from Willow Street residents. May I assume you haven't been to visit Miss Parchester lately?"

I shook my head. "What kind of complaints, Peter? Is she doing something to cause problems?"

Grinning, he headed for the door. "I wouldn't dream of spoiling this particular surprise. Can I come by tonight if I bring a pizza and a six-pack?"

I agreed and watched him as he crossed under the portico and headed up the sidewalk in the direction of the campus. I tried to decipher his cryptic remarks, but I had no luck and was cheerfully diverted when that rarest of creatures, a customer, appeared with a fat wallet and a hunger to put some romantic intrigue in her life.

At five o'clock I closed the store and retreated to

the office to wait for Caron and Inez, who were no more than fifteen minutes late. After a spirited argument, I allowed my darling daughter to climb into the driver's seat. Caron's sixteenth birthday loomed as alarmingly as my fortieth; she anticipated not only pink balloons and overnight popularity but also a shiny red sports car. My attempts to save her from debilitating disappointment thus far had been ignored.

"This car is a slug," she said as we pulled out of the parking lot. "Rhonda Maguire's getting a new car. She can't decide if she wants a convertible or a four-wheel drive."

Inez leaned over the seat and said, "The only reason she wants a four-wheel drive is that the boys on the football team are always drooling over them. Rhonda thinks they'll drool over her if she has one."

I closed my eyes as we lurched into the traffic flowing up Thurber Street. "Rhonda ought to be introduced to Miss Parchester's basset hounds. They'll certainly drool over her." I leaned my head against the seat and listened to the ensuing derogatory comments regarding Rhonda Maguire's latest foray into perfidy, which centered as always on her attempts to ingratiate herself with a certain junior varsity quarterback.

"What's going on?" Caron said irritably.

I opened my eyes and frowned at the cars inching around the corner to Willow Street. On the street itself, traffic was barely moving. Those on foot were making noticeably better progress; as I stared, a group of children cut across the nearest yard and jostled a more staid couple in matching Bermuda shorts. Fraternity boys who'd arrived early for rush week were drinking beer and telling what must have been hilarious jokes as they walked up the sidewalk.

"How many people did Miss Parchester invite to

tea?" Inez asked with such bewilderment I could almost hear her blinking.

"Just us, as far as I know," I said, equally bewildered by the scene. Willow Street runs through the middle of the historic district. At one time, the mostly Victorian houses were the residences of the highest echelon of Farberville society, including the honorable Judge Amos Parchester. Now some of the houses had been subdivided into apartments, while others struggled like aging dowagers to maintain their facades. I couldn't conceive of any reason why the street was worthy of all this interest, but clearly something odd was happening; something, I amended, that was causing a lot of complaints to be made to the police department.

Caron continued past the corner. "I'm going to park behind the library so we won't get stuck later—when it's time to go to the mall. You Do Remember that we're going to the mall, don't you?"

"Yes, dear," I said, trying not to concoct any wild hypotheses about Miss Parchester's involvement. As we walked up the sidewalk, I was relieved to see that the crowd was gathering in front of the house beyond hers. A great tangle of shrubbery blocked my view of whatever was taking place, but from the expressions of those farther up the sidewalk, it was a doozy.

"Claire," Miss Parchester trilled from her porch, "I've already put on the kettle. Oh, and I see the girls are with you. What a lovely little party we'll have." She clasped her hands together and beamed at us as if we'd done something particularly clever by finding her house.

She may have been impervious to the traffic jam and the swelling crowd, but I wasn't. "What's going on next door?" I said as I herded the girls toward her house.

"It's rather complicated," she said. She ushered us

inside and closed the front door. "And annoying, I must admit. As you know, I am a staunch defender of our constitutional rights, but I'm not sure our forefathers took this kind of thing into consideration when they penned the document."

The living room had not changed since I was last there, unless the dust was thicker and the scent of camphor more pronounced. Stacks of yellow newspapers and faded blue composition books still teetered precariously, and the moth-eaten drapes still blocked most of the daylight. Miss Parchester appeared to be wearing the same cardigan sweater, frumpy dress, and fuzzy pink bedroom slippers.

Once we'd been supplied with tea and cookies, I repeated my question. Caron and Inez nodded, one forcefully and the other tentatively.

Miss Parchester sighed. "About a year ago, old Mr. Stenopolis died of a heart attack. He was well into his eighties and quite a neighborhood character. I remember as a child when he and Papa would exchange angry words concerning Mr. Stenopolis's disinclination to keep his grass mowed and his sidewalk swept. Papa was on the state supreme court, as I must have told you, and often entertained distinguished visitors."

"Who lives there now?" I said before we were treated to a lengthy recitation of Papa's accomplishments in the realm of jurisprudence.

"Mr. Stenopolis left the house to his nephew, Zeno Gorgias. The young man moved in two weeks ago. He's certainly charming and personable, but he has some ideas that are . . . unconventional. Mr. Stenopolis once told me that Zeno is a nationally renowned artist whose paintings sell for a great deal of money."

"Why did he move to Farberville?" Caron asked. "It's so utterly middle-class and boring. If I were famous, I'd live in New York or Los Angeles or some-

place where people don't sit around and drink"—she
noticed my ominous expression—"diet sodas all day."

Miss Parchester smiled sweetly at her. "He said he
was tired of all the pretentious, self-appointed critics
of the art world. He was living in Houston when he
learned he'd inherited the house and came to have a
look at it. It is a lovely old house, although Mr. Stenopolis never threw away so much as a tin can or a piece
of string. The last time I was inside it, I was appalled.
Every room was piled high with rubbish, odds and
ends of scrap metal, jars, broken appliances, magazines, wads of aluminum foil, and so forth. I told Mr.
Stenopolis that it was a firetrap, but he simply
laughed. He had a very infectious laugh."

I tried once more to nudge her into the present.
"This artist named Zeno moved in two weeks ago.
What's he done that has lured such a crowd?"

Miss Parchester's blue eyes watered and the cup
clinked as she placed it in the saucer. "He told me
that he's exploring what he calls 'interactive environmental art.' People are supposed to be startled into
reacting to his stimuli." She took a tissue from her
cuff and dabbed her nose, then sniffled delicately and
said, "He's been very successful in his goal. So far
he's relied on word of mouth, but he mentioned that
he's been in contact with the local television station,
as well as the newspaper. Before too long everyone
in Farberville will be in our heretofore peaceful neighborhood, trampling flowers, discarding litter, making
it impossible for any of us to take our cars out of
our driveways."

"Isn't that a public nuisance?" asked Caron, who
has committed an impressive number of misdemean-
ors in the past and therefore been obliged to take
more than a cursory interest in the law.

"I should think so," Miss Parchester said sadly, "but
the authorities have refused to become involved. I'm

in a muddle myself. I'm adamant in my support of freedom of speech and of religion, but walking to the grocery store is a taxing chore, as well as bending over to pick up litter or trying to salvage my zinnias. Nick and Nora are so distressed by all the confusion that they won't come out from under the back porch. I've considered joining them."

I set down my cup and saucer and gestured at the girls. "Perhaps we'd better take a look for ourselves, Miss Parchester."

Caron and Inez leapt to their feet, and we were thanking our hostess when the front door banged open and a man literally bounded into the room.

"Miss Parchester," he said, snatching her hand and noisily kissing it, "I have come to beg a favor of you. Do you have an extension cord that I might borrow?"

She tried to give him a stern look, but her cheeks were pink and she was twittering like a debutante. "Let me introduce you to my three dearest friends, Zeno. Then I'll see if I can find an extension cord in the garage."

While she rattled off names, I coolly studied him. He had long, black hair that hid his ears and flopped across his forehead when he moved. And move he did, as if he'd been wound too tightly or had imbibed an excessive amount of caffeine. His hands darted through the air and his feet scarcely made contact with the carpet. His expression shifted continuously, which is why it took me a moment to put his age at thirty despite his sweaty T-shirt, sandals, immodest gym shorts—and the Mickey Mouse beanie perched on his head. How it managed to remain on his head was as much a mystery as what he was doing next door.

"I am enchanted," he said to me, lunging for my hand.

I put it behind my back. "Welcome to Farberville, Mr. Gorgias."

He threw back his head and laughed so boisterously that I glanced uneasily at the light fixture above his head. "No one calls me anything but Zeno, my dear Claire. When I die, there will be only one word on my tombstone: *Zeno*. It will be the perfect summation of my life." Abruptly sobering, he spun around and caught Caron's arm. "And what do you wish as your epitaph?"

"I don't know," she mumbled.

He may have intended to try the same ploy with Inez, but she was well out of reach and still retreating. "I am sorry I cannot stay," he continued, "but I must find an extension cord. Everything is at stake— everything!"

Miss Parchester announced she would look and shuffled through the kitchen and out the back door. Caron and Inez clutched each other and warily watched him from behind a settee. If it would not have been misconstrued as an act of cowardice, I would have joined them. In a nanosecond.

"So you are a widow," Zeno said, turning back to me. "It is a crime against nature for a woman to sleep alone, you know. This is what my grandfather told me when I became a man." He shoved back his hair and gave me a disconcertingly wicked grin. "Or maybe it's a line from a movie. Who cares?"

"Why do you say I'm a widow?"

"I love women, from rosy little babies to the oldest crones with hunched backs and gnarled hands. I study them very closely. Women are more complex than men, more analytical, more likely to allow an occasional glimpse of their souls. Also, Miss Parchester told me the tragic story of how your husband was killed in a collision with a chicken truck. I wept as I envisioned the bloodstained feathers fluttering down the desolate mountain road."

Before I could respond, Miss Parchester returned

empty-handed. "I can't think where else to look, Zeno," she said. "I'm sure I have one somewhere, but it's been years since I last saw it."

He put his hands on her shoulders and kissed the tip of her nose. "Don't worry, my darling. After all, art should be spontaneous, and it has been dictated by fate that I shall have only one stereo speaker today. Tomorrow I may have two, three, or even a hundred!"

He bounded out the door.

"Goodness," I said as I sank down on the sofa and took a sip of cold tea. "He's energetic, isn't he?"

Caron snorted. "If you ask me, he's psychotic. He just admitted he doesn't know the difference between real life and the movies." She flung herself beside me and continued making vulgar noises to express her low opinion of Zeno, or, more probably, adults in general.

"I'm glad I don't live near him," Inez contributed, her eyes as wide as I'd ever seen them. "Does he always just barge in like that, Miss Parchester?"

"He said that doorbells limit the spontaneity of the encounter, since both parties are warned in advance. Zeno is enamored of spontaneity, among other things. It's refreshing, but also tiresome. There have been times after his visits when I've taken to my bed to recuperate, or been obliged to pour myself a glass of elderberry wine."

I didn't point out that she found other occasions to seek solace in the bottle, one of which had required some dedicated sleuthing on my part. "I guess we'd better see what Zeno is doing," I said as I stood up.

We were thanking Miss Parchester again when the doorbell rang. It's possible that at least one of us flinched, but the door stayed shut as Miss Parchester went across the room. She opened it, then gasped and stumbled backward, knocking over a pile of old year-books and a spindly floor lamp.

A young woman stood on the porch. Her streaky

blond hair was cropped at odd angles, reminding me of the roof of a thatched cottage—after a windstorm. Her eyes were large and dark, her lashes thick with mascara, her mouth caked with scarlet lipstick. Her ample body was flawless except for a few freckles scattered on her shoulders and a puckery white scar that might have come from an appendectomy.

I could arrive at this judgment at the approximate speed of light because she was wearing only the bottom half of a string bikini and silky pink tassels on her breasts.

TWO

Have y'all seen Zeno?" she asked in a low-pitched Southern drawl that made every vowel a diphthong and every word a sequence of inflections. Her expression was remarkably bland, considering her attire (or lack thereof).

"He was here a few minutes ago," I answered, since Miss Parchester was hyperventilating so wildly she was incapable of a response. "He wanted to borrow an extension cord."

The girl put her hands on her hips. "Well, if he shows up again, tell him to get himself back real quick. We got all kinds of trouble brewing."

I willed myself not to stare at the tassels that were swinging like fluorescent pendulums. Such things may be commonplace in New Orleans, but not in Farberville, where community standards are draconian at best. "And you are ... ?"

"Melanie Magruder. I met Zeno the other night at the bus station, and he hired me to participate in his productions. Sleeping in bus stations isn't near as much fun as you'd think, so I took the job. I just didn't plan on being threatened by a bunch of Bible thumpers. I'm an actress, not a target for religious fanatics."

Miss Parchester regained a degree of dignity and

nudged me aside. "May I offer you a cup of tea, Miss Magruder?" she said as if addressing royalty rather than what might well prove to be an alien life-form. "The water's still hot, and it won't be any bother to add some to the teapot."

"Thanks, but I don't think so, honey. I'd better keep looking for Zeno before the riot starts." Wiggling her fingers in farewell, Melanie went down the stairs and out to the sidewalk. Her hair seemed impervious to the breeze as she continued across the street to talk to a bronzed young man pushing a lawn mower.

Caron and Inez, who'd been momentarily paralyzed, hurried to the doorway to assess the yardman's biceps and triceps. From their reverent whispers, I gathered he was getting a rave review.

I patted Miss Parchester's shoulder. "I'm beginning to understand why you're upset with your new neighbor."

"What would Papa do in this situation? He was so concerned about constitutional rights that he once defended a snake handler out in a far corner of the county, citing freedom of religion. He won the case, but his client died of snakebite the very next Sunday. There is such a fine line between an individual's rights and the responsibility of society to protect its members from harming themselves."

I admitted my lack of expertise in such matters. This time the girls and I made it out to the porch, where we paused to inspect the thickening traffic jam. We could, if we wished, go to the sidewalk and turn left toward the library parking lot. The girls could be deposited at the mall within fifteen minutes, and I could be in my apartment in thirty, sipping scotch and watching the local news.

And wondering what on earth Zeno was doing on Willow Street.

We went to the sidewalk and turned right, falling into line with several giggly girls and a grim older man in a gray three-piece suit and dark red tie. In some inexplicable way, he exuded animosity. Recalling Melanie's remark about religious fanatics, I did not protest when he pushed past me.

Zeno's inheritance was a three-story jumble of gingerbread, gables, turrets with brass weathervanes, and a need for a fresh coat of white paint. Windows in the upper stories were cracked or covered with cardboard, and a gutter dangled in front of the jagged remains of a round stained-glass window in the center of the third story.

The view of the yard was blocked by a solid mass of backs. Caron and Inez deftly slithered between them and disappeared; I took the more mature approach of standing on my tiptoes and peering over shoulders, but I was too far back to see anything. The murmuring that arose from the crowd was amiable, as if we were gathering for a picnic in the park or in line for a movie. It faded as a new sound drifted out from the house.

After a few shocked seconds, I recognized it as the panting and moaning of a woman engaged in a sexual encounter. She sounded as though she was enjoying it very much. The audience was not, however. The amiable murmurs became squawks of incredulity. Horns were honked in protest. Hairs on the backs of necks bristled. The more prudish listeners covered their ears and fled.

"Mother!" called Caron, waving at me from the edge of the yard. "Over here!"

I retraced my steps, fought my way through Miss Parchester's shrubbery to join them—and froze as I took a look at Zeno's front yard. My immediate impression was that he'd transplanted a cemetery, but then I realized the dozen headstones were carved out

of slabs of Styrofoam instead of marble or granite.
Gaudy plastic flowers decorated some of them; balloons and streamers were attached to others. Two
pastel-blue coffins were partially buried in a vertical
position. A third, massive, black one was on the brick
sidewalk, the lid opened to display a mannequin
dressed in a clown suit and a sunbonnet. A hand-hewn
cross tilted at a precarious angle; from the horizontal
bar a teddy bear swung from a noose, its button eyes
round with panic. Stuffed dogs and cats suffered a
similar fate along the front of the house. The trees
were draped with strings of Christmas lights, unlit at
the moment but potentially blinding.

Zeno's pièce de résistance rose in front of a bedraggled japonica bush. It was a wooden stage a good ten
feet high, with a rickety ladder propped against it to
provide access for those unconcerned with broken
bones. The backdrop was a painted depiction of a lush
tropical garden. In the middle of the stage was a live
apple tree, its roots encased in a burlap bag.

The front door opened, and Melanie Magruder
came down the steps. Her costume had been augmented with a large construction-paper leaf attached
to the bikini bottom and a rubber snake draped
around her neck. She scampered up the ladder,
plucked an apple from the tree, and held it aloft as she
began to grind her hips in time with the increasingly
passionate noises from what was apt to be a stereo
speaker. The tassels swung back and forth, then almost mystically made full revolutions.

Zeno came from behind the house and surreptitiously started taking photographs of what must have
been a diverting array of expressions. The majority
tended to be outrage, I noticed apprehensively. Caron
and Inez were amazed, if somewhat appalled, but
many of the people near us were clenching their fists
and muttering threats. The man in the three-piece suit

who'd brushed by me on the sidewalk appeared to be on the verge of an apoplectic fit; I felt as though I should escort him to Miss Parchester's house for a soothing cup of tea.

The unseen woman reached a climax in an absolute cacophony of shrieks, graphic incitements, and exhalations. Melanie's tassels spun like propellers and her upturned face was glazed with ecstasy. Zeno darted around the yard, his camera clicking steadily.

There was a final shriek and then silence. Melanie slithered down the ladder and collapsed across the nearest grave. The string bikini did little to impede a panorama of her generous buttocks. Her head was turned toward us, and as I stared, she winked at me. I regret to say I almost lost my balance and had to grab Caron's shoulder to keep from falling.

"Thank you, thank you!" Zeno yelled at the crowd. "Now you must allow your superficial impressions to seep inwardly until you have extinguished any inborn fear of your own sexuality. Life is the springboard of passion; death is its climax. Only art is eternal."

"You should be arrested!" said a young woman as she shoved her way to the front of the crowd and shook her fist at Zeno. She had brown hair pulled back in an uncompromising ponytail, pasty skin, and eyes that were blinking furiously. A drab smock hung well below her knees; her shoes were the sort favored by field sergeants.

"Blasphemer!" she continued in a voice crackling with rage. "The Bible says, 'He that shall blaspheme against the Holy Ghost hath never forgiveness, but is in danger of eternal damnation.' The story of the creation of mankind is not meant to be reduced to a pornographic parody! I demand that you cease right this minute!"

Zeno responded by taking her picture several times.

"You are a wretched, wretched sinner! How dare

you expose the rest of us to this—this blasphemy?"
She turned to confront the crowd through red, over-
flowing eyes. "And how can you stand here while this
sacrilege takes place in front of you? You saw that
naked woman and heard those obscene noises. How
can you just stand here?"

The crowd pretty much agreed that they couldn't
and began to leave. The woman sank to her knees
and hid her face in her hands, her shoulders jerking
as if she were receiving jolts of electricity. I was about
to go over to her and do what I could to calm her
down when a man came running across the street and
knelt beside her.

"Tracy," he said as he rubbed her back, "you
shouldn't be here. You're making a spectacle of yourself and embarrassing both of us. I want you to get
up right now and come home with me."

She awkwardly complied. He wiped her face with a
handkerchief, then took her arm and led her across
the street. Every third step or so, he looked back with
laserlike intensity; if looks could indeed kill, Zeno and
Melanie would have been reduced to tiny piles of
ashes. Eventually the couple went into a small house
next to the one directly across the street.

I elbowed Caron, who was doing a fine imitation of
a pillar of salt. "Ready to go to the mall, dear?"

"Don't you find all of this A Little Peculiar?"

"Of course I find it peculiar, but it has nothing to
do with us. I would imagine the police will put a stop
to it on the grounds of disturbing the peace or creating
a public nuisance."

"No, they won't," said a male voice.

I found myself gazing at the three-piece. He was
perhaps as old as sixty, with skimpy white hair and a
thin mustache above thinner lips. His nose was squatty
and pitted with pores, and his jowls were loose enough
to flap in a strong wind. He was no longer a walking

case of animosity, but he wasn't a likely candidate for Miss Congeniality, either.

I grimaced. "It seems as though they should. This kind of thing surely is against the law."

"Are you an attorney?"

"Are you?"

"I am Anthony Leach, and I have served at the bar for over thirty years. This morning I consulted the city prosecutor, who has determined that this—this nonsense does not violate any local ordinances. He was not unsympathetic, but he refused to file charges."

Caron, who is as self-righteous as any fifteen-year-old, gave Leach a beady look. "What about those disgusting noises? Anyone with the intelligence of a liverwort could figure out what that was about."

"Disgusting, but not explicit," he replied. "Pornography is a hazy area, and the courts are reluctant to infringe on an individual's constitutional rights."

"What's your interest?" I asked.

He pointed at a redbrick house across the street from Miss Parchester's. "I regret to say I live there. This used to be an agreeable neighborhood, convenient to my office, the courthouse, the library, and the grocery store. The students are reasonably quiet and considerate. The rest of us are professional people or retirees. We were all living compatibly until this crackpot moved in."

"Eventually he'll get bored and go onto something less intrusive," I said, edging away from him until I bumped into Inez.

Spittle gathered in the corners of Leach's mouth and his complexion darkened. "I've been trying to sell my house for some time. Ten days ago I finally found a potential buyer who fell in love with the neighborhood. This buyer was on the verge of making an offer when she drove down Willow Street yesterday. I can hardly blame her for changing her mind. Hell, I couldn't give the house away now."

I was about to offer to take it off his hands when Zeno came down the stairs. He vanished around the far side of the house and then returned seconds later with a stepladder. Melanie appeared with a cardboard box. She had put on a loose work shirt, but the tassels had not been replaced with a brassiere and the snake was looped casually around her neck.

"Now what?" demanded Caron. She poked me for emphasis, but all I could do was shake my head.

Zeno positioned the ladder beneath one of the maple trees, then noticed us and waved. "Did you enjoy your first encounter with interactive environmental art, Claire? Did the juxtaposition of intimacy and inanimateness compel you to set aside any dogmatic assumptions?"

"He's not only a psychotic," Caron said under her breath. "He's a moron, too."

Zeno climbed the ladder and hung a set of brass wind chimes from a branch. "You must come back at dusk on Saturday. We are going to have our first venture into son et lumière. All the lights will be on, as well as some spotlights and strobe lights to add energy. Melanie will make another tape, so they will compete with each other to seduce the audience." He reached down to take a second set of wind chimes from Melanie, who seemed rather bored. "Everyone assumes art is visual," he continued as if we were a captive class, "but we must cater to all the senses. Now I make some auditory art, eh?"

The wind chimes began to clink vigorously. Despite the noise, I could hear Anthony Leach grinding his teeth as he stalked away. In contrast, Caron and Inez loosed a stream of well-articulated criticism all the way to the car and then all the way to the mall.

Inez's mother was bringing the girls home, so I was

in my bathrobe when Peter arrived at my apartment, which consisted of the upstairs half of a duplex across from the college campus. In winter I can see the building where my deceased husband had toiled in the English department. He'd been annoyed when the building had been condemned and the department relocated to a sanitized concrete block building that lacked odd little rooms with couches and deadbolts.

Peter and I met at the door and spent a few minutes expressing pleasure at seeing one another. Once I'd readjusted my bathrobe and we were settled on the sofa with pizza and beer, I described what we'd seen on Willow Street, then said, "Isn't there some local ordinance about obscene noises?"

"There's a sound ordinance, but it deals primarily with the decibel level. If this guy plays the tape at more than sixty-five decibels, he can be ordered to desist. If he refuses, he can be fined. The prosecutor sent one of our men there today with a sound-level meter. The tape may have seemed loud because of the shock value of its content, but it wasn't in violation. There's also a provision about disturbing or annoying a reasonable person of normal sensitivities—"

"That's the one."

"—but the prosecutor won't use it because the definitions are too vague. A civil suit charging violation of constitutional rights could bankrupt the city."

"Miss Parchester is a reasonable person of normal sensitivities," I said sulkily. "Being forced to listen to coitus uninterruptus has to be disturbing and annoying."

He polished off a piece of pizza and reached for another. "Half the people in the neighborhood have claimed the same thing, but the prosecutor's not going to risk an enormous judgment against the city. Even if the city won, the legal fees would be staggering."

"Why isn't Zeno's yard a public nuisance?" I asked,
although without a great deal of optimism.

"That ordinance has to do with creating an un-
sightly or unsanitary condition. Zeno insists that it's
art. He may be the only person in town who sees it
that way, but once again we're back to vague definitions and the threat of a lawsuit." He put down his
beer and grinned at me. "All this talk about the tape
is giving me an idea. How long do we have before
Caron might interrupt us?"

I fended him off with the last of the pizza. "What
about Miss Parchester's rights to life, liberty, and the
pursuit of happiness? She can't get her car in or out of
the driveway when Zeno's brought in a crowd. People
trespass in her yard and wreak havoc on her zinnias.
Doesn't she have the constitutional right to zinnias?"

Peter accepted the rejection with only a faint frown.
Retrieving his beer, he said, "The chief will put a couple of men on traffic control for the next production,
but short of blocking the street to everybody except
residents, nothing's going to do any good until the
general population gets jaded and stays home."

My rejection having been only temporary, we
amused each other in an adult fashion until Caron
came pounding up the steps. We were at opposite ends
of the sofa when she came into the living room, stared
suspiciously at our damp faces, then flung a small sack
in the corner and flopped down across a chair.

"Rhonda was at the mall," she announced with a
grandiose sigh. "She bought so much stuff she could
barely carry it. I, on the other hand, could find nothing
in my size that wasn't too tight. I might as well put
on a bikini bottom and tassels and look for an unoccu-
pied stage. How much do you think Zeno paid that
weird woman?"

"Not enough," I said quickly. "You've got a couple

of weeks until school starts. You'll be able to find something in your size that fits if you keep trying."

Peter had yet another odd look on his face when he left. Men will never understand the ideological implications of shopping.

I avoided the historic district the remainder of the week, devoting myself to ordering stock for the advent of the semester and making excuses to my accountant, who seemed obsessed with quarterly tax estimates.

It was business as usual right up until Friday afternoon, when Caron and Inez came racing into the store. Inez managed to skitter to a halt, but Caron careened into the science fiction rack and went down under a flurry of lurid covers.

"You're not going to believe this," she gasped as she sat up and examined her elbows and knees for mortal wounds, then stood up and unconcernedly stepped over the debris. "I can hardly believe it myself."

"I believe you're going to pick up those books," I said in a wonderfully controlled voice.

She gestured imperiously at Inez to help her. When they were done, she limped to the counter. "It's really, really exciting. We're going to be on television tomorrow night. You've got to rent a VCR, Mother, so we can make a copy of the broadcast and have a party so everybody can watch it again."

"We have a VCR," Inez said, "but my father hasn't figured out how to tape stuff. He says he's electronically challenged."

Caron's limp vanished as she began to pirouette in front of the counter. "I'm going to be so incredibly famous that Rhonda will beg me for my autograph. I may make her pay for it, or maybe—"

"Why are you going to be on television?" I asked.

"I'm not sure I will," Inez said. She took off her glasses and wiped them on her shirttail, replaced them, and gazed at me with the solemnity of a jury foreperson with inauspicious news regarding the life expectancy of the defendant. "My parents aren't like you, Mrs. Malloy. They're kind of old-fashioned, even for librarians."

It was flattering to know I hadn't been condemned to a rocking chair, but I did not have a warm glow. What I did have was more akin to the stirrings of an ulcer. "Why are you going to be on television?" I repeated.

"Maybe even a major network," Caron said. Resuming her piteous limp, she went into the office and started rummaging through desk drawers.

I waited until she emerged with my last bar of chocolate. "I'm beginning to get irritated, Caron. For the third and final time, why—"

Her hand stopped halfway to her mouth. "We ran into Zeno up on the square. I was trying to find some decent jeans and he was taking photographs of feet. He said you can tell a lot about people by their shoes."

Inez gazed modestly at her worn sneakers, one of which was untied. "He said I'm very compassionate."

"Because you can't keep your shoes tied?" I said, mystified.

"It means I look at people's faces rather than at the ground. Looking at the ground means you're introspective and don't care about anybody but yourself."

Caron swallowed the last bite of candy and regained center stage, her preferred habitat. "Only a bufflehead would buy into that babble, Inez. I keep my shoes tied, and I'm compassionate. Remember when I thought Rhonda's creepy little brother put a slug down the back of my shirt? Anybody else would have ripped out his hair, but all I did was knock the holy—"

"Television!" I said desperately.

She licked her finger, then gave me an ingenuous

smile. "Zeno needs two more actresses for his sound-and-light show. He's paying us fifty dollars each."

My knees buckled so abruptly that I barely made it to the stool. "Are you out of your postpubescent mind? There is no way you're going to take off your clothes and climb up on a stage to have an intimate relationship with a rubber snake! I already have a reputation in this town for getting involved with murder. I am not going to add the stigma of being the mother of the Willow Street Stripper."

"Oh, Mother," she said, somehow managing to extend her lower lip at the same time. "I am not going to Take Off Anything. I can't believe you would think I would, much less stand on that stupid stage and act vulgar. Our roles are a lot more civilized."

"Yes?" I said.

"That's right," said Inez. "Zeno promised that we would be completely dressed, except maybe he'll have us go barefoot. People who go barefoot all the time are highly artistic."

I opened the drawer below the cash register to hunt for a roll of antacids. "If you're not taking on the roles of Eve's licentious kid sisters, what precisely are you going to do?"

Caron began sidling toward the door, snagging Inez's arm along the way. "We get fifty dollars and we don't so much as bare our belly buttons," she said as she backed into the table of fraternity and sorority knickknacks, winced, and revised her course. "I'm going to spend it all on clothes, so it'll save you some money. Besides, we get to be on television. Don't you think that's neat?"

My jaw was dangling unattractively as they took off up the sidewalk, no doubt heading for the nearest telephone to arrange for representation by the William Morris Agency. I'd felt smug earlier in the week when I'd said it was none of our concern. Now it seemed it

was. I considered what would happen if I flatly refused
to let Caron participate. In spite of—or at least in the
intervals between—her bouts of emotional turbulence,
I loved my daughter and did not want her to resent
me well into the next decade. Which she would, if she
obeyed me. If she acted more in character and climbed
down the drainpipe (metaphorically speaking), I'd be
forced to take stern parental retaliation that would
cause her to resent me well into the next decade. It
was clearly the antithesis of a win-win situation.

I'd eaten all the antacids by five o'clock, but acid
was still roiling in my stomach. My best friend, Luanne
Bradshaw, was out of town and therefore unavailable
to give me advice in the beer garden across the street.
Peter had mentioned an evening seminar. My aged
hippie science-fiction freak had ambled in earlier; his
unfocused eyes and general incoherence had pre-
cluded him from the role of Dear Abby. My accountant would zero in on the monetary aspect.

A confrontation was in order. After all, I was a
mother, not a mouse.

THREE

Traffic was sluggish on Willow Street as rubberneckers slowed down in front of Zeno's house, but it was only a trickle compared to what it had been earlier in the week. I muttered an Anglo-Saxon oath as I envisioned the chaos that would overwhelm the neighborhood in twenty-four hours. Miss Parchester very well might end up under the back porch with her basset hounds, a decanter of elderberry wine, and a straw.

Zeno's yard had been transformed into an elephant's graveyard of gutted appliances, each painted a resplendent shade of orange, pink, yellow, or a combination of all three. A dazzlingly red iron bedframe dominated the brick sidewalk; reposing on it was the mannequin, currently attired in a tuxedo and a Viking helmet. The old rugged cross was now the old rugged lavender cross. Dozens of sets of wind chimes clinked and clanked.

I found a parking spot farther up the block and was approaching the house when I heard angry voices across the street. I paused out of prudence (okay, curiosity) as the ponytailed woman came to the edge of the sidewalk, accompanied by the young man who'd come to her assistance. His face was as pasty as hers, although he had the cheeks and overbite, as well as the paunch, of a chipmunk. He wore a dark suit of discount store origin and carried a shabby briefcase. His shoes were indicative that he was not a compassionate person, at least at the moment. He appeared to be of college age, but there was something unduly sober and repressive about him that made it seem unlikely he was a beer-swilling fraternity boy.

"You have to put a stop to this blasphemy, Joshua," the woman said loudly, although well within the allowed decibel limit.

"What am I supposed to do about it?" he blustered. "I've tried to reason with him since the day he moved in. I offered to pray with him, but he laughed in my face. Do you expect me to burn down the house?"

He tried to take her arm, but she pushed away his hand and stepped into the street. Without looking at him, she said, "If you won't do something, I will."

I drifted toward the topic of their conversation, but I kept an eye on the couple. If I were perceived to be Zeno's confederate, I might be knocked to the ground and lectured about blasphemy. My knees are much too comely for crude encounters with concrete.

Joshua grasped her shoulder so tightly I could see his fingers digging into her flesh. "I'm your husband, and you took a solemn vow to love, honor, and *obey* me. I'm ordering you to go back in the house, damn it—and you will obey me!"

"Don't you dare use profanity with me!"

"Joshua! Tracy!" called Anthony Leach as he hurried toward them. Following him at a more decorous rate was a middle-aged woman in a floppy black hat, from under which billowed shoulder-length blond hair. Her mouth sagged downward in a frown; harsh creases implied it was her typical expression. She wore a black T-shirt and black sweatpants; black athletic shoes completed a relentlessly monochromatic ensemble. She held a cigarette in one hand and a martini glass in the other, and was dividing her attention between the two, with only occasional glances at Leach's back.

It looked as if the neighborhood vigilantes were about to have a conclave (although the woman in black might have been more comfortable at a coven). Appointing myself Miss Parchester's emissary, I made my way through the traffic and arrived at the curb at the same time as Anthony Leach. The blond woman halted several feet away.

"What is it, Mr. Leach?" asked Joshua.

"I've done the paperwork for a civil suit. The judge is more likely to grant a temporary restraining order if it's a class action with all of us as plaintiffs. I've already got Miss Parchester's signature, as well as those of the graduate students on the corner, Colonel Culworthy, and old Mrs. Fernlift, who thinks Nazis are holding rallies. Mrs. Hadley here is the only hold-out, but she says she'll consider it if everyone else signs." He was about to continue his sales pitch when he noticed me. He did so without delight. "I've seen you before, haven't I? Who are you?"

Joshua and Tracy stared narrowly at me. The blond woman looked at me over the rim of her glass. All four of them seemed to be anticipating a response.

I wished I had a glib one, but I didn't. "I'm Claire Malloy. I own the Book Depot down on Thurber Street next to the railroad tracks. Miss Parchester is a friend of mine. She's deeply distressed at what's going on."

Unimpressed with my compassion, Leach turned his back on me. "I need everybody's signature before I try to find a judge. Just sign on any of the lines and put the date next to it."

"Why are you reluctant to sign it, Mrs. Hadley?" demanded Tracy. "Do you think Mr. Gorgias has a right to offend the Christians of this community by making a mockery of our religious beliefs?"

The woman under attack dropped her cigarette and

ground it out with her heel. "He has a right to freedom of speech. As a writer, I have an obligation to
oppose censorship of any kind, even if I personally
object to the message."

"You're a writer?" I said, forgetting I was not a
card-carrying resident of Willow Street and thus a less
than welcome addition to the conclave. "What do
you write?"

"Mrs. Malloy," said Leach, "this is not career day
at the high school. We don't have time to—"

Mrs. Hadley disagreed. "I write mysteries. My
twenty-third came out this last spring and received
glowing reviews. *Publishers Weekly* described it as
'well-plotted and intriguing.' The *Library Journal*
said—"

Leach flapped a document at her. "Mrs. Hadley,
will you please give your attention to the matter at
hand? Are you going to join the suit or not?"

She took a pen from him and, with a sigh, scribbled
across the bottom of the final page. "I feel as if I'm
adding my name to Salman Rushdie's death warrant,
Mr. Leach. Let the records reflect I did this under
protest, and don't ever let the Authors Guild hear
about it. I'd be expelled for my treachery, if not
hunted down and stabbed through the heart with a
quill." She handed the pen to Tracy. "I can understand why you're offended. However, you'd best be
careful about imposing your beliefs on others. One of
these days you might find yourself in the minority."

"Never," Tracy said without hesitation. "My husband and I have dedicated our lives to spreading the
true word of God. After Joshua graduates from the
Bible Academy in December, we'll be posted to Af-
rica or Central America, where he'll teach school and
I'll be a nurse's aide. Both of us will have the opportunity to—"

"Sign the paper!" said Leach. He spoke with such

urgency that we all stared at him. "I have another potential buyer," he added as a sheen of sweat formed on his forehead. "If Willow Street is featured on the news tomorrow night, he won't even bother to come by."

Tracy sniffed. "I'm sorry that you're motivated by greed rather than spiritual concerns. Joshua and I will pray for you, just as we did when you allowed that boy to mow your yard on a Sunday. 'Remember the sabbath day, to keep it holy.' He was practically naked, which made it worse. Yes, Mr. Leach, rest assured that we will pray for you."

"Do that," Leach growled as he jabbed his finger at the document.

The couple signed and went inside, perhaps to spread the cream cheese on bagels before they kneeled in an attempt to save souls. Leach nodded curtly at Mrs. Hadley, shot a dark look at me, and walked toward his house.

"You've written twenty-three mysteries?" I said, getting back to the more intriguing issue. "I'm a compulsive mystery reader, but I'm afraid I'm unfamiliar with your work. Do you use a pen name?"

"That's not an author's favorite question. Come have a drink, Claire. I do so enjoy the company of booksellers; they tend to be as frustrated with publishers as we writers are." She slid her arm through mine and yanked me into motion. "Call me Jasmine—and promise not to ask me how you should go about getting an agent. I prefer State Farm, myself, but it's a matter of individual taste."

I was nonplussed enough to be led down the sidewalk. It was inconceivable that I could be unaware of a prolific mystery writer who lived in Farberville. Inconceivable and humiliating. "Have you lived here long?" I asked.

"Quite some time," she murmured as she stopped

in front of a dilapidated house directly across from Zeno's. "But I'll have to move if this madness continues. My apartment is arranged so that the living room and the bedroom that doubles as my office are in the front, and the kitchen and bathroom in the back." She gestured at the second story, and when she spoke, there was enough bitterness in her voice to momentarily unnerve me. "My desk is in front of that window. Every single time I glance up from my word processor to consider a scene or search my mind for the precise word I want, I find myself looking at this visual aberration—or at Zeno adding to it. The wind chimes are never quiet. The viewers who are affronted by the religious symbolism express themselves belligerently. The ones who are amused bray and make crass jokes. Car doors slam incessantly."

"Have you tried to write at night?"

"The Christmas lights flicker all night, even after the traffic has dwindled. Last week I was so spellbound that I stood at the window and counted the damn things. I'd reached two hundred before I realized what I was doing and pulled down the shade. He plays that blasted tape at odd hours, and as I said, the wind chimes are never quiet." Her hand jerked as she lit a cigarette. She inhaled deeply, squinting as the smoke stung her eyes. The wrinkles on her face deepened like fissures on a precipice. "And if I were to stay up all night writing, when could I sleep? I'm already so frazzled and exhausted that I'm well behind schedule, and I can't afford to move until I turn in the completed manuscript and receive a payment. I'm a prisoner here, and I find that unbearable."

"I'm sure your publisher will understand. Who is it, by the way?"

Rather than enlightening me, Jasmine stared over my shoulder. A black Cadillac pulled to the curb across the street and stopped. The few pedestrians

abandoned their preoccupation with Zeno's yard and
lined up on the sidewalk to discover who was hidden
behind the tinted windows.

"What's he doing now?" growled Jasmine. "Bringing in more so-called actresses from strip joints?"

"Maybe it's a cardinal with a papal writ to desist,"
I said. "Tracy may have been on the phone with the
pope."

"I doubt the threat of excommunication will have
any more effect on Zeno than Leach's class-action suit
or Tracy Dwain's self-righteous diatribes."

I was about to agree, when the passenger's door
opened. A women emerged, stooped to speak briefly
to a companion inside, and then turned to face what
Jasmine had described as a visual aberration.

Her back was to us, so I couldn't see what was apt
to be a horrified expression. I'd caught a quick glimpse
of elegant feline features when she stepped out of the
car; she did not look the type to burst into laughter
and accept a beer from the fraternity boy who was
openly ogling her. He was liable to be out of his
league. Her black hair was piled in an elaborate
French roll and held in place with a gold barrette. Her
beige suit had been designed by someone with a Gallic
surname. She appeared to be in her twenties, but she
had the savoir faire of a seasoned gossip columnist.

The driver opened his door and squirmed out from
behind the steering wheel. He was vastly less impressive in a short-sleeved shirt and blue jeans that
strained against his substantial rump. Wiping his forehead with his wrist, he went to the sidewalk and began
to shake his head. The woman, who was several inches
taller than he, bent down to whisper in his ear. He
responded by shaking his head more vigorously. I
wasn't sure if he was in shock or had moved on to
denial.

Zeno came out onto his porch, carrying a dripping

paintbrush and a gallon paint can. He stopped so abruptly that yellow paint erupted out of the can and splashed on his bare feet. "Ruthanne, what a surprise," he called with none of the exuberance I'd seen earlier. "I didn't expect to see you and Harry."

Propriety should have kept me where I was, but I was too far away to easily hear what might evolve into a diverting exchange. I told Jasmine that I wanted to check on Miss Parchester, crossed the street, and found a reasonably unobtrusive post at the corner of her yard.

"Well, I didn't expect to see this," Ruthanne said, wafting her hand at the assemblage of appliances, coffins, and so forth. Her strained smile exposed tiny white teeth. "What are you doing, Zeno? Operating a landfill in the middle of a residential neighborhood?"

He shifted uneasily. "Art does not exist solely within the confines of a gallery or museum. This is a commentary on the extinction of technological—"

"I need to speak to you in private, Zeno," she said. She conversed once again with her companion and then started for the porch. The crowd parted to allow her to pass, closing ranks as she and Zeno went inside the house.

Harry opened the trunk and took out an extensive collection of matched luggage and a lone canvas bag, then leaned against the car, dejectedly watching the front door. His face was as round and plump as his rump, and his thin, brown hair had begun a premature retreat that artful combing could not conceal. He looked more like a pampered lapdog than a Mafia hit man, but recent events on Willow Street had proved almost anything was possible. In my capacity as an emissary, I decided it was appropriate for me to determine who he and Ruthanne were.

"Hello," I said as I approached him. "Welcome to Farberville."

"Thanks."

"Are you a friend of Zeno's?"

He finally tore his gaze away from the door. "I'm Harry Tillington, his agent. And you?"

"Claire Malloy. I have a dear friend who lives next door. I was on my way to visit her when you arrived." I waited for an explanation, but it was not forthcoming. "Is the woman with you also an agent?"

"Ruthanne is Zeno's wife," he said with a small smile that made it clear he was indulging me in my not-so-subtle thirst for knowledge. "She had a call last night from some lawyer here who's threatening to bring a lawsuit. She and Zeno are ... estranged, but she felt as though she'd better come find out what's going on. When she called me, she thought the lawyer was crazy. I suspect she's changed her mind by now. I have, anyway."

The wind chimes on the nearest tree began to clatter convulsively, as if we were in an earthquake. As Harry, the remaining gawkers, and I stared, two bare legs plunged through the foliage. I wasn't nearly as astounded as Harry when the rest of Melanie Magruder appeared. She dangled from a branch, kicking her legs and cursing, then fell to the ground and sprawled on her back like a hapless turtle.

"His wife?" she drawled as she sat up and disengaged a twig caught in her hair. "He didn't tell me about any wife. What's she doing here?"

Harry shrugged. "She's come to discuss whatever it is *he's* doing here and how best to avoid a lawsuit. If I may be so bold, what were you doing in that tree?"

"Adjusting a spotlight." She looked at me. "Is he telling the truth? What would Zeno be doing with a wife like that?"

"I have no idea," I replied, although I admitted to myself that she had posed a legitimate question. Zeno had abandoned the Mickey Mouse ears, but he currently was dressed in ragged cutoffs and a soiled, baggy undershirt of the type favored by swarthy peasants. His arms and legs were dappled with paint, and his cheeks were dark with several days' growth of whiskers. At least one foot was bright yellow.

His wife was dressed for a cocktail party at a posh New York gallery. She had the look of someone who never perspired at the height of summer, even if clad in mink. Her pedicured toenails might be red, but her feet would never be yellow.

However, her cheeks were flaming as she came out the door and hurried down the steps. Zeno came running after her, his hands outstretched.

"Ruthanne," he said imploringly, "you've got to—"

"No, I don't," she said as she took refuge behind Harry. "I've put up with a lot of bullshit from you over the last two years, Zeno. I've closed my eyes to your bouts of drunkenness and endless affairs. I made excuses and broke appointments for you." Keeping her hands clamped on Harry's elbows, she pushed him forward. "Harry's tired of apologizing for you, too. He was the one who had to call the gallery in Athens to cancel the show because you'd done nothing but dig trenches in the backyard for six months."

Zeno dropped his hands and grinned at the spectators as if they were his closest friends. "It was an allegorical representation of man's futile attempts to bring order into the anarchy of—"

"Zeno!" Ruthanne bounced her forehead against Harry's back hard enough to dislodge a hairpin, took several breaths, and said, "For God's sake, let's not go into that at the moment. I realize that you hate Houston and that I should never have talked you into moving there. I'll put the house on the market and stay there until it sells. Harry's agreed to find you a studio in Santa Fe. When I'm able to move, I'll hunt for a proper house with a big backyard. An enormous backyard. Acres and acres of backyard. You can dig the Panama Canal for all I care!"

"It'll be great, Zeno," Harry said with a noticeable lack of enthusiasm. "I can stop by and see how you're doing, make sure you've got everything you need, even buy your groceries and pay your bills until Ruthanne comes. You won't have to do anything but paint and enjoy the sunsets. How 'bout it?"

Zeno's grin disappeared. "Ruthanne is right when she says I hate Houston, but she is wrong when she says I am moving back to Santa Fe. Uncle Stenopolis's house is the sole surviving link with my family. When I walk through it, I can hear him singing the old songs. I can feel the tromping of his feet as he dances with the ghosts of his past." Slowly snapping his fingers, he began to hum what sounded like the score of *Zorba the Greek*.

Ruthanne shoved Harry aside and went over to Zeno. They were of equal height, but even though Zeno was a good deal bulkier, I would have preferred him as a wrestling opponent. Her sharply sculpted features were accentuated by her anger; it was easy to picture her raking claws across his face.

"Please, Zeno," she said, attempting to suppress her anger, "give our marriage another chance. Once we're settled in Santa Fe, we'll have fun like we used to. I won't get involved in too much charity work, and I won't entertain the people you find so pompous. If you want to go out drinking with some of your old friends, I won't object. It'll be great, Zeno."

"I will not leave this house," he said.

She dropped her wheedling tone. "Then you give me no choice but to petition the court to be named your legal guardian, since you're clearly a danger to yourself and the people who live around you. The hearing will last three minutes. I'll show the judge photographs of all this and of the interior." She looked around in search of a sympathetic audience. "You wouldn't believe what it's like in there. Every room is crammed with newspapers, magazines, and boxes of books. One stray spark and the whole neighborhood will go up in flames."

Harry grabbed Zeno's arm. "Do you have any completed work in there?"

"Half a dozen canvases," he said, shrugging.

"Half a dozen? Are you crazy, Zeno? What if there is a fire? What if someone breaks in and steals them? Do you realize how much they're worth?"

Zeno patted him on the head. "Don't get so excited, my little agent. They're tucked away in a back room where no one would find them—and they're insured. My devoted wife made sure of that before I left Houston. She probably made sure I have plenty of life insurance, too. If I refuse to behave like a good boy, I may be worth more dead."

Ruthanne raised her hand as if to slap him but then heard a collective gasp from the crowd and thought better of it. "You can either accompany Harry to Santa Fe and resume your career, or you can spend ninety days in a mental institution, digging trenches in the sandbox and working on paint-by-number kits. Ninety days, Zeno—that's how long they can keep you for evaluation. By the time you're released, I will have sold this house and moved all your things to Santa Fe. I have your power of attorney and I can do it. Trust me when I say that I will."

"Can she do that?" Melanie said to me. "It doesn't sound fair. I mean, doesn't Zeno have a right to live where he wants and create whatever fool art keeps him happy? What business is it of hers?"

Ruthanne turned to look at her. "It's my business because I'm his wife. It's none of your business because you're nothing but his current slut. In any case, you'll be long gone in ninety days. If you have a problem with that, I have some unsavory associates in Houston who'll make sure of it."

Melanie crossed her arms, and when she spoke, her voice was husky with menace. "Zeno, honey, tell this blood-sucking bitch to beat it before I feel obliged to drive a wooden stake through her heart."

"Let's go, Harry," Ruthanne said disdainfully, if a bit shrilly. She waited until he opened the door of the Cadillac, and then she disappeared into its interior. Harry replaced the luggage, gave Zeno an impotent look, and went around to the driver's side.

Someone in the crowd began to clap, and a few male voices expressed disappointment that a brawl had not evolved. I realized I was trembling in the aftermath of all the hostility, as though it had been directed at me. I was relieved when the car pulled away from the curb.

Zeno watched its departure, his shoulders hunched and his eyes narrowed. Once it turned the corner, he relaxed and said, "Let us not worry about such things. Come, Melanie, I have decided to paint the front of the house yellow so that it will radiate sunlight even in the dark." Despite his blithe dismissal of Ruthanne's threat, his feet moved heavily as he went around the iron bedframe and onto the porch. He picked up the brush, then carefully laid it across the rim of the paint can and went inside.

Melanie remained beside me, her hands on her hips and her head cocked. "Can she really have him packed off to the funny farm like she says?"

"I suggest Zeno hire a lawyer and ask that very thing. Do you have any idea what Zeno has planned for tomorrow night? He's hired my daughter and her friend, but I'm going to forbid them to participate if he wants them to do anything ... unsuitable."

"I can't tell what he has planned from one minute to the next. He's what you might call unpredictable."

I watched her go up the steps and into the house. As much as I wanted to confront Zeno, I didn't have the heart. His neighbors were conspiring to put a stop to his behavior via a class-action suit. His wife and agent were conspiring to do the same via a competency hearing. For all I knew, the prosecutor may have been unscrewing the back of the sound-level meter to tinker with its internal organs.

Jasmine was no longer outside her house, thus preventing me from tactfully grilling her about her books. There were other ways to explore this minor puzzle, however, and the idea of doing so on my own sofa appealed. I'd started for my car when I heard my name called.

Miss Parchester came to the edge of the sidewalk and waved. "Could I interest you in a nice cup of tea?" she said, swaying dangerously and giggling as hiccups slipped out. "I want to tell you about the time dear Papa defended a snake handler. The snake died the very next Sunday, you know."

I took her arm and steered her toward her door. "A cup of tea would be very nice, Miss Parchester. I can't imagine anything I'd enjoy more than a cup of tea."

FOUR

I was so distracted the following day that I could make no sense of the local newspaper—or make any headway with the crossword puzzle. Willow Street was awash in hostility, with high tide scheduled for sunset, when a respectable percentage of the local population would arrive for our very first son et lumière show. Word of mouth can be amazingly effective in a town the size of Farberville, particularly when one of the words is *camera*. Religious groups might be painting picket signs and beating their plowshares back into swords, while fraternity boys opened the first kegs of the day in anticipation of the revelry. Anthony Leach no doubt was at the golf course, chasing down judges in hopes of a temporary restraining order. Ruthanne Gorgias and Harry Tillington might be on the back nine, intent on a similar quarry. I assumed the police were devising a strategy to deal with a crowd that not even a visit from the president could draw.

Caron had spent the night with Inez, which was a shrewd move on her part. If she could dodge me all day, she could claim afterward that I'd not specifically forbidden her to participate. That she might make this claim from a jail cell was enough to send me to the mirror to search for fresh gray hairs. I envisioned headlines more lurid than those in any tabloid; all of

them began: DAUGHTER OF BOOKSELLER CLAIRE
MALLOY . . .

By midafternoon I was reduced to totalling my
checking and savings accounts to determine how much
money I could scrape together for bail. Not enough,
I concluded gloomily. For the first time in years, I
rather wished Carlton were around so that I could
abdicate responsibility and take refuge in some remote
cabin. The fact that I could entertain such a heretical
thought added to my despondency. Our marriage had
not been intolerable, but I'd discovered that self-
sufficiency was more appealing than compromise
(a.k.a. capitulation on my part). The last thing I
wanted was for Carlton to come through the door to
complain about some imagined slight in the English
department and leave me with a list of errands to
run. He'd always been too busy to run them himself;
seminars occupied his days, distaff students his
evenings.

It was in this state of mind that I greeted Peter
Rosen when he came into the Book Depot. "What do
you want?" I snapped, then realized what I'd done
and tried to manufacture a smile. It was not my most
bewitching to date.

"A date for the movies tonight?" he said, sensing
the presence, if not the precise location, of emotional
land mines. He can be very perceptive on occasion.
Carlton would have stepped over my bloodied body
on his way to the bedroom closet to see if I'd alpha-
betized his clothes.

"Aren't you going to be occupied fingerprinting innocent parties who've been lured into crime by the
specter of financial gain and stardom?"

Peter thought this over for a moment. "I have to
attend a very dreary banquet honoring various civic
groups for their commitment to law and order. It
should be over by eight o'clock at the latest. Of

course, afterward I'll have to drop by the station to put away the thumbscrews and hose down the rack, but that shouldn't take too long. We can make the second show, or better yet, rent Dirty Harry movies and make our own popcorn."

I refused to be distracted by his attempted levity. "Do you have a separate facility for juvenile offenders, or are they thrown in cells with prostitutes and drug dealers?"

"What's this about?" he said as he cast aside caution and came over to the counter. "I'll presume you're worried about Caron. Has she done something that might require the services of a lawyer? It won't be an admission of female frailty to accept some advice once in a while. Even with all my masculine infallibility, I have to consult the manual every time I load my camera."

It was most certainly an admission, but I went ahead and told him about the two newest recruits in Zeno's upcoming production. "They don't know what they're supposed to do," I added, "but Zeno has a forceful personality and the tunnel vision of either a genius or a megalomaniac. He may be plotting a full-scale attack on the basic tenets of Judeo-Christian theology. If they're overwhelmed by his enthusiasm . . ." I dribbled to a stop, unable to elaborate on the images that had haunted me all day.

He caught my hand and squeezed it in a paternalistic manner I would have found disturbing if I hadn't already been so disturbed about a more tangible problem. In a tone that barely escaped condescension, he said, "Don't underestimate them, Claire. Caron and Inez have too much sense to do something that will get them arrested. If nothing else, they know darn well that they'd have to get along without mousse and conditioner."

"They stole five cartons of frozen frogs from the

high-school science department, didn't they? Do you honestly believe they paused for one measly second to consider the consequences?"

Peter's mouth quivered, but he managed not to smile. "Okay, so maybe they have a history of impulsive behavior. Do you want me to talk to them about what might constitute public indecency or disorderly conduct?"

"I suppose so," I said as the foreboding phrases echoed like massive church bells. Instead of asking for whom they tolled, I called Inez's house and asked to speak to Caron.

Mrs. Thornton is a faintly bewildered woman who has never quite assimilated the extent of her daughter's escapades. "She's not here. They got up much earlier than usual and said they were going to Rhonda Maguire's house to swim."

"Did Inez say anything about their plans for this evening?"

"Only that she and Caron would be sleeping at your house. Is there a problem, Mrs. Malloy? Caron's welcome to stay here again tonight."

I asked her if she was aware of what had been happening on Willow Street and, when she admitted she was not, laid it out in meticulous detail. I then repeated what the girls had said to me the previous afternoon. Once she quit gasping, I said, "A member of the police department has volunteered to talk to them. I'll call them at Rhonda's, and if they're not there, I'll call you back."

"I'll wait for your call," she said, having assimilated at record speed both the potential peril and the likelihood the girls would not be at Rhonda Maguire's.

I hung up, grimaced at Peter, and called the Maguire home. Mrs. Maguire informed me that Rhonda had gone to the mall for the day and that no one was lounging beside the pool. Inez's mother agreed to start calling their other friends in hopes Caron and Inez had not gone so deeply underground that we couldn't rout them with anything short of a backhoe.

"Can you put out an APB?" I asked Peter.

"Of course I can't. They haven't done anything wrong."

"They haven't done anything wrong—yet."

He was already backing away. "Then you don't want to catch a movie later?"

"I shall devote the evening to reading up on due process," I said, then bent over my calculations until I heard the bell above the door tinkle as he left. For the remainder of the afternoon, I checked periodically with Mrs. Thornton, who was having no success. No one answered the telephone at home. No one burst through the door with outlandish remarks about fame and fortune. The customers who wandered in sensed the voltage in the air and refrained from making small talk.

At five o'clock I closed the Book Depot and then wasted half an hour and half a gallon of gas driving around the part of town encompassing Inez's house, Rhonda's pool, and our apartment. None of the pedestrians I spotted had a mop of red curls and a guilty slouch. Once at home, I took a shower and changed into slacks and a cotton sweater, an outfit I felt was appropriately dignified for the posting of bail and the proffering of stern maternal discourses.

I fixed myself a drink and slumped on the sofa to watch the local news. The final segment featured a certain street in the historic district. A bit of footage showed Zeno dragging the black coffin across the porch while babbling cheerfully about the implications of "interactive environmental art." This was followed by a short interview with Anthony Leach, who admitted he'd not been able to get a restraining order but vowed to keep trying. The city prosecutor mumbled

about the relevance of freedom of speech and ducked
out a doorway. The segment concluded with the promise of a fun-filled event for the entire family.

As dusk approached, I took a circuitous route to
the library parking lot, locked my car, and joined the
parade up Willow Street. At the corner, a uniformed
police officer barked orders at the cars and trucks ma-
neuvering for entry from both directions. Cannier citi-
zens whizzed by on bicycles, motor scooters, and roller
blades. Dogs strained at leashes, as did runny-nosed
toddlers determined to trample zinnias.

In front of Jasmine's house were two dozen som-
berly clad protestors, each holding a sign. The milder
messages characterized Zeno as the Antichrist. Most
of the protestors looked as if they'd been bused in
from a backwoods nursing home, but a few were as
young as Joshua Dwain. Lips were tight and expressions laden with accusation. No one pushed through
them, or even walked in front of them. Tracy and
Joshua were not among them.

Jorgeson, who was Peter's partner in matters of
crime warranting the scrutiny of the CID, sat on the
low wall in front of Anthony Leach's house. He held
a metal box that I suspected was a sound-level meter.
It was somewhat heartening; if Zeno violated the
sound ordinance, it was possible Jorgeson could stop
the show immediately. Or, I thought with a sudden
chill, he could arrest the entire cast and call for the
paddy wagon (if Farberville had such a thing).

It was impossible to get close enough to Zeno's yard
to see what modifications had been made (as in two
more lavender crosses or a table set for thirteen). I
went back to Miss Parchester's yard and was preparing
to wiggle through the bushes when Jasmine materialized at my side.

"Ruthanne came back this afternoon," she said as
she held aside a branch and gestured for me to pre-

cede her. "She and Zeno had a screaming match on the sidewalk. I finally turned off my word processor and took refuge in the kitchen with Ernest and Julio."

"Are Ernest and Julio your cats?"

"The Gallo brothers. I lost an entire afternoon at a time when my editor is talking about revoking my contract and demanding I return the advance. As if I could!"

I stepped over an empty whiskey bottle and a nest of beer cans, then looked back at her. "Can they do that?"

"My editor will be the first to tell you that she's not operating a charity for wayward writers. If Leach can't get the restraining order, I don't know what I'll do. Something, though."

A mouthful of foliage prevented me from responding. I was still spitting out forsythia leaves as I arrived at the edge of Zeno's yard and forced myself to look around for Caron and Inez. Neither they nor Melanie were visible. No fresh crosses had been added, which made me feel slightly encouraged. The stage was still adorned with the apple tree, however, and there were two large speakers on the front porch.

"What on earth . . . ?" murmured Jasmine.

My encouragement vanished like a drop of water in a hot skillet. "What?" I asked, peering frantically at the scene. "What on earth—what, Jasmine?"

She had a peculiar expression, thoughtful rather than appalled, and she seemed to be staring at the side of the house instead of the front yard. In a vague and unconvincing voice, she said, "I was musing out loud about Zeno's goals for tonight. I would imagine the presence of television cameras will only encourage him to be even more outrageous."

Abruptly, spotlights erupted from various hiding places in the trees and under the porch, as did a strobe light at the foot of the iron bed. The strings of tiny white Christmas lights flickered on and off; if Jasmine had continued counting, her total easily would have surpassed two thousand. The lumière had begun, apparently.

The front door opened. I held my breath as Melanie came onto the porch, dressed once again in tassels, the almost invisible bikini bottom with its paper fig leaf, and the limp rubber snake. Cheers and boos hailed her as she came around a coffin and down the steps, assumed a provocative pose for the benefit of innumerable cameras, including that of the local television station, and then started toward the stage. The speakers came alive; as Zeno had promised, this time there were two tapes that assailed us with a pant-pant here and a moan-moan there.

The crowd grew rowdier and, for the most part, angrier. Children shrilly demanded to know if the snake was real, while fraternity boys whistled and hooted. I couldn't see the protestors across the street, but I doubted they were nodding their approval.

The lid of the coffin flew open and Zeno jumped out. His ankle-length black cape and ghoulish makeup startled everyone into silence. "Death is the ultimate cosmic orgasm!" he yelled, waving his arms so that the cape swished like silken wings.

"Blasphemer!" screamed a voice from across the street. There was such rage in the single word that the crowd swung around to stare. I recognized Tracy's now familiar battle cry.

A roar drowned out whatever else she was screaming as she began to cross the street. The sound grew louder as a motorcycle sped between the lanes of cars. Warnings were shouted from the crowd. Tires squealed. Across the street, Jorgeson was on his feet, waving his arms above his head.

A single headlight flashed on the maple tree, then swung down. Metal slammed into metal. The motorcycle's engine whined into silence, and for an agonizing moment, all that could be heard was the heavy breathing from the tapes.

The crowd surged toward the curb. I fought my way back to Miss Parchester's yard, then ran across the street and caught up with Jorgeson as he shoved aside the protestors, ordered drivers to stay in their cars, and kneeled next to the back bumper. From my perspective, I could see only Tracy Dwain's leg bent at an unnatural angle.

Jorgeson looked back at me. "Call 911, and be sure to warn them about the traffic jam. Then go down to the corner, tell the officer what happened, and wait for the paramedics."

Jasmine grabbed my arm and dragged me toward her house. "Call from my place!" she shouted over the hysterical outbursts from the crowd.

Somehow we made it upstairs. She pointed at a telephone, and after I'd made the call, reappeared with several blankets. We stumbled back downstairs. As frantic as I was to know Tracy's condition, I ran down to the corner and explained the situation to the officer. He seemed to grow younger and more panicked with each word. I was on the verge of suggesting he sit on the curb and put his head between his knees when we heard a siren.

He regained control of himself and waded into the traffic to clear a path for the ambulance. It took nearly ten minutes of directing cars into driveways and the library parking lot before the ambulance arrived at the corner. Clearing a path up Willow Street was patently impossible. As soon as the paramedics pulled out a gurney, I led them to the site of the accident. Jorgeson had been joined by several other uniformed officers, who were keeping the crowd at a civilized distance. Joshua Dwain stood on the sidewalk, dazedly watching the paramedics as they moved between the cars and surrounded his wife.

Breathing unsteadily, I retreated into Jasmine's yard and looked at Zeno's house. The spotlights and strobe had been turned off, as well as the speakers. Melanie was gone, but Zeno stood on the dark porch, still wearing the cape.

The scene eventually quieted down. Tracy was wheeled down the hill, with Joshua hovering over her. The policemen took down the names of the calmer witnesses and sent away a great many others. A red motorcycle was wheeled to the curb and unceremoniously dropped. An officer knelt to measure a skid mark, while another interviewed the driver of the car that had been hit by the motorcycle after it had slammed into Tracy.

Jorgeson was making notes in a small book as he came back to the sidewalk. I allowed him to finish and then said, "How badly is she hurt?"

"Hard to say," he said, wincing. "Her head hit the pavement pretty hard, and she lost a lot of blood. If the paramedics could have gotten to her more quickly . . ." He gestured at the traffic that only now was beginning to move. "Moot at this point, I guess."

"What about the motorcyclist?"

"I sent him to wait in my car. He's just a kid who wanted to see the circus. He should have been going slower and paying more attention, but all the witnesses agree that the victim dashed into his path from between two parked cars. He may not even be charged with anything. I'd better take him to the station and get started on the paperwork."

"Officer!" called Anthony Leach as he came from the direction of his house. "I just arrived home from a last-ditch effort to find an amenable judge, and heard people talking about an accident."

Jorgeson told him what had happened, then said,

"If you'll excuse me, I need to arrange for a van to collect the motorcycle and transport its driver to the station."

"This is outrageous," Leach blustered, blocking Jorgeson's way. "The person who's responsible is that maniac across the street. If you people had done your duty and arrested him for—for destroying the neighborhood, none of this would have happened. Tracy and Joshua Dwain may be more fervent in their religious belief than most of us, but they've always minded their own business. Zeno Gorgias was aware of what he was doing. He might as well have aimed a gun at Tracy and pulled the trigger!"

Jorgeson and I stared as Leach covered his face with his hands and began to cry in a thin wail. I was trying to think how best to oblige Jorgeson to assume responsibility (and he likewise, I'm sure) when Melanie Magruder came across the street. She'd changed into conventional clothing and restrained most of her hair beneath a crocheted cap; she would have merited only a few second glances at a bus station.

"What's his problem?" she demanded.

"He's upset about Tracy," I said diplomatically.

"We're all upset about her," she said, giving Leach a contemptuous look. She shifted it to Jorgeson. "Is she gonna be okay? I heard some folks say there was a lot of blood on the street where she was lying."

"It depends on her condition when she gets to the hospital."

Leach jerked his hands off his face and lunged at Melanie. "Murderess!"

"Pervert!" she shrieked at him.

A certain amount of scuffling and acrimony ensued. Melanie was more than willing to take on Leach, who was staggering as if he were on ice. Jorgeson at last beckoned to a uniformed officer, who pinned Leach's arm behind his back and marched him away. I hung on to Melanie and explained why she should not attempt to relocate a particular part of Leach's anatomy. Jorgeson described the penalties for disorderly conduct, and was launching into assault and battery when he remembered he had more pressing concerns, rolled his eyes at me, and walked away in what I assumed was the direction of his car.

I let go of Melanie's arm. "I suggest you go back to Zeno's and stay out of sight for the next few days. Leach isn't the only person who will blame you and Zeno for Tracy's accident. The popular sentiment's likely to be that her carelessness was caused by your sacrilegious attack on her beliefs."

"You buy into that?"

I thought for a moment. "No, I don't. A philosophical doctrine that can't withstand ridicule is pretty flimsy. The problem is that fanatics are notoriously humorless. I doubt there were any really good jokes bandied about during the Spanish Inquisition." I started to walk away, then stopped and looked back. "How's Zeno taking this?"

"He flipped out. First he said he was going to the hospital, but then he said maybe he'd go over to the hotel where his bitchy wife is staying to tell her some fool thing. The last I saw him, he was sitting in a coffin in the front room, guzzling ouzo and talking to his dead uncle."

"Is anyone else in the house?"

"There could be a whole battalion hiding in there." After a belligerent look in the direction of Leach's house, Melanie crossed the street. She was starting up the brick sidewalk when the broad black Cadillac came around the corner and rolled up the hill with the muted menace of a shark closing in on a flabby swimmer. Melanie's pace increased, and she was inside before the car stopped at the curb and the passenger's door opened.

Ruthanne Gorgias wore shorts and a blouse, but the overall effect was still that of a model preparing to pose on the beach at Cannes. "You, over there!" she called to me. "I'd like to speak to you."

I had no business getting more deeply involved, as Peter Rosen would be the first to point out, but I wondered if she'd had any luck with her scheme to pack Zeno off to be evaluated. Jasmine had mentioned a screaming match earlier in the day; she hadn't elaborated, but it was hard to imagine the topic had concerned which moving service to hire. As I obligingly started toward her, Harry Tillington climbed out of the driver's side and stared at me. He, too, was dressed in shorts, but he was not going to grace the cover of *Vogue* anytime soon.

"Do you live in one of these houses?" he asked as I veered around the hood.

Before I could concoct an explanation for my presence, Ruthanne said, "Harry heard the most dreadful story on the radio about a woman being struck by a motorcycle in front of this house. The announcer implied that it was Zeno's fault."

"He didn't say that," Harry said soothingly, although his chubby face was crinkled with worry. "It wasn't like Zeno was operating the motorcycle."

"That's right," said Zeno as he came down the porch steps. The cape had been discarded, but smudges of black and white makeup remained beneath his eyes and at the edges of his face. Rather than ghoulish, he looked as though he were in the terminal stage of a disease. "I was not operating the motorcycle, but I am responsible for what happened. Had I not created this situation, the woman would not have run into the street. I intentionally goaded her because I relished her unique interaction with my art."

"Don't be absurd," said Ruthanne. "You're not responsible for this accident, and you'd damn well better stop saying you are. If the woman dies, her family could sue us for millions of dollars. I am not going back to an attic apartment and a diet of beans and rice, nor am I going to resume a scintillating career as a clerk in a department store. You have a reputation now, Zeno. We have to protect it." She tugged on Harry's arm with such fervor that I expected it to come free in her hands. "Tell him how much damage will come from a lot of negative publicity."

Harry glanced at me, then pulled her behind the car for a private conversation.

Magnanimously deigning not to have my feelings hurt, I went over to Zeno and said, "Tracy could have ignored all this and stayed inside to pray for a well-aimed bolt of lightning. Fundamentalists believe in free will. She chose to exercise hers, with tragic results."

"It is no use to offer platitudes, Claire. My art is responsible, and I am responsible for my art. I will go to the hospital and tell her this. Furthermore, I will offer her a large sum of money to compensate for the pain I have caused her and her husband. They can use it to build a mission in the jungle." His expression brightened as he considered the scenario. "Then in a sense my art will interact with a culture that relies on aboriginal perceptions of nature and—"

"Zeno," Harry said, inserting himself between us and adroitly nudging me off the sidewalk, "don't get carried away with this. You can offer to cover the woman's medical expenses as a gesture of neighborly goodwill, but that's it. Any further payment will constitute an admission of guilt that she can utilize in a lawsuit. Your work sells for a good price, but you can't afford a multimillion-dollar judgment and a lot of bad publicity. Tomorrow morning we'll just gather up your completed canvases and go to Santa Fe. When

Ruthanne receives the hospital bills, she'll send a check."

"No, I will give her everything I have," Zeno said excitedly, now thoroughly consumed by his newest brainstorm. If he'd been wearing the cape, he might have flapped into the sky. "As penance, I will quit painting and teach art in some dismal junior college, where the students openly aspire to become commercial artists." He pushed Harry out of the way and charged toward Ruthanne, who promptly darted behind the car. "You must divorce me, of course, so you will not be dragged into this degradation. It is only fitting that I suffer alone."

Ruthanne shook her head. "I control the corporate checkbook, Zeno, and I say you're going to stop this idiocy at once and do what you're told. Harry and I will be back in the morning to arrange for your things to be shipped to Santa Fe. And another thing—make sure that slut is gone before we arrive." She got into the Cadillac and slammed the door.

Harry slapped Zeno on the back. "Don't worry about this. Ruthanne and I have it under control. You just get some sleep and start packing in the morning."

"On Monday I will hire a lawyer who will take away from Ruthanne the power of attorney so that I can follow through with my wishes to give everything to the injured woman. The remaining paintings can be sold to endow a scholarship in her name. I haven't decided what I'll do after that, but in any case I'm finished with Ruthanne—and with you, Harry. I won't need an agent anymore."

Harry flinched. "You can't stop painting. You have a show scheduled for next spring in San Francisco. It's going to do some serious damage to your reputation if you back out now."

"I have made my decision," Zeno said with the

teary anguish of a Shakespearian king aware of his imminent demise in Act V.

The car window slid down. Her voice thick with venom, Ruthanne said, "Then I hope you make lots of new friends at the mental institution, because you're going to be there for a long, long time. Get in the car, Harry."

Seconds later the car rolled away from the curb. Zeno made a childish face at the taillights, kissed me on the cheek, and went inside his house.

I was alone on the sidewalk, and it seemed that it was ready to be rolled up for the night. The glare of spotlights had been replaced with the fuzzy glow of streetlights; the only noises were those of indigenous backyard fauna and the incessant tinkle of the wind chimes. If Caron and Inez had been present earlier, they'd had ample opportunity to sneak away during the last hour. Lights were on in Jasmine's apartment, but the blinds were drawn and I saw no silhouetted figure hunkered over a computer. Leach's house was dark. Miss Parchester's porch light was on; the rest of the house was dark.

I drove slowly down Thurber Street, watching for Caron and Inez among the rednecks roving from bar to bar in pursuit of ephemeral pleasures via transitory sexual relationships. I didn't see the girls, to my relief. On weekend nights, Caron is not allowed to set foot on this particular stretch of downtown Sodom without prearranged permission. Resolving not to think about what would happen when she turned sixteen, I pulled into my garage and went upstairs.

In the living room, I hesitated, glancing at the telephone. I wanted to talk to someone about the accident—specifically, Peter. I couldn't categorize Tracy as a martyr, but neither could I dismiss her sincerity or her self-imposed moral imperative to act on her beliefs. Secular humanism had collided with religion; the result had been tragic.

I finally decided I was too tired and confused to deal with the issues. After I'd changed into my bathrobe, I turned on the television in an effort to banish the unpalatable images. I flipped through the channels until I found a dependable old movie, and I was dancing on a rainy Parisian street when the telephone rang.

"Mother," Caron said, her voice precariously close to tears, "you have to come pick us up right now— and bring some clothes."

"Where are you?"

"At the animal shelter."

"And your clothes?" I said rather calmly, considering the essence of the conversation thus far.

"It's long story. Just come get us, okay?"

I had a hunch it was going to be not only long, but also very interesting.

FIVE

I drove across town to the Farberville animal shelter, an unimpressive concrete-block building at the edge of the industrial park. The only vehicle in the parking lot was a small truck with a metal cage on its bed. A cool breeze rustled weeds along the fence, and from the woods behind the building a whippoorwill cried for a companion. An unseen dog barked apathetically. The very serenity of the scene added to the surrealism of the moment.

Carrying the shorts and shirts I'd taken from the floor of Caron's room, I walked across the gravel, took a deep breath, and went inside to find out how my daughter and her best friend had ended up at an animal shelter—without their clothes. I was very low on theories.

A sturdy woman in a khaki uniform stood behind a counter. Eschewing conventional pleasantries, she said, "We're supposed to close at nine o'clock, but I thought I'd better wait for you. The girls are in the office. I'd appreciate it if you got them out of here as quickly as possible."

I would have preferred a few details before I confronted them, but she picked up a key ring and went through the doorway that led to the kennel, where only a few inmates offered a greeting. I remembered the rows of steel mesh cages from a previous visit, when I'd been hailed as a senator by a delusional drunk. This visit had the possibility of being equally bizarre. Determined to be nonjudgmental until I heard their story, I opened the office door.

Two gorillas stood up and turned toward me. "What took you so long?" demanded one of them, the voice so muffled I could scarcely understand it.

The clothing tumbled out of my hands. I'd steeled myself to find them in their underwear—or wrapped in blankets. Nothing in my nearly sixteen years of motherhood had prepared me for this. Dr. Spock had not covered any topics that were remotely relevant, nor had the magazines in the pediatrician's waiting room. Discussions with other mothers had centered on sexism in the nursery schools, the political correctness of cloth diapers, and the exorbitant cost of child care.

The nearer gorilla grabbed her head and grappled with it until it came off to expose a more ordinary countenance. Caron's cheeks were flushed, but she was smirking at me as if I had an extraordinarily foolish expression on my face. "Surprised?" she said.

Inez pulled hers off and smiled more timidly. "Do you need to sit down, Mrs. Malloy? You look a little bit pale."

I may have looked a little bit pale, but I felt as if all the blood had been drained from my body in preparation for embalming. "Would you care to explain?" I said weakly.

"I have to lock up now," said the animal-control officer as she emerged from the kennel. "There's no time for them to change. My husband's here and we want to make the second show."

"So you mentioned several times," Caron said. She scooped up the clothes and walked past me. Inez trailed behind her. They both looked so solemn I felt as though I should hand them diplomas and wish them success in the world of silverbacks. I shrugged at the officer and went out to the car.

"Now will you explain?" I said as we drove away.

Caron slithered down in the seat and snorted. "It's Utterly Ridiculous. Zeno had this really screwy scheme about how we were going to come running outside, pounding on our chests and making grotesque noises.

"He said it would symbolize something or other about the conflict of Darwinism with religious mythology," added Inez.

Caron turned around and glared. "He made no sense whatsoever. Anyway, we went into this squalid back room to get dressed. I wanted to keep my clothes on, but it was too hot inside the suit. It weighs an absolute ton. It's no wonder gorillas are an endangered species. They probably faint and fall out of trees all the time." She made several explosive noises to describe her scenario.

"So you put on the suit," I prompted her.

"And went into the front room to wait for our cue. I was telling Inez it was just as well nobody could recognize us when there was that awful accident out on the street. We decided we didn't want anything more to do with Zeno and his idiotic symbolism, so we went back to change into our clothes. Zeno must have locked the door, because we couldn't get it open. It was getting so crazy out in front that we finally just climbed out the kitchen window and crawled over the fence into Miss Parchester's yard."

Inez sighed. "We were going to call you from her house, but those basset hounds started jumping all over us and slobbering. We went over the fence into the alley, but we were almost run down by some car that didn't have its headlights on. We panicked and—"

"*You* panicked," Caron interrupted contemptuously.

After a moment of deliberation, Inez chose the less confrontational path and resumed her story. "We tried Colonel Culworthy's backyard, but his dog snapped and snarled until we made it to the next yard. Pretty soon we were on Washington Avenue, and—"

"And some stupid man thought we were bears," Caron interrupted again. "Like there's been a bear in Farberville in the last hundred years! He called the animal shelter, and that woman came in a truck and caught us in an alley. She claimed we were frightening people on purpose, and she made us go with her to the shelter. She was going to call the police, but she changed her mind and let me call you."

"Why did she change her mind?" I asked.

"Oh, you know," Caron said as she put on the gorilla head and hung out the window to wave at a car filled with college boys.

I glanced in the rearview mirror in hope Inez might be more forthcoming, but she'd followed Caron's lead and was waving at the same car.

Feeling like a carpooling Dian Fossey, I delivered Inez to her house and drove home. Caron dashed up the steps and was in the shower by the time I reached the kitchen. I was too dazed to call Peter and regale him with the story—which was so ludicrous that I wasn't sure I'd still believe it in the morning.

I'd started for my bedroom when the telephone rang. Although I assumed it was for Caron, I returned to the living room and picked up the receiver.

"I'm so glad I finally caught you," said Miss Parchester. "Papa was always unflagging in his support of certain constitutional rights, but he did have reservations about the contemporary interpretation of the second amendment. He was not positive that the right to keep and bear arms was not strictly limited to the establishment of a well-armed militia. Then again, he did enjoy hunting ducks with his cronies. I don't know what he would have done, but I myself am a little nervous. He has a gun, you see, and he's waving it very recklessly."

I hoped she wasn't referring to Papa. "Who has a gun, Miss Parchester?"

"Joshua Dwain. He's standing in front of Zeno's house and, from what I can understand of his shouts, intends to kill him. I'm sorry to have to say this, but the neighborhood simply hasn't been the same since Zeno moved here. Nick and Nora have been barking for more than an hour. I switched on the back porch light and sat with them for a long while, but the very second I went inside, they started barking again. I've never heard them sound quite so ferocious. I find their behavior very odd."

I was not interested in discussing canine psychology at a time when errant bullets might penetrate her living-room walls. "Miss Parchester, I want you to call the police, and then stay in the kitchen until they arrive."

"I hate to get the poor boy in trouble with the authorities while his wife is in the hospital." She paused, hiccuped, and then said, "I do believe I hear another voice outside. I'd better investigate. I enjoyed our little chat, Claire. Do come by for tea soon."

I stared blankly at the buzzing receiver. Joshua Dwain, with a gun. Another voice. Miss Parchester to the rescue. The one thing Willow Street did not need was more blood on the pavement.

I called Peter and gnawed on my lip until he answered. When I finished relating the gist of Miss Parchester's call, he exhaled unhappily and said, "I'll have him picked up and held until he cools off. Jorgeson said he didn't see Caron and Inez in Zeno's yard. Are they safely at home?"

"Yes, but let me tell you about it tomorrow. Right now I'm afraid Joshua Dwain is going to hurt someone."

Peter promised to arrange for a patrol car and hung up. I dialed Miss Parchester's number and listened to a dozen rings before acknowledging that she had gone outside and not yet returned. I could imagine her weaving up the sidewalk, dressed in a bathrobe and pink slippers, determined to expound on the Judge's opinions regarding the ambiguous wording of the second amendment. Joshua Dwain might be even less overjoyed than I to deal with her. And he had a gun.

I decided to drive to Willow Street, park at the corner, and make sure Joshua had been disarmed and carted away to a nice, quiet holding cell. At the same time, I could make sure Miss Parchester was back home rather than drinking ouzo with Zeno and Uncle Stenopolis.

It was possible that Peter would not approve of this outing. If given half a chance, he might turn officious and order me not to set foot out of my apartment.

I gave him no chance whatsoever.

A police car was parked in front of Zeno's house, its blue light flipping eerily on the metallic skeletons in the yard. The house itself was dark, and worthy of a title role in a B-grade horror flick. Two officers stopped conversing as I came up the street and joined them. Neither looked old enough to be out this late without parental consent, but it was not the moment to mention as much.

"Do you live around here, ma'am?" asked one of them, trying to sound authoritative despite his obvious uneasiness.

"I'm the one who called Lieutenant Rosen to report the presence of a young man waving a gun and shouting threats. Did he leave?"

"We don't know," the second admitted. "This has to be the right house, but there wasn't anybody hang-

ing around when we got here. If there'd been gunfire,
we would have had reports by now."

His colleague took off his hat and ran his hand
across his stubbly hair. "We were just talking about
whether we should ring the doorbell. It looks like everybody in there is asleep. I'd hate to catch hell for
disturbing them over some wacky report of an armed
man."

"My report was in no way wacky," I said stiffly,
refusing to allow myself to question my source. Miss
Parchester had been in her cups when she called, but
her excursions into fantasyland tended to focus on
Papa's estimable career and unerring opinions. She'd
sounded lucid when telling me about Joshua. "The
man with the gun lives over there," I said, pointing at
the Dwains' house. "There are lights on. Why don't
you find out if he's at home?"

"Maybe we ought to call in for further instructions,"
said the stubbly one.

I resisted an urge to shake my finger at them.
"You're not going to win any promotions for standing
here all night. Isn't this covered in your training? Go
knock on the door and politely ask him if he was in
this precise location half an hour earlier, shouting
threats to kill the man who lives here."

"Where were you half an hour earlier, ma'am?"

I hesitated, then said, "I was on the phone with
Lieutenant Peter Rosen. He assured me that he would
send someone to disarm Joshua Dwain before . . ." I
was casting about for a tactful phrase when I realized
there was a vague acridity in the air. Wrinkling my
nose, I tried to identify it. I heard a sinister crackle
behind me, and spun around to gape at Zeno's house.
The downstairs windows had been black when I arrived; now two of them were orange.

"Fire!" gasped the more astute of the officers. He
dived into the car and began gabbling into the radio.

He was less than professionally detached, but he was getting across the pertinent information.

Glass shattered and flames shot out, licking at the ceiling and pillars of the porch. The crackling grew louder and the orange glow intensified as it raced throughout the ground floor. The roof of the porch caught fire, and the flames attacked the eaves on the second floor. Other windows exploded from the interior heat. My face and bare arms tingled.

The officer shouted something at me, but I ignored him and ran to Miss Parchester's front door. I rang the doorbell, rattled the knob, and repeatedly yelled her name until the living-room light came on.

She peered through the pane, then opened the door and gave me an admonishing frown. "I realize I invited you for tea, Claire, but I was thinking about some afternoon next week."

Smoke swirled down on me, stinging my eyes and burning my throat. "A fire!" I said. "It's liable to spread in this direction. You've got to come with me, Miss Parchester!"

She leaned forward and sniffed the air. "Yes, I believe you're right. Just let me put on some proper clothes, then we'll fetch Nick and Nora and be on our way. Did you think to call the fire department, Claire? They do like to be notified when—"

"Are the dogs in the backyard?" I said as I charged past her. When she failed to answer, I went through the kitchen and out to the porch, where the two basset hounds were whimpering. They followed me through the living room and, in their eagerness to cooperate, nearly knocked Miss Parchester out of her fuzzy pink slippers as they galloped out the front door.

"What about their leashes?" she said, reeling in the doorway.

I spotted two leashes on a nearby table, grabbed them, and propelled her outside. The smoke was thicker, the crackles and crashes louder. Sparks drifted by like lazy fireflies. I took Miss Parchester's arm and pulled her toward Leach's redbrick house; we arrived on his porch just as fire trucks squealed around the corner. Nick and Nora scampered behind Miss Parchester and watched the fire from between her legs.

"Oh, my goodness," she said, her hand on her chest. "I warned Mr. Stenopolis that the house was a firetrap. This is such a pity. It really is a fine old house."

"Not for long," I said as I strained to spot Zeno and Melanie among the neighbors gathering on the more prudent side of the street. The scene was more chaotic than the one earlier in the evening. Firefighters shouted at one another as they disengaged hoses and dragged them toward the side yards. More police cars arrived, their blue lights clashing with the red ones of the fire engines. The roar of the fire was louder than any motorcycle. The front porch crashed in a crescendo of sparks.

The door behind us opened, and Anthony Leach stumbled onto the porch. He'd pulled on a bathrobe, but it gaped to expose an expanse of gnarly gray hair and liver spots. "What's that maniac done now? Is this more of his so-called art?"

Miss Parchester clucked at him as if he'd disrupted a lecture. "Zeno is not a maniac, Mr. Leach. He may be somewhat unconventional, but he would never—"

"He's a maniac," Leach countered.

"He is not."

"He's burning down his house."

"That does not mean he's a maniac."

I left them debating Zeno's mental equilibrium and crossed to the yard next door. Nero had fiddled while Rome burned, but Jasmine was merely smoking a cigarette.

"What are you doing here?" she asked me as I approached her. "Don't you have a home of your own?"

"Have you seen Zeno and Melanie?"

"Are they inside?"

I groaned as part of the roof collapsed. "Once the fire started, the ground floor was engulfed in less than a minute. They could have gone out the back door or climbed out a window."

"Maybe," she said without emotion.

The house was now ablaze from the bottom of the basement to the tops of the turrets, but the firefighters seemed to have the fire contained, if not controlled. I watched in horrified silence, unable to convince myself that Zeno and Melanie had escaped and were somewhere nearby. At some point, Miss Parchester abandoned her argument with Leach and joined us. Nick and Nora snuffled behind her, their tails drooping and their expressions as glum as my own.

"And how are you this evening, Jasmine?" Miss Parchester said as if she were about to pull a teapot out of one pocket and lemon cookies out of another. "This is a shame, isn't it?"

Jasmine nudged me and pointed. "There's Zeno talking to the policemen, and Melanie is behind him."

"Is he going to be arrested?" asked Miss Parchester. "Perhaps I ought to have a word with the police officers. They might be as inclined as Mr. Leach to assume that Zeno is unbalanced. I'm sure that if he started the fire, he did so unintentionally."

I caught her arm before she could toddle away, and said to Jasmine, "I think Miss Parchester could use a cup of tea. Could you ... ?"

Jasmine escorted Miss Parchester and her basset hounds up the stairs to her apartment. Once it was clear that the fire would not spread, I walked back to my car and drove home, having done more than my share of good deeds for the day. I might have been caught up for the entire month, I decided as I fell into bed, too exhausted to do the necessary computations.

Peter arrived on the doorstep the following morning, armed with warm doughnuts and a fat Sunday newspaper. I supplied him with coffee, then curled up next to him on the sofa and said, "I presume you heard about the fire?"

"Yes, I heard about the fire," he said, gazing blandly at me. "I was somewhat bemused when I read the preliminary report. The officers at the scene said that they were harangued by an unidentified woman who claimed to have spoken with me on the telephone. Before they could ascertain her identity, she fled."

"I did not flee. I was worried about Miss Parchester, so I hurried to her house to persuade her to move to a safer site until the fire was under control."

"Which leads us to the issue of why you were there in the first place. Do you truly feel competent to disarm a hysterical man purportedly waving a gun? Do you have some training in martial arts that you've thus far failed to mention, or were you going to rely on your beguiling smile and powers of rhetoric?"

A momentary distraction was in order. "Speaking of last night, let me tell you what happened to Caron and Inez," I said. I related the story between muted eruptions of giggles that I hoped would not be overheard down the hallway. Caron does not respond well to aspersions on her estimation of her own dignity, which in her mind compares favorably with that of Queen Victoria. "At least they weren't charged with anything," I concluded. "They said the animal-control officer changed her mind for some reason."

"She probably didn't want to mess with the paperwork." He took out the sports section and sat back like an old married man. "Any more coffee?"

I'd deftly steered the conversation away from the less amusing events of the previous evening, but now it seemed as if he'd dismissed them entirely. I tried to conceal my frustration as I went to the kitchen and refilled his cup. "Was Joshua Dwain charged with anything?" I asked as I returned.

"This morning he admitted he'd gone to Zeno's house and shouted some nasty threats, but he claimed he didn't have a gun. His wife lost a dangerous amount of blood before they could get her to the hospital, and she's in critical condition. She's still unconscious, possibly in a coma. Dwain was so upset about it that the police officer let him go with a warning."

"I can hardly blame him," I said as I imagined the small cubicle in intensive care and the pale, motionless figure lost beneath tubes and needles. "Joshua didn't strike me as an overly emotional sort, but those are the ones with a surprising amount of latent anger and potential for violence. Something like this could have stripped away his facade." When Peter failed to lower the newspaper, I flicked it with my finger and said, "Is it possible that he crept into the house and started the fire?"

The pages rustled. "The arson investigators are there now. By the way, the uniformed men have orders to arrest you on sight, so I heartily recommend you stay away until the investigation is completed. We have a separate facility for juveniles, but we throw meddlers right in the tank with prostitutes and drug dealers."

"All I did was ask a simple question."

The pages rustled more loudly. "It looks as though the college will have a good football team this season. They've got a linebacker—"

"I'm sure they have lots of linebackers."

"He's nearly three hundred fifty pounds and—"

"That's gross," Caron announced as she walked through the room and into the kitchen. The refrigerator door opened. "Everything in here is either green or blue. I may vomit."

I was about to suggest she do so in proximity to the commode when Peter's beeper chirped. He arched his eyebrows at me until I stalked into the kitchen, hissed at Caron to be quiet, and then positioned myself next to the doorway to eavesdrop. What was said at the other end of the telephone could have been illuminating, but Peter's responses, mostly mutters and terse questions, were unsatisfactory.

As soon as he hung up, I came back into the room. "Shall I make another pot of coffee so we can have a leisurely conversation about linebackers?"

"I have to go." He tucked the beeper in his pocket and gave me a perfunctory kiss on the cheek. "I'll be tied up all day, but maybe we can rent a movie tonight. Have you seen *Gorillas in the Mist*?"

"I heard that!" Caron howled from the kitchen.

After he was gone, I called Miss Parchester, motivated not out of curiosity but by a purely charitable desire to assure myself that she was home. She was not. Jasmine Hadley was not listed in the directory, and I had a feeling Anthony Leach would not appreciate—much less share—my concern for Miss Parchester.

I was speculating about the significance of Peter's "Who?" and "Any ID?" when Caron came in and grabbed a doughnut.

"Someone has to drive Inez and me to Zeno's house so we can give back the gorilla suits," she said between bites. "Maybe it had better be one of Inez's parents. I'd hate to have to fend for myself while you hang out with prostitutes and drug dealers."

"Peter was making a minuscule and unamusing joke," I said coolly and then told her about the fire. "Zeno has more serious problems than gaps in his wardrobe. I may drop by to visit Miss Parchester later today. If he's around, I'll ask him what he wants you to do with the gorilla suit. In the meantime, just hang it in the closet."

She took the last doughnut and started for her bedroom. "Well, at least there won't be any more silly shows on Willow Street. Zeno went out with a bang, didn't he?"

"He certainly did," I said to the empty room. The neighborhood would resume its amiable ambiance, with only the charred remains of Zeno's house to remind them of the ordeal. It was a prime location; Zeno would have no difficulty selling the lot once it was cleaned up. Miss Parchester's zinnias would flourish. Anthony Leach would sell his house. Jasmine Hadley would resume writing her mysterious mysteries. If all went well, Joshua Dwain would graduate and take his wife away to some remote jungle mission, with or without Zeno's beneficence to keep them supplied with malaria tablets and religious pamphlets. It was impossible to predict what Zeno would do.

And it was impossible to sit on the sofa, speculating about the fire and Peter's phone call. I told Caron that I was going to the store to work on orders, but by the time I reached the car, I had a much dandier idea.

The Farberville hospital parking lot would be crowded later in the day, when visitors recently released from church arrived with flowers and balloons. At the moment, the pious were nodding in their pews and the only flowers and balloons were locked inside the dimly lit gift shop.

A woman in a gray smock found Tracy's name on a computer screen and told me that the patient was in the intensive care unit. Although I doubted I would be allowed to visit her, I might find Joshua in the waiting room and be allowed to convey my sympathy and hopes for a happy conclusion. I was about to push the elevator button, when I saw a figure lurking behind a plastic rubber tree. My finger poised in midair, I stared until I recognized Ruthanne's chauffeur.

Harry emerged and gave me a sheepish smile. "I was just on my way to the cafeteria to get some coffee."

"Are you here to visit Tracy Dwain?"

"Not exactly."

I studied his badly wrinkled clothes, unshaven cheeks, and red-rimmed eyes. "You look as if you've been here all night, Harry."

"I have," he admitted. "Ruthanne's afraid that Zeno will show up. He may be overwhelmed with remorse now, but he isn't legally responsible for the accident. He'll come to realize that after he's had a few days to calm down. In the interim, I'm playing guard dog. Right after we left last night, I dropped Ruthanne off at the hotel and came here." He glanced at his watch. "I guess I'd better call her and find out what she wants me to do. She was going to try to set up an appointment with that attorney this afternoon to pursue this competency thing."

"Do you approve?"

He considered my question with an increasingly gloomy expression. "I don't know," he said at last. "Maybe Zeno needs a kick in the ass to get him back on track. Ruthanne's tried everything short of chaining him to an easel, and I've spent more time in Houston trying to cajole him into working than I have tending to business in Santa Fe. She and I kept telling each other his latest obsession wouldn't last, but now I just don't know. Artists, like Saint Bernard puppies, should not be loosed on society without a degree from obedience school and a muzzle." He took a handful of change from his pocket. "If you'll excuse me, I'd better call her."

I suggested that he sit down, then told him about the fire. He looked at the stains on the carpet for so long that I was glad we were within seconds of medical assistance. I was about to offer to bring him a glass of water, when he said, "Zeno probably decided to burn down the house to spite Ruthanne."

"To spite Ruthanne?" I said, surprised. "This makes it easier for her to coerce him into moving to Santa Fe. If the fire was set intentionally, she has a better motive than he does."

"There were six canvases in the house. Zeno's become very popular in Europe. His last sale was for a hundred thousand dollars."

"A hundred thousand dollars?" I sat down next to Harry, wishing someone would offer me a glass of water—or something stronger. "I'd heard he was well known, but . . ."

"Those canvases would have brought more than half a million dollars. I don't know how much they were insured for, but it may be only a fraction of that. Insurance companies are weak on aesthetics."

He looked so depressed that I wanted to pat him on the head. I didn't know if he was thinking of the lost art or the lost commission, but it seemed inappropriate to offer condolences in either case.

"I'm going to try to visit Tracy," I told him as I stood up. "I was told this morning that she's in critical condition."

"Oh, hell," Harry said, slumping further into the upholstery. "If she doesn't make it, Zeno will be even more determined to give her husband every last penny. I'm going to be stuck here until he's taken away in a straitjacket. I'd better call Ruthanne right now and let her know all this. Could you possibly wait here until I get back?"

"Sorry, Harry, but this is between Zeno and Ruthanne. I'm not going to stop anyone from doing anything."

He struggled to his feet, gave me a disappointed

look, and went around a corner. Congratulating myself on my sanctimonious position, I punched the elevator button.

When the doors slid open, I found myself facing Miss Emily Parchester.

"How nice to see you," she said, taking my arm and heading into the lobby as if we were on a sylvan path. "Did I mention last night that I thought I saw bears in my backyard? Nick and Nora were barking, and I—"

"Wait a minute," I said as I gently disengaged my arm. "I'm not ready to go just yet. I want to see how Tracy is doing."

"She's not allowed any visitors except for her husband. I gave him a jar of peach compote, and he promised to save it for her." Miss Parchester's eyes clouded with pity. "She's in a coma, you know. Joshua overheard one of the paramedics say that they might have been able to stabilize her if they'd arrived sooner, and this made him very angry. He tried to convince me he didn't have a gun last night, but I know what I saw."

I fell into step with her, and we were almost out the door when she said, "I do hope Joshua will not be charged with murder at a time when his wife needs him so very much."

"Murder?" I said, nearly bumping my nose on the glass door as I tripped on the rubber mat.

"As I was leaving this morning, I saw a body being removed from the wreckage of the house, and I heard one of the police officers say they'd discovered it in a coffin. I found that very curious."

So did I.

SIX

As I drove to the Book Depot, I mentally ran through the list of everybody's whereabouts. In that no one appeared to be missing, I had no candidates for the corpse in the coffin. Someone in the crowd could have slipped inside the house, courtesy of an open window in the kitchen. Tracy's accident had taken place shortly after seven o'clock, so the trespasser would have had to remain undetected in the three-hour interval before the fire forced Zeno and Melanie to evacuate. This was not inconceivable. If a battalion could hide in there, so could one wily burglar with designs on half a million dollars' worth of art (or Caron Malloy's insanely expensive athletic shoes).

Jorgeson's car was parked next to the Book Depot, and he was standing by the back door, a sooty handkerchief in his hand. Streaks across his forehead gave him the look of a disgruntled bulldog. His jacket and trousers were flecked with ashes, and his shoes were caked with black gunk. It was not challenging for someone with my deductive prowess to surmise where he'd spent his morning.

I pulled in beside him. "I'm closed today, but business has been so poor that I'll sell you a book anyway. How about a cozy mystery with a bumbling British chief inspector, a shrewd amateur sleuth, and a couple of cats?''

Jorgeson put away the handkerchief. "I need you to come to the station and make a formal statement. Your daughter said you'd be here.''

"She's a loquacious child," I said as I thought about the implications of his presence. Arson was the realm of the fire department's investigative team; murder belonged to the CID. "Whose body was discovered this morning, Jorgeson, and was it really in a coffin?''

"Lieutenant Rosen told me not to discuss any of this with you, Ms. Malloy. He was very definite about it. Why don't you take your car to the station so I won't have to bring you back when you're finished?''

I cut off the engine and made sure he was watching as I dropped the car keys in my purse. "I don't believe I'd better do that until I consult a lawyer. It's been intimated that Anthony Leach has office hours on Sunday. Perhaps I'll give him a call and find out when he can accompany me. If he's booked for today, we can come tomorrow.''

"I am not going to give you any unauthorized information. Your statement's not a high priority. I was just trying to tie up a few loose ends while we wait for a report from the medical examiner. If you want to come tomorrow, give your statement to Sergeant Lydia King." He gave me a small smile. "She's been warned about you, too.''

"This will be on the local news in a matter of hours," I said, politely disregarding his final remark. "Arson and murder make a good story, particularly on a slow weekend. I can wait until five o'clock to learn the details, if Lieutenant Rosen so desires.''

"Whatever," he said as he headed for his car.

"Have you identified the body?''

"Are you coming to the station now?''

Lieutenant Rosen had trained his minion well in the

dainty art of negotiation. "Yes, Jorgeson," I said. I retrieved my keys and jangled them.

"An hour ago Zeno Gorgias identified his wife's body. The cause of death has not yet been formally declared, but she had a head wound."

It occurred to me that Harry wasn't going to have any success in his efforts to call Ruthanne at the hotel. Ironically, she was in the same building as he was— but in the basement rather than the lobby. "What was she doing at Zeno's house?" I asked.

"That is a question Lieutenant Rosen is asking Mr. Gorgias at this moment." Jorgeson got in his car and drove away, apparently confident I would follow him with the doggedness of a private eye.

I did, of course, but operating on automatic pilot as I recalled the conversation on the sidewalk after the disastrous son et lumière. Ruthanne's parting shot had been a vow to carry through with the competency hearing. Had she returned to plead with him one last time—or to burn down the house? It made less sense than Caron's telephone call from the animal shelter, I concluded as I parked in front of the police station and went inside.

Two hours later I emerged, slightly nauseous from the oily coffee and poor ventilation in the interview room. Jorgeson had withstood my cleverly couched questions and obliged me to repeat every conversation I'd had with any and all of the Willow Street residents, Caron and Inez, Ruthanne, and Harry. Jorgeson had pretended to be unimpressed when I produced Harry's current whereabouts, but he'd halted the interview and left the room for a minute.

Fragments of the conversations ricocheted in my mind like bullets from a drive-by shooting. I had more questions than I'd had before the interview. The most intriguing one was: Who had joined Joshua Dwain on the sidewalk half an hour before the fire? Miss Parchester had heard a voice and gone to investigate, but I'd failed to ask her later whom she'd seen. This was an oversight that could be resolved by dint of a telephone call, since I wasn't inclined to find out whether Peter was bluffing. In the past, he'd gone so far as to have my car impounded simply because I had made a small, unsanctioned visit to a crime scene. Peter's disapproval didn't worry me so much as the idea of finding myself among those who'd recently—or repeatedly—been fingerprinted.

I would call Miss Parchester from the bookstore. If she wasn't home, I'd dutifully devote the rest of the afternoon to activities that might lead to something other than a shudder from my accountant. I was starting the car when I heard my name called.

Melanie Magruder came down the sidewalk, flashed white teeth at me, and climbed into the passenger's side. Her clothes were filthy, her shoes as gunky as Jorgeson's. The only part of her relatively clean was her face. Without makeup, she looked only a few years older than Caron.

"Thanks for the ride," she said. "They offered me one, but I told them I'd been surrounded by uniforms too long already. The only other time I've seen so many grim faces was at my grandmother's trial. She caught her boyfriend with his pants around his ankles, and he was nowhere near the outhouse."

"Where would you like me to take you?" I asked.

"Now that's a problem," she said as her head fell back against the seat. The blond hair enveloped her face; all I could see was the tip of her nose and an occasional flutter of her eyelashes. "Last night we borrowed sleeping bags from some students and slept in Miss Parchester's garage. That's okay for one night, but I don't want to make a habit of it and end up needing weekly visits to a chiropractor. Then again, all I have are the clothes I'm wearing, since I didn't

stop to pack my bag and find my purse on the way
out the window. I don't have a nickel to my name."

"Maybe your family can help," I said as I drove
toward Thurber Street. "You can call them from the
bookstore if you want."

"They're dirt poor and proud of it. No, I'll think of
something before too long. I just hope I don't starve
to death waiting for Zeno to get back from the police
station. They wouldn't tell me anything, or even let
me speak to him before I left. They are not friendly
folks, the Farberville police."

"Let me buy you some lunch. Then I'll take you to
Willow Street to wait for Zeno. I'm sure his agent will
lend him some money until he can get to the bank in
the morning."

We went to a nearby restaurant. The brunch crowd
had departed, and we were able to sit in a booth away
from the few remaining diners. I was still queasy from
the session in the interview room, but Melanie clearly
was not and ordered enough for both of us.

"Why did Ruthanne return last night?" I asked her
as she tore into a packet of crackers.

"That's what the cops kept wanting to know. The
thing is, Zeno and I had an argument, and I went
upstairs and locked myself in one of the bedrooms.
When I left him, he was into a second bottle of ouzo.
The next thing I know, I'm smelling smoke and the
floor is real warm. I climbed out on the roof over the
back porch and jumped down. A broken leg seemed
a lot better than being roasted like a chicken."

"How did Zeno get out of the house?"

"He said he tried to go through the storage room,
but the door was stuck. He finally climbed out a window in the kitchen. I grabbed him and steered him
away from the house. He didn't make much sense at
first, but watching his house burn to the ground had
a sobering effect."

"And what about Ruthanne?"

Melanie opened another packet of crackers and began to crumble them. "He didn't know she was in the house. Otherwise, he would have made some dumbass attempt to rescue her so he could get his picture on the front page. He's into that."

I was about to point out a wee inconsistency when the waiter arrived with a laden tray. I waited until he was out of earshot and then said, "How could he not know she was there? He had to have let her inside."

"Honey, he was so drunk he didn't hear that crazy boy screaming out in the front yard." She paused to wipe a trickle of grease off her chin. "He said he went to this little room where his uncle used to play records, and went to sleep."

"It's a good thing he woke up and managed to escape," I said, watching her carefully as she finished the hamburger, licked her fingers, and started in on the first of two pieces of pie. "You obviously heard Joshua Dwain. Did you go downstairs?"

"No."

She'd spoken too quickly to be convincing, but I let it go for the moment and tried a new tack. "What do you think caused Zeno to wake up?"

"Same thing as me."

"The smoke?"

Melanie glanced briefly at me. "Yeah."

I persisted with a few more questions, but she became reticent and finally rebellious—despite my munificence in matters of lunch. As we left, I told her I wanted to stop at the bookstore to make a call before I took her to Willow Street and found myself in handcuffs. When we arrived, I asked her to wait in the front and went into the office to call Miss Parchester and find out if the coast was clear.

If she'd gone home from the hospital, she'd left once again on another mission. I decided I could deposit Melanie at the library should the CID still be in the midst of taking photographs and sifting soot. After a brief detour to powder my nose, I returned to the front room.

Melanie was gone. As was, I ascertained from an inspired search, the money in the cash register. I rushed outside and stopped under the portico to look both ways. Although she had only a few minutes' head start, she'd vanished down one of the side streets. I was feeling less than munificent as I tried to figure out how much she'd stolen. The sum was more than I usually kept over the weekend because I'd failed to go by the bank Friday afternoon. It wasn't much— perhaps a hundred dollars—but it was more than enough to buy a bus ticket. To where, I did not know.

Jorgeson's boss might not be amused when he learned that I'd grilled a suspect over lunch and then afforded her the means to leave town. However, he would be even less amused if I didn't let him know, so I dutifully reached for the telephone.

I'd predicted Peter's reaction with uncanny accuracy. I listened to his sputters for a long while, then said, "She was broke and hungry, for pity's sake."

"She's no longer broke and hungry, is she? Now she's merely missing, thanks to the generosity of Ms. Malloy," he retorted with unnecessary coldness. "She was in the house at the time the fire broke out. We had hoped to discuss it further with her."

"Before or after you charge Zeno with murder?"

This innocent question set off yet another tirade. I tried several times to interrupt him, but he was not cooperative and I finally replaced the receiver. I was in no way meddling. Surely it was reasonable of me to be concerned with Miss Parchester's continued safety in a neighborhood fraught with arson, murder, and bears.

I was also deeply annoyed by Melanie's duplicity—

and determined to retrieve my money. I locked the
store and drove to the bus station in the south part
of town. It was even less imposing than the animal
shelter; the landscaping consisted of litter plastered
along the edge of the squat building and a runty tree
with half a dozen withered leaves. There were no
buses in the parking lot, but the lingering redolence
of fumes suggested one had recently departed, with or
without Melanie Magruder.

Inside, the plastic benches were dotted with flies
and yellow jackets feasting on sticky soda spills. Behind a glass window, a man with a gaunt face, a mail-
order toupee, and stooped shoulders was bent over a
magazine. The cover suggested that the interior consisted primarily of photographs of unclad female flesh
accompanied by monosyllabic captions.

He gave me an unfriendly look as I came across the
room. "No more buses today," he said waspishly.
"And no loitering, either."

"I can assure you that I am not going to loiter. I'm
trying to find a young woman with cropped blond hair
who might have appeared within the last half hour.
Have you seen her?"

"If I tried to remember everybody who came
through here on the way to nowhere, I'd be too busy
to sell tickets. Like I said, no loitering." He looked
down at the magazine and made a sucking noise that
was particularly offensive.

On the wall behind him was a board with information concerning the comings and goings of buses. One
destined for Chicago supposedly had departed only
fifteen minutes earlier. If Melanie had hitched a ride
shortly after pilfering the cash register, she might have
been able to buy a ticket at the last second and catch
the bus. I frowned at the clerk, wondering if I could
bring myself to choke it out of him. His neck was
likely to be as dirty as his mind.

I was still debating when I noticed a car pulling in beside mine. It had a telltale blue bubble on its roof, as well as a painted badge on the door and an antenna that might have allowed communication with another galaxy. I was doing nothing illegal, mind you. The bus station was a public place, and I was a member of the public, entitled to inquire about buses.

However, Peter was on a rampage, and discretion seemed in order. I ducked into the ladies' room, by far the dirtiest one I'd ever been in. The smell was pungent enough to be sliced and diced. The graffiti scratched and scrawled on the partition of the single stall was primitive and sadly unimaginative. Hoping I was not in danger of an infection (or an infestation), I pressed my ear against the door and tried to hear what was being said at the counter.

The clerk was a good deal more effusive than he'd been a minute earlier. "Nobody got on the bus to Chicago," he said loudly. "Nobody got off, either. The driver came in, signed the log, took a piss, bought a candy bar from the machine over there, and pulled out on schedule. The next bus leaves at four in the morning for Shreveport. If this woman shows up, I'll call the police station and let you fellows know."

"Shit," hissed a voice behind me.

Clutching the stained rim of the sink, I turned around. No one had materialized, nor were feet visible under the door of the stall. This did not mean I was in the throes of an auditory hallucination, however. I myself had taken refuge in an airport ladies' room in the past, and I knew the procedure. I also knew the identity of the hisser.

"You can't stand on the commode forever, Melanie," I said softly. "You might as well come out of there before you soak your shoe in what's apt to be worse than factory sludge."

"It sure isn't anything I'd drink, no matter how long I was lost in a desert. Are the police still out there?"

I eased open the door, then closed it and said, "No, they've gone. Come out or I'll go tell the clerk that he's harboring more than vermin and viruses in here. He might carry through with his promise to call the station."

"The jackass better not," she said as she emerged, as blasé as a wealthy matron in a Saks Fifth Avenue fitting room. "He and I made a deal. So, what're you doing here? Going sightseeing in Shreveport?"

"What makes you so sure that I won't call the police? After all, you stole money from me."

Her eyebrows shot up like a McDonald's logo. "You think I stole money from you when you were kind enough to buy me lunch? I feel awful that you thought for one minute that I'd do something like that. I may have borrowed a few dollars, but I am planning to pay you back at my very first opportunity."

I held out my hand. "Opportunity knocks, Melanie."

She turned to study her reflection in the cracked mirror. "My hair is so bad it's a wonder those college boys gave me a ride down here. You got a comb in your purse?"

"Yes, and I also have a dime, which is what I need to make a call at the pay phone outside this door."

Before I could make good on my threat, Melanie flung herself across the door and spread her arms. "You don't want to call anybody. I can't give you back the money, but if you'll drive me over to Willow Street, I'll get it from Zeno. It's real important that I talk to him before the police ask me any more questions."

"Talk to him about what?"

"About what happened to Ruthanne. He's a good man, a little weird at times, but lacking a mean bone in his body. I don't think he'd kill that bitch and burn down his own house, but I need to make sure before the police get hold of me for more questioning. There's something I didn't tell them earlier. They're gonna find out, though, and keep me locked up until Zeno's trial. Y'all have the death penalty in this state, don't you?"

For the first time, she sounded more like a frightened teenager than an actress who was contemptuous of her audience. I held up a finger and said, "Let's do this in order. Why can't you return the money you took from the cash register? You haven't had time to do anything with it, except maybe buy a candy bar."

"I bought a ticket to Shreveport."

"How much was that?" I said sternly.

"Fifty-nine dollars."

"And the rest of it?"

She jabbed her thumb at the door. "Like I said, the jackass and I have a deal. It didn't come cheap, and I had to let him peek at my tits just so I could keep ten dollars for food. I could have kept more, but I wasn't about to let him touch me."

I'd been slightly nauseous earlier; now I had to close my eyes and will my stomach to stop lurching. "Okay," I said when I felt calmer, "I expect to be repaid. What is it that you didn't tell the police?"

"I have to talk to Zeno first. If you'll help me find him, you can get your money immediately. Once the police get hold of me, there won't be any way I can repay you for a real long time. I'm serious when I say they'll keep me in custody as a material witness."

I weighed my alternatives. The more civic-minded one was to deliver Melanie Magruder into the viscous fingers of the Farberville police. Peter would not congratulate me, but he might stop sputtering in the foreseeable future. Then again, a bona fide bounty hunter might be able to collect a hundred dollars, but I lacked credentials. And Caron would realize before too long that her new shoes were black globs of rubber.

I decided to take the middle road. "Okay, Melanie," I said, "first I'll try to retrieve my money from that man out there. If I don't have any luck, I'll drive you to Willow Street. If Zeno's there, you can talk to him about whatever is bothering you—and make arrangements for him to repay me. Then I am going to take you to the police station so that you can turn yourself in and tell the police whatever it was that you omitted earlier."

"I don't know about that . . ."

"You don't have much of a choice. I can call the police right now and do my best to prevent you from leaving until they arrive, or you can agree to what I've proposed. I cannot allow you to take off again; I'm too enamored of my freedom."

"All right," she said, sighing.

I trusted her about as far as I could carry her on my back, but I led the way into the waiting room. The prince of porno pretended not to notice me as I walked to his cage and said, "This woman needs a refund for the ticket she bought a few minutes ago."

"Can't do it." His nose still planted between the pages, he took a pad from a drawer and shoved it at me. "She can fill out a form and send it and the ticket to the main office in Dallas. They'll mail a check in six to eight weeks."

"She'd also like you to return the money she gave you. The police will not be pleased to learn that you accepted a bribe and lied to them."

"All she gave me was fifty-nine dollars for a ticket to Shreveport. If she says differently, she's lying to you." He closed the magazine and glanced at Melanie, who was sidling toward the door. "Yeah, I forgot she was in the restroom. I reckon I'd better call the police station and tell them to come back and arrest her."

Leering, he went through a doorway behind him and slammed the door.

I doubted he would call the police, but I decided not to pursue my demand that he return the bribe—if indeed he'd received it. I was not an accomplished liar, but Melanie had proven herself to be a professional with an innate talent far exceeding that of Caron Malloy. And, to be candid, I was curious to find out what she'd failed to say in her statement that she thought would incriminate Zeno. For Miss Parchester's sake, of course.

Melanie was waiting in the car. Once we were headed for Willow Street, she said, "Do you think they're gonna charge Zeno with murder?"

"Yes," I said bluntly. "The police tend to adopt the most obvious scenario. Ruthanne came to the house and needled Zeno until he lost his temper. He bashed her on the head, then started the fire either by accident or to destroy the evidence. He may be able to plead temporary insanity or diminished responsibility, but he'll be inconvenienced in any case. No more son et lumière shows for you, no more paintings for Harry to sell to art connoisseurs."

Melanie grumbled but said nothing. I turned the corner onto Willow Street and saw with relief that there were no police cars parked along the curb. Out of caution, I parked in front of Miss Parchester's house. "I don't see Zeno," I said as I opened the car door. "He may still be at the police station."

Everything had a patina of fragile gray ashes, except for the bright yellow tape the police had tied between metal rods to deter souvenir hunters and amateur archaeologists. Zeno's house was an unlovely heap of charred wood, blackened appliances, sodden rubble, and metal frames from which tatters of fabric hung like Spanish moss. The cross had been toppled; it was now an asymmetrical X marking an unknown spot. The stage was nothing more offensive than the remains of a campfire. The surviving wind chimes tinkled an uneasy dirge.

"Maybe Zeno's around back," said Melanie. "There were some boxes of old clothes in the storage room, and he may be trying to salvage them."

"He may be homeless at the moment, but he's not destitute," I said as I followed her through the side yard, not quite on her heels but well within reach of her shirt collar. "He certainly doesn't have to root through this to find a pair of socks. If he's not at the police station, he may be at the mall with Harry, buying whatever he needs. Or at a real-estate agent's office, buying Anthony Leach's house."

She stopped so abruptly I ran into her. "Where's he gonna get money to buy a house? He spent his last couple of hundred dollars on wind chimes, paint, and spotlights."

"He's a rich man, Melanie."

"Zeno?" She put her hands on her hips and laughed. "I had to pay for the ouzo because he was flat broke."

"Harry Tillington told me that Zeno's paintings sell for a hundred thousand dollars."

"Don't give me that shit! I don't know anything about art, but I know when I'm looking at smudges and spatters. My little niece paints better pictures than those, and she's in third grade. At least her trees have trunks and her cows have four legs."

"That's what Harry said this morning."

She sagged against the fence, her fingers digging into the honeysuckle vines. In a hoarse voice, she said, "A hundred thousand dollars? Are you telling me that those paintings in the storage room were worth that kind of money? They were just stacked in a corner— stacked like kindling, I guess. Zeno told me I could have one if I wanted, but I told him I didn't. Sweet

Jesus, I could be buying myself a BMW and a bottle of wine with a cork."

"It doesn't matter now," I said. "Let's find out if Zeno's here and then go on to the police station."

The backyard was muddy and cluttered with debris. The roof had crashed atop what had been the back porch, and whatever had been in the rear of the house was now under many feet of shingles, rafters, and sections of walls and floors.

Melanie sighed plaintively as she kicked a piece of glass. "The back door was right there, and it led into the storage room. There were all kinds of cans of kerosene and gasoline, as well as paint. I heard them exploding when I jumped off the roof."

"Was the door usually locked?"

"You've met Zeno. Does he seem like the kind of person who'd go around locking doors? As far as I know, he doesn't have a key for any of the doors."

I recalled Caron's story. "But one was locked last night. My daughter and her friend changed into the gorilla suits in one room, but when they tried to retrieve their clothes, they couldn't open the door. You told me that Zeno had to crawl out the kitchen window."

Melanie's eyes narrowed as she considered what I'd said. "There was a bolt on the inside of the storeroom. It was so rusty that it's hard to believe it could be moved, but maybe it was. But who'd bother with it? If Zeno did it, he'd have had to go all the way around the house to come inside. Locking it wouldn't keep someone from waltzing in from the backyard. Maybe the door was just jammed." She shook herself as if she'd been splashed and then added, "I'm going to poke my head in Miss Parchester's garage to make sure Zeno's not there. I'll be right back."

Before I could make a grab for her, she climbed over the fence with admirable agility and dropped behind the honeysuckle. I caught sight of bobbling blond hair as she trotted across the yard. In a matter of seconds, she'd gone past the garage and disappeared around the corner of the house.

I went to the fence as Nick and Nora waddled out of the forsythias by the gate. Both of them had steak bones in their mouths and mildly guilty expressions. "Nice work," I told them tartly. "Is this the way you fend off bears, too?"

They thumped their tails enthusiastically, no doubt thinking in their poorly constructed canine brains that I, like Miss Parchester, would reward their lack of vigilance with T-bones and syrupy praise. They'd have better luck awaiting aliens from Jupiter.

Which would not be a bad place to be when Peter found out I'd let Melanie escape a second time.

SEVEN

More than mildly irritated at myself for not reacting more quickly, I went to the sidewalk in front of the house and looked around for Melanie. Every yard offered hiding places galore behind shrubbery, trees, and high porches. Cars were parked along the street and in driveways. I knew of at least one alley; there were likely to be others. It was a wonderful arena for a game of hide-and-seek, but I wasn't willing to play. Melanie thus far had conned me out of a free lunch, a hundred dollars, and a ride to Willow Street—which meant the score was zip to three. I'd have more success playing chess with a melancholy man named Vladimir.

I went to Miss Parchester's house and determined that she had not returned. I wasn't especially worried that she'd absconded to the foggy, boggy moors, never to be seen again. She was too devoted to Nick and Nora to disappoint them at dinnertime. Filet mignon was likely to be on the evening's menu.

As I left her porch, I saw Anthony Leach come out of his house. His white linen suit was significantly more stylish than the bathrobe of the previous night, and his white hair was deftly combed into a pompadour. He paused at the edge of the porch to speak to his yardman, who was in the act of flagrantly violating a commandment by pruning a bush on the sabbath. Leach then continued to the sidewalk and stood with his arms crossed, openly gloating at the rubble.

"Mrs. Malloy!" he called genially. "How are you today?"

His question was perfunctory, but I crossed the street and said, "I'm still spinning from all the excitement last night, and I've heard there was more this morning. Were you at home when the body was discovered?"

"Yes, there were a great many policemen over there earlier this morning. They left only a few minutes ago. I could see very little from my living-room window, and there's been nothing on the radio. Do you know the identity of the victim?"

"Zeno's wife, Ruthanne."

"I knew that man was a menace! I warned her of that when I first spoke to her on the telephone."

"You called her in Houston, didn't you?" I asked, scanning my memory for the pertinent conversation. "How did you locate her?"

He licked his fingertip and smoothed his mustache with the practiced gesture of a riverboat gambler. "It took only a bit of research, Mrs. Malloy. We in the legal profession are accustomed to tracking down sources. In that Zeno Gorgias is a well-known painter, he is listed in certain reference material at the library. The most current entry noted that he resided in Houston, and it took only a single inquiry to ascertain his telephone number. Mrs. Gorgias was most gratified when I called to let her know what was happening here on our quiet little street, and she promised to come immediately." He did his best to assume a mournful expression, but his lips were twitching so ardently the mustache was in danger of flying off. "Had I but known this would end in tragedy, I'd never have suggested she come to Farberville."

I believed that as much as I believed he would never evict a widow from a two-room shack to collect a legal fee. "At least Zeno won't have to worry about the class-action suit, will he? It's all immaterial now that he no longer has a stage."

"Oh, he'll have other things to worry about," said Leach, lapsing back into complacency. "I'm on my way to the hospital to confer with Joshua Dwain. It can be argued that Zeno created a public disturbance that ultimately led to the accident. I'm going to take the case on a contingency fee simply to make sure Zeno can never afford to rebuild that house and resume his blasphemous displays—if he's not found guilty of murder and sent away for thirty years, that is."

"All I said was that Ruthanne's body was found, Mr. Leach. Why do you assume she was murdered?"

"Is that a leading question, Mrs. Malloy? The facts of the case strongly suggest murder. Yesterday Ruthanne Gorgias made threats that angered her husband, and this morning she was found dead inside his house." His finger again drifted to his mustache as he gazed pensively over my shoulder. "Of course, the girl might have done it. She was living in his house, taking his money, and concerned that she might find herself out on the street. Her motive isn't as strong, but she may be as vicious as she is immoral. I'm surprised she isn't in custody at the moment."

"How do you know she's not?" I asked, uncomfortably aware of the perspiration spreading across my back. If he'd seen Melanie arrive in my car, he would be more than delighted to pass it along to the CID. The tidbit would trickle up to the senior officer on the case.

"Moments ago I saw her sprinting down the street. She's easily recognizable, even when she's wearing clothes."

"So she is," I agreed brightly. "By the way, were you at home last night when Joshua Dwain appeared in front of Zeno's house? From what I've heard, he had a gun and was threatening to kill Zeno."

Leach gave me a shocked look. "My client with a gun? I think not, Mrs. Malloy, and what you just said could be construed as slander. Joshua has acknowledged that he shouted some unpleasant things, but he did not have a gun and he did not threaten anyone with bodily harm. We can all sympathize with his action. His wife is in a coma and may not survive; if she does, she faces extensive reconstructive surgery on her leg, as well as months of painful physical therapy. The two of them were planning to devote their lives to serving the less fortunate of our fellow human beings. The tragedy occurred as a result of deliberate, malicious provocation, and I have no doubt the jury will hold Zeno Gorgias fully responsible. Punitive damages, as well as actual ones, should run into millions of dollars." He walked away briskly, rubbing his hands together as he no doubt mentally rehearsed a closing argument worthy of an operatic death scene. The only element missing was any hint of genuine compassion for the Dwains.

I kept an eye out for Melanie as I drove back to the Book Depot, but she once again had vanished. The patrol cars were already under instructions to watch for her; calling Peter with an update would only affect his blood pressure—and not for the better. I was opening a catalog when I realized Leach had not answered my question. Unless he'd gone to bed, it seemed likely that he had heard Joshua's shouts. Miss Parchester had heard them. Melanie had heard them, too, and she was in an upstairs bedroom at the time. Jasmine was likely to have heard them from her desk by the window.

Envisioning her at a desk reminded me that I'd not

yet determined if she truly was a mystery writer. I dug
out *Books in Print* and futilely searched for her name.
If she was telling the truth, her twenty-third book had
been published less than six months ago. Why was she
being coy? Even the tweediest academics at the college were eager to trumpet the publication of slim
volumes of poetry, biographies of justly neglected
dramatists, and convoluted "literary" novels in which
nothing much happened.

Nothing much happened for much of the afternoon,
either. I continued to call Miss Parchester's house, and
she continued to fail to answer the telephone. A re-
morseful Melanie Magruder did not appear beneath
the portico. Peter did not call to apologize, but I
hadn't been holding my breath in anticipation. A blue
tinge does not become me.

I'd turned off the light in the office when I heard
pounding on the front door. As I hesitated, the doorknob rattled and the pounding intensified.

"Okay!" I shouted as I went back to the front room,
picked up the nearest lethal weapon (a volume of
Books in Print), and unlocked the door.

"My dear Claire," Zeno said, enveloping me in a
hug that emptied my lungs and lifted me off my feet.
His shirt reeked of smoke and sour sweat, as did the
black hair tickling my nose. It was obvious Miss Parchester's garage lacked bathing facilities.

Fighting back a sneeze, I wiggled out of his arms
and retreated behind the counter. "It's a shame about
your house, Zeno—and about Ruthanne. The police
told me her body was found this morning."

"I feel terrible about that. We were married not so
long, only two years. When I met her at a gallery, I
never before had seen a woman with such graceful-
ness. She was like mercury, silvery and supple. I
wanted to paint her, to carve her in marble, anything
to capture her ethereal beauty. Only when Harry

jabbed me did I realize that she, this embodiment of Diana, the goddess of the hunt, was speaking to me."

The last woman I'd heard described as a contender for deification had proved to be closely akin to a black widow spider. However, he'd had a traumatic couple of days, so I merely said, "I'm truly sorry, Zeno. Have the police come up with any ideas why she was in your house when the fire started?"

His ebullience disappeared as if someone had flipped off a switch. Gesturing helplessly, he said, "If they have, they are keeping it a secret. I wish I could tell them, but I was drinking too much because . . ."

"Because of Tracy's accident?"

He sat down on the floor and wrapped his arms around his knees. After a few moody sighs, he looked up with the poignant expression of a dieter trudging past an ice-cream shop. "I wanted my art to seize that tiny fraction of a second that it takes stimuli to race from the eye to the brain. I am willing for my art to jar people into exposing their biases and examining their preconceptions about the very nature of art itself. I do not force them to confront it, though. I make the statement; people are free to react to it or disregard it."

"Tracy felt as if she had an obligation to stop you," I said, unimpressed by his sophomoric art-department jargon. "She was exercising her freedom, too. The accident with the motorcycle was a fluke; the officer at the scene told me the driver was just a kid who wasn't paying attention."

"Because he was interacting with my unique creation." Zeno lay back on the floor and folded his hands on his chest. His eyes closed, he intoned, "Am I the life and the resurrection?"

"I don't think so. Have you seen Melanie since you were released?"

"Ruthanne was lying in the coffin in the front room

when they found her this morning," Zeno said in the same sepulchral voice. "She'd been hit on the head. The police were very eager to find a weapon."

"Did they?"

"I doubt they would have released me if they'd found it in the house. As things stand, I was given orders to remain available while they continue their search."

I leaned over the counter and said, "Have you seen Melanie?"

He opened one eye to look at me, and then closed it. "Not since we were taken to the police station many hours ago. Why do you ask?"

I gave him a synopsis of my encounters with her. "She may be hanging around Willow Street, waiting for you. On the other hand, she may be hitchhiking to Kalamazoo by now. What do you know about her?"

"That she is an artiste."

"An artiste from where?"

"I do not encumber my spirit with the past. I did not ask her any questions, and she did not offer any information."

"She told me that she met you at the bus station. What were you doing there, Zeno?"

"Taking photographs of the travelers slumped in their seats. There is so much to be read in their scuffled shoes. Melanie intrigued me, so of course I told her she could stay at my house and become a part of a bold, new experiment in artistic expression. She is very passionate, very energetic. I like that."

"I'm sure you do," I said, hoping no one was at the display window watching me converse with what might be misconstrued as a corpse in front of the counter. "Tell me what happened last night after Ruthanne and Harry drove away. You went inside and eventually had an argument with Melanie, right? Was it a very passionate and energetic argument?"

"I don't remember what it was about, but I'm sure it was nothing worthy of either of us. After she went upstairs, I played music and dreamed of dancing around a roaring bonfire on the beach. Then I opened my eyes and saw the bonfire in the next room. I was so frightened I could hardly think and went blundering through the kitchen to try to get out through the storage room. The door wouldn't budge, so I climbed through an open window and fell on my head. Luckily, Melanie was there to drag me away from the house."

"Did you lock the door right before the show was to begin?"

"Lock it with what?"

"You kept half a million dollars' worth of paintings in an unlocked room. Weren't you worried that someone could come in through the back door and steal them? All you had to do was call a locksmith or install a deadbolt."

"I do not concern myself with money," he said grandly. "At first when my paintings began to sell, I let Harry handle the contracts, the taxes, all the inconsequential details. When I wanted money, he gave it to me. Ruthanne took over when we married. She arranged the corporation, kept inventories on the computer, made investments, talked with the bankers and the brokers all the time. She became very obsessed with money and no longer drank and danced. Her lovemaking became perfunctory. After a while, I found someone with whom to savor the important things in life."

"Is this what caused the estrangement?"

"I should think it was when she found me in bed with the cook. Rosalee was a robust woman without inhibitions, with hair the color of a raven's feathers, with skin like a field of wheat. Ruthanne came into the room at a most unfortunate moment." He smiled at the memory, then realized I was less than moved by his tacky little tale of infidelity and made an attempt to look penitent. "After that, I lived in my studio for many months, with Ruthanne checking on me as though she were a prison warden. When I learned that Uncle Stenopolis had left me his house, I decided to move here. Now the house is gone."

"As is Ruthanne," I reminded him.

"And I feel terrible." He stood up and approached the counter. I could by no means read his mind, but I had a feeling he was contemplating how best to arrange for a bed for the night.

"Have you talked to Harry?" I said. "If your wallet was burned in the fire, you must need money. He can get some out of an ATM or cash a check at his hotel."

"I called the hotel, but he wasn't there. I left a message telling him to meet me at the house later this afternoon. I want to see if anything of my Uncle Stenopolis's survived the fire."

"Do you need a ride?" I said pointedly.

He grinned at me as if I'd proffered a lewd invitation. "No, my truck was parked on the street last night, so it was not damaged by the fire. I always leave the key in the ignition, which is lucky for me, since I did not have time to grab anything before I went out the kitchen window. Would you like to take a ride with me sometime, dearest Claire? We could go up into the mountains and read Sappho's poetry to each other in the moonlight."

I'll admit I considered his proposal. He was probably ten years younger than I. Technically, I wouldn't be robbing the cradle, but I might be accused of poaching in the playground. There were other considerations, too. Before I could decline, the door opened and the primary consideration came inside. He wasn't exactly scowling, but he wasn't making any pretense of being pleased to see me. In fact, he managed not to see me at all. "Mr. Gorgias," he said, "I need you to come back to the station."

"Am I to be charged?" asked Zeno.

"I can't say at this time. Shall we go?"

Zeno glanced at me (proving I wasn't totally invisible) and then said, "I am supposed to meet my agent in an hour. Afterward, I will present myself at the police station."

Peter shook his head. "We need you right now. If you wish, you can use the telephone at the station to cancel your meeting. It's likely that this will be a lengthy interview, Mr. Gorgias. It might be wise to arrange to have your lawyer present."

"The only lawyers I know are the one who handled Uncle Stenopolis's estate and Anthony Leach. Mr. Whitbred has since retired, and Leach may not care to represent me. For some reason, he has taken a strong dislike to me."

I decided to find out if I was inaudible as well. "I'll try to get hold of Franklin Adamson, Zeno. He's one of the best criminal lawyers in town. If he can't represent you, he can recommend someone else."

Peter took Zeno's arm and led him toward the door. "Ms. Malloy is always eager to help in an official investigation. Today, for example, she managed to spend time with two crucial witnesses, although she misplaced one of them." The door closed on whatever other aspersions he was offering.

I called Franklin Adamson and explained what I knew of the situation. He confessed that he'd seen the segment on the local news and would have attended the son et lumière if he hadn't been obliged to host a dinner party. He agreed to meet Zeno at the police station.

The preliminaries having been covered, I said, "Let me ask you something, Franklin. What do you know about Anthony Leach?"

"Are you checking references or suggesting I make deprecatory remarks about a fellow member of the bar?"

"The latter."

"There are some rumors," Franklin said reluctantly. "Recently, a client filed a complaint with the state ethics committee that Anthony refused to turn over the proceeds from a judgment. It wasn't the first complaint of that nature, but it may be the strongest thus far. I wouldn't care to be in partnership with him. His wife seems to agree with that; she filed for divorce and moved out on him last month. Guess I'd better head for the police station."

I thanked Franklin for the gossip, which was interesting if not profoundly intriguing, locked up the bookstore, and went out to my car. As I started the engine, I found myself brooding over Peter's trifling remarks. I had not "misplaced" Melanie. And it was not my fault that Zeno had burst into the store and opted to confide in me, if that was what he'd done. He'd regaled me with highlights (and lowlights, if such things exist) of his relationship with Ruthanne and her transformation from Greek goddess to Uriah Heep. It was hard to know how much of his version was true; he was too busy being a self-proclaimed genius to be an accurate observer of anyone else. He'd claimed not to remember the argument with Melanie or Ruthanne's arrival. But she had arrived sometime before the fire, and she had been hit on the head. Putting her in a coffin was a macabre touch that might have appealed to Zeno's twisted artistic style. Then again, someone else might have come to the same realization and set the scene to make him look guilty.

I should have gone home. If Peter had not annoyed me quite so much, I would have gone home. I would have fixed myself a drink, microwaved an entrée, and found out if Caron and Inez were up to anything out-

landish, unscrupulous, or illegal. Then I would have
curled up with a good book and, at the appropriate
moment, turned out the light and fallen asleep.

Instead, I drove to Willow Street with the honorable
intention of meeting Harry so that I could tell him
that Zeno had been taken to the police station. The
black Cadillac was not parked in front of the remains
of Zeno's house, but I was almost an hour early. So
many witnesses, so little time, I thought as I glanced
at all the pertinent houses, not sure where to start
meddling.

I tried Miss Parchester first, but she did not come
to the door and her living room was dim. Anthony
Leach's car was not in his driveway; he was likely to
be at the hospital, scheming with Joshua Dwain to sue
Zeno for a trillion dollars. Even if Joshua was home,
he might not be in the mood for a cozy chat about
the gun that only Miss Parchester claimed to have
seen. He and his lawyer had denied its existence.

It was time to accept an earlier offer of a drink. I
went up the interior stairs and knocked on Jasmine's
door, wondering how violently writers reacted when
interrupted in the middle of a sentence of deathless
prose. I'd been in her apartment for only a minute
the previous evening and, in my haste to communicate
with the voice at the end of the 911 number, had
noticed almost nothing. If she collected weapons for
purposes of research, she didn't leave them scattered
around the telephone or displayed in cases on the wall.
This did not mean that she might not keep a gun atop
her printer and a butcher knife in her desk drawer.

I knocked again, discovered the door was not
locked, and tentatively opened it an inch or two. "Jasmine? It's Claire Malloy." In response, I heard a tiny
intake of breath. She could be ill and unable to speak,
I told myself as I tightened my grip on the doorknob.
It was more likely that she was pretending she wasn't

home so I would go away, but I could not do so with a crystal-clear conscience. Gritting my teeth, I went inside.

Her living room was furnished in a fashion reminiscent of Miss Parchester's, although dust was less prevalent and the odor more difficult to interpret. Thick stacks of paper were piled on the sofa and coffee table, but they were more likely to be manuscripts than essays written by students now old enough to be grandparents. Unopened mail was scattered on an end table; the majority of the envelopes had cellophane windows.

"Jasmine?" I called again as I went across the room and hesitated by a closed door that, based on what she'd said, led to her office. More than anything, I hoped I'd find her sitting in front of her computer, an annoyed look on her face. But why hadn't she simply told me to go away? It might not have worked (I am a determined meddler), yet it was an obvious response to an unwelcome guest.

As I opened the door, I sensed movement behind it. Clamping down on my lip, I stayed where I was and stared at the figure slumped across the desk. Jasmine's hair no longer flowed in a blond profusion. It was darkened with blood and that which Hercule Poirot called "little gray cells." Her head had fallen on her outstretched arm, and her fingers were wrapped around a coffee mug; the other arm hung limply. The computer screen was as empty as her eyes. To say I was dumbstruck would have been an understatement.

The door crashed into me, sending me stumbling backward. I did what I could to maintain my balance, but I was clipped by a table and I landed on the floor with a thud. I scrambled to my feet and was heading for the front door when I heard the sound of a gun being cocked. It was not a pretty sound.

"I'd prefer that you don't leave just yet," Melanie said. She was trying to be ever so casual, but there was enough muted hysteria in her voice to make me worry that her finger might slip on the trigger. Slip or otherwise.

I stopped and forced myself to turn around. As I'd feared, she had a gun. It was pointed at me in a bobbly sort of way, which foreboded ill for my anatomy.

"Melanie," I said. I intended to elaborate, but my mind was blank and my mouth as dry as an AA meeting.

"I didn't shoot her."

"Of course you didn't," I croaked.

"I just got here a few minutes ago. About the time I saw what had happened to her, I heard someone coming up the stairs. The gun was lying there, so I picked it up in case . . ."

"I am not returning to the scene of the crime, Melanie," I said with admirable control. "Put down the gun before it goes off by mistake."

She thrust her chin forward and scowled at me. "So you can call the police? They won't listen to me for ten seconds before they throw me in a cell. I'll have some public defender who's been out of law school for a whole day, and end up being found guilty of everything all the way back to original sin. No, thanks."

"Put down the gun."

"Yeah, I may just do that. First, I want you to go back in there with that dead woman."

That was low on my list of preferences but several slots higher than being shot in the face. "I'll do what you want," I said, "but you're making a mistake. If you're telling the truth, you won't be charged with anything. Running away will only make you look guilty." Shooting me would compound it, but I decided not to say so in case she interpreted it as a suggestion. Instead, I managed a shaky laugh. "You don't think I shot Jasmine, then came back to see if she'd recovered and wanted to offer me a drink?"

"I don't know what you've been doing, honey, but you sure do hang around this neighborhood a lot. You haven't missed much of anything, have you?"

"I bought you lunch. Murderers do not buy lunch for other people. I did not call the police from the bus station, nor did I call them after you ungraciously ran off earlier this afternoon." I turned on the full maternal fury. "I have done nothing but accommodate you, Melanie. Would you please reciprocate by putting down the gun?"

"Get in there," she said, unaffected by my performance.

I came across the room and stopped again in the doorway, appalled by the sight of Jasmine's body. Two hands hit my back, and this time I went stumbling into the office. As I crashed into a bookcase, the front door slammed. Footsteps pounded down the stairs.

Damn. I'd lost her again.

EIGHT

After I'd explored a lump on my forehead and concluded I was bruised but not bloodied, I forced
myself to look more carefully at the body. It appeared
that Jasmine had been shot in the head, although I
couldn't see the wound from my perspective and I
sure as heck wasn't going to poke my finger in her
hair. I knew where the most likely weapon was—well,
I knew where the most likely weapon *had been* before
Melanie made one of her increasingly typical exits. If
she'd been truthful, she'd only picked up the gun
when she heard me come up the stairs. She hadn't
mentioned if it had been near Jasmine's dangling
hand, indicative of suicide—or across the room, indicative of something altogether different.

In either case, the room was sweltering and the
stench was worse than the rest room at the bus station.
I hurried into the living room, reached for the telephone, and abruptly realized that someone could be
hiding in another room. Rather than take roll, I skit-
tered down the stairs, nearly breaking my elegant neck
in the process, and made it to the front yard. Melanie
had vanished, naturally. Leach's car had not returned.
Miss Parchester's interior was still dim. The police had
not arrived to continue their search of Zeno's blackened rubble.

After much disjointed thinking and hand-wringing, I decided to try the Dwains' house next door. If I had no luck, I would continue up the street until I found someone willing to call 911. I cut across the grass and went up the steps to the porch. Before I could ring the doorbell, Joshua Dwain opened the door.

"What do you want?" he asked warily.

"I need to call the police. Jasmine Hadley's dead. I think she was shot."

"Is this one of Zeno's vile stunts to keep the entire neighborhood in hysterics? Is he paying you to knock on doors and make preposterous statements so he can leap out from behind a tree with his infernal camera?"

"No! Either call 911 or let me in so that I can do it." An image of Jasmine's blood-caked hair flooded my mind. I leaned against the nearest pillar and rubbed my face as though I could erase the image, but it persisted with the tenacity of an abscessed tooth. Her eyes were wide and flat, her skin waxy, her mouth slack. For the first time, I understood the source of the repugnant odor I'd noticed in her apartment.

I sank down on the top step and put my head between my knees. "Call 911, Joshua," I said in a hoarse voice.

"Yeah, okay. You wait here."

I waited, since the only other thing I was apt to do was fall down the stairs and do further damage to myself. He returned almost immediately.

"They want more details," he said.

"I don't have any more details."

"Who shot her?"

I abandoned the idea of swooning and looked over my shoulder at him. "You may not be a rocket scientist, but do try to understand what I'm saying: Jasmine Hadley is dead of very unnatural causes. Share this with the dispatcher. I will speak to the police when they arrive; I strongly suggest they do so immediately. Got that?"

His mouth tightened and his chubby cheeks ballooned until he resembled a pugnacious groundhog. "I will pass it along," he said with such disapproval that the words hung in the air like dialogue in a comic strip. He slammed the door for emphasis.

Five minutes later a police car cruised sedately up the street. Joshua came out to the porch and made noises under his breath; my best guess was that he was praying I'd be pilloried for perpetrating a hoax.

I went to the edge of the yard and waited for the uniformed officers to get out of their car. To my relief, they were not the two quasi-adolescents who'd been sent the previous night to disarm Joshua. One was a grandfatherly type, the other a middle-aged woman. Neither looked especially friendly, but they weren't delivering a pizza.

"I found the body," I said to get the conversation started. "It's in the upstairs apartment of this house."

The woman assessed me for a moment. "And you are?"

I told them my name and then tersely explained everything that had happened. Joshua, who'd followed me, hissed when I mentioned Melanie's name, but I ignored him and finished my narrative with only a hint of shrillness.

"What happened to your forehead?" she asked.

"I bumped it when I was pushed into the bookcase," I said. "Don't you think you'd better send for backups to search for Melanie? She's had more than fifteen minutes to get away."

"Tell 'em she's armed and dangerous," the male officer said to his partner as she went to their car. He looked at me with a slight frown, as if I, too, might be armed and dangerous. If I'd been in a better mood, I might have been flattered. "Now, Ms. Malloy, I'm sure we'll have more questions for you before we're through, and you're looking a little pale. Why don't you sit in the back of our car?"

"Why don't I sit on the porch right over there until you're ready to ask me questions?" I said. When his frown deepened, I winced and added, "I'm feeling awfully queasy. Fresh air's the only thing keeping me from losing my lunch. If you really want me to sit in your backseat, where it's hot and stuffy, I will. Just promise not to get upset if I ... well, you know."

His imagination was in working order. "Okay," he said gruffly. "Make sure you don't leave."

Joshua and I returned to his porch. Before he could continue inside, I said, "Did you see anyone go into Jasmine's apartment this afternoon?"

"No, Mrs. Malloy, I did not. I was at the kitchen table, studying for a summer-school exam. The only window looks out on our backyard." He reached for the doorknob. "I don't know what your role in this is, but I don't have to answer any more of your questions. Why don't you go on home and mind your own business?"

I'd heard that sentiment so often that I didn't bother to respond to it. "Miss Parchester was positive she saw a gun in your hand last night when you were threatening to kill Zeno. If you didn't have a gun, how were you going to do this—with your bare hands? Does the Bible Academy have classes in karate for Christians? Or is it jujitsu for Jesus?"

My taunts proved to be productive. He jerked to a stop and glared at me. "I was crazed with grief. I came back from the hospital to pack a bag for Tracy and found a letter she'd received from her sister, who's a missionary in Honduras. As I read it, all I could think was that Zeno was responsible for what happened to Tracy and that he deserved to be punished for depriv-

ing her of the opportunity to do God's work. I did
not have a gun—but if I had, I might have used it.''

"You aren't familiar with the commandment that
says: 'Thou shalt not kill'?''

"Yes, Mrs. Malloy, I am," he said drily. "I am also
familiar with the passage in Ecclesiastes that says
there is 'a time to kill, and a time to heal; a time to
break down and a time to build up.' Last night was
my time to break down, but this morning I received
counseling from our minister and began a healing process. I have prayed for the strength to forgive Zeno,
and in time I will come to accept whatever happens
as God's will."

I ignored the piety and said, "Miss Parchester also
heard another voice outside while you were there.
Who was it?"

"Ruthanne Gorgias came in a taxi. It's a shame she
didn't live long enough to have Zeno institution-
alized."

"She'd be the first to agree with you. What did she
say to you last night?"

He looked away, but not before I'd seen indecision
flicker across his face. I couldn't remember if one of
the commandments covered lying, but if it did, I had
a feeling he was going to violate it. In a voice that
suggested at least one rehearsal, he said, "At first she
was all sugary and said how sorry she was about what
had happened and how she and Zeno wanted to pay
the hospital bills. I told her that I wouldn't accept a
penny of his filthy money. She dropped the act and
said if I didn't leave she'd call the police and have me
arrested. I went home."

"Did she say why she was there?" I asked.

"Zeno sent her a message at the hotel that he
wanted to talk. She seemed to think he was going to
back down and do what she wanted."

I sat down to think this over. If Zeno had sent

Ruthanne a message, he hadn't mentioned it to me. Neither had Melanie, but she had admitted they had had an argument that sent her upstairs. This might have been the cause of it. Zeno's capitulation would put her back at the bus station, suitcase in hand, debating between Chicago and Shreveport. Or she might have seen him as something more significant than a meal ticket. She and Zeno hadn't seemed particularly enamored of each other, but she might have been hiding her emotions. Or she might have known more about his wealth than she'd pretended.

Joshua cleared his throat and said, "I'm going to the hospital. If the police want to speak to me, they'll have to go there or wait until I come home."

"How's Tracy doing?" I asked gently.

"The doctors are unable to say. She went into shock in the ambulance and hasn't regained consciousness. If they could have gotten her to the emergency room more quickly..." He stopped to wipe the corner of his eye, then did his best to reassemble the disappointed smile of a Christian confronting a lapsed convert. Despite his efforts, it would not play in Peoria—nor would I care to meet him in a dark warehouse. "It's too late for suppositions, isn't it? I'm going to the hospital."

He was driving away as more patrol cars parked in front of Jasmine's house. Another car turned into the library parking lot at the bottom of the hill. A man with a medical bag arrived in a station wagon and went into the house. Several minutes later, a familiar car pulled to the curb. I'd known it would, but I'd been nurturing a very feeble pipe dream that Peter had been too busy grilling Zeno to leave the station.

"And yet another corpse?" he said as he came into the yard and gave me a discouraged look. "You're beginning to rival Jessica Fletcher, and she finds one every week just before the second commercial."

"She outwits the police just before the final one."

"What happened to your head?"

"I bumped it in Jasmine's apartment."

"Ah, yes," he said, lifting a finger as if he'd finally remembered an insignificant detail, "Jasmine's apartment, also known as the scene of the crime. Just what were you doing there?"

"On Friday Jasmine invited me for a drink, but it didn't work out. This afternoon I dropped by to take her up on her offer. She's a mystery writer, and you know how much I love the genre. I can assure you we were not going to discuss anything more sinister than her books."

"How silly of me to have assumed anything else. For one brief moment, I wondered if you had come to Willow Street to conduct a small investigation."

"Only into her pen name."

His eyes turned cold and his face a shade of red that brought to mind Miss Parchester's much-abused zinnias. "Claire, you have got to stay out of this. Someone killed Ruthanne Gorgias and set the fire. Now Jasmine Hadley has been killed. One of the parties involved is lurking in the bushes with a gun. And you insist on sticking your nose into what is a very dangerous situation."

"So you mentioned earlier," I said stiffly. Before he could explode (which he clearly was about to do), I stood up and said, "I think I'll go home and watch the show we were discussing, then stick my nose in a novel. Please tell the officers who responded to the original call how to get in touch with me."

His jaw quivered for a moment, and his expression indicated a goodly amount of inner turmoil. However, he repressed it well and stalked away to confer with the increasing number of police officers in Jasmine's front yard. I didn't want to be nearby when he heard how Melanie had again slipped through my hands as if I lacked opposable thumbs.

As I arrived at my car, Harry Tillington pulled up, studied the scene, and said, "What's going on? Has Zeno done something else?"

"Zeno's at the police station and liable to be charged with Ruthanne's death. I arranged for a lawyer. As for all this"—I gestured at the activity behind me—"it's pretty complicated. Jasmine Hadley was shot."

"Who?"

I was about to elaborate when I realized Peter was watching us. If he'd had a forked tongue and hooded ears, he would have borne an alarming resemblance to a cobra. "Listen, why don't we go someplace else to talk? The police can get testy when civilians clutter up their crime scenes."

"Lieutenant Rosen looks more than testy."

"He and I are friends—or we used to be, anyway. He's a bit disgruntled that I'm here."

"Come back to the Drakestone Hotel with me," Harry said. "I think I'm going to need a drink while you explain all this."

It sounded like a splendid idea.

The Drakestone Hotel wasn't much, but it was the best Farberville had to offer upscale visitors (and Ruthanne surely was the uppiest in a long time). Like Willow Street, it had seen better days and a classier clientele, but all hope had not yet been abandoned. There were silk flowers in the lobby, cordial smiles on the faces of the staff, and a portly concierge dozing at a small desk.

Harry's room was dowdy, but the air conditioner provided a refreshing change from the August heat. He made a quick trip to an ice machine, then produced a bottle of scotch and two glasses. "Okay," he said after he'd fixed the drinks and we were sitting on a remarkably uncomfortable sofa, "who was this person who was killed and is this why Zeno's at the police station again?"

I told him what I'd told the police. "I don't know how Jasmine's death fits into all this," I continued. "Maybe she was responsible for Ruthanne's death and was overcome with remorse, but she struck me as more cynical than anything else. If she were inclined to murder someone, she'd probably take notes and use it in her next book. What if she was looking out her window last night when Ruthanne arrived? When Joshua told me about it, he sounded evasive. Something else could have happened on the sidewalk or on the porch."

"Could the Hadley woman have seen Melanie open the front door and invite Ruthanne inside? That would give Melanie a damn good motive to kill her."

I shook my head. "Jasmine must have been interviewed by the police earlier today. Why wouldn't she have told them whatever she saw? Both Melanie and Zeno were allowed to leave the police station this afternoon, so Jasmine didn't implicate either of them."

"But now you think Zeno's going to be charged," Harry reminded me.

"When Ruthanne appeared last night, she told Joshua that Zeno had sent her a message here at the hotel. Joshua surely told this to the police. It's hard to believe Zeno sent the message, though. Last night I didn't get the impression he was going to pack up and move to Santa Fe."

"He's impulsive, as you must have noticed by now, and changes his mind more rapidly than the rest of us change television channels. I suppose he might have come up with some extravagant notion of covering the Mission of San Miguel in aluminum foil or repainting the Painted Desert. I wish he'd expend some of his energy on canvases."

"You seem to know him better than anyone else. Do you believe he sent the message to Ruthanne, knocked her unconscious, and lit the fire?" I asked.

"I don't know." Harry glanced at my untouched glass, then went across the room and poured himself another drink. As he sat back down, he said, "I've been Zeno's friend for nearly ten years, as well as his agent. He has a temper and he's lost it more than a few times. He's been arrested for brawling in bars, but I can't see him striking Ruthanne or any other woman. He's too much of a romantic for that."

"He admitted he was drunk. According to what he said, he was in a back room pretending to be Zorba the Greek and didn't even know Ruthanne was in the house. He's not big on locking doors. She could have let herself in, but then what did she do for the next half hour—dust?"

"I don't know," he said, staring dejectedly at me.

I took a swallow of scotch and let it dribble down my throat as I tried to envision Ruthanne entertaining herself in what must have been by her standards a loathsome environment. Several swallows later, I conceded defeat and moved on to other equally murky problems. Before too long, my glass was empty and I was totally confused.

Harry appeared to have fared no better and was in danger of sighing to death. To distract him, I said, "Tell me about Zeno's past. You've known him for ten years?"

"He came here from Greece when he was a kid. He was bright enough to discern what it takes to succeed. Please don't quote me, but in the art world, it's how you personally are perceived as much as how your talent is perceived. He conned his way through a degree in fine arts, schmoozed at cocktail parties, and found a wealthy patroness to pay for a spacious studio in Santa Fe and appearances at all the de rigueur events in New York and Paris. His behavior was just scandalous enough to titillate the connoisseurs—without offending them."

"Then he's a fraud?"

"As you said, he's playing Zorba. Maybe it's a role, but it's a role that suits him and he revels in it. That doesn't mean he's a cold-blooded killer beneath all that innocent exuberance. He's incredibly generous and compassionate. He insisted on buying me a new car when the first big sale came through, and he's sent a couple of promising disciples to Europe. Once Ruthanne took control, she put a stop to it, of course." He hung his head and resumed sighing. "I still can't believe she's dead. She was quite as dynamic as Zeno, although in a more cultured way. You should have heard her when she thought she'd found a discrepancy in the account. I don't know why she bothered to call me; I could have gone outside my office and heard her all the way down in Houston. Zeno was too much in awe of her to risk messing up her hair, much less harming her."

"The only other person in the house was Melanie. She doesn't seem very cold-blooded, either. Admittedly, she hasn't seemed too concerned about committing less serious crimes, and she certainly has a knack of showing up in the wrong places at inopportune moments, but she just doesn't strike me as a calculating murderer. I've encountered a few along the way, and, at least in retrospect, I realized there was something about them that was—I don't know—different from the rest of us. I may be proven wrong about Melanie, but I don't think so."

"You've encountered a few?" Harry said, nervously watching me.

"Less than a dozen."

After a few uncomfortable moments, he must have concluded I was not the village sociopath. "What about this man who was outside the house?" he suggested. "Someone who makes death threats might follow through with them a few minutes later. He claims that he went home, but he could have dragged Ruthanne inside the house, killed her, and started dropping matches on all the piles of newspapers." He stopped and shuddered as if the air conditioner were sending out a mist of acid rain. "And on the paintings in the storage room. They represented two years of work. Even if Zeno's never charged with any crime, he may or may not continue to paint, what with his fixation with his son et lumière shows and photographs of feet. The gallery in San Francisco will not be amused if I don't produce what our contract specifies. Artistic photos of laceless sneakers won't cut it."

"When I talked to him this afternoon, he was already reconsidering his responsibility. He may back off his plan to give the Dwains all his money and do penance in a community college," I said soothingly, then returned to the more important topic. "But do I believe Joshua Dwain killed Ruthanne? He might have, I suppose. The religious right has some peculiar ideas about violence and retribution. He himself used the phrase 'crazy with grief.' That doesn't explain why he would attack Ruthanne, though, since she was trying to put a stop to Zeno's antics."

"What if he stormed into the house to set the fire and she tried to prevent him? He might have shoved her too hard, or snatched up something and bashed her."

I put down my glass and picked up my purse. "It's possible, Harry. You'd better find out if you need to go to the police station to give the lawyer a retainer. I've never met one who would disrupt a Sunday afternoon out of a high-minded desire to see justice done."

As I rode down in the elevator, I remembered what Franklin had said about Anthony Leach. A small lightbulb blinked on above my head as the elevator doors slid open in the lobby. Leach was frantic to sell his house, perhaps more so than the ordinary seller—yet there was no FOR SALE sign in his yard. And his wife had filed for divorce. I'd never gone through a divorce myself, Carlton having spared me that particular indignity, but I'd had friends who were certifiable by the time the judge signed the decree. The issue that seemed to bubble to the top of the unsavory mess was always money, overshadowing custody of children, pets, or season basketball tickets. Was Leach so frantic to sell the house and dispose of the proceeds that he would kill a potential client?

It was not a question I could pose tactfully to my friend Franklin or to Leach himself. It was worthy of thought, though, and it received plenty as I drove home.

Caron sat in the living room amid soda cans, bags of cookies and chips, and an indecipherable assortment of cosmetics. The television was turned to MTV, where scantily clad members of unspecified gender gyrated and lip-synched.

"Peter called," she announced. "He wasn't very nice when I told him I hadn't seen you since this morning and had no idea where you were. I am not your social secretary, for pity's sake."

"No, you're not," I said as I went into the kitchen and put on the teapot. I was confirming Caron's previous assessment of the contents of the refrigerator when she came into the kitchen.

"I'm going to Inez's house," she said.

I looked at her over the refrigerator door. "Did anyone else call?"

"Miss Parchester called while I was taking a shower. I stood there and dripped all over the floor while she rattled on like the boiler at the bookstore. Why does everyone think I'm supposed to know where you are

Every Minute of the day? Doesn't anyone think I have my own life to lead?"

"What exactly did Miss Parchester say?"

Caron made a face so that I could appreciate the extent of the ordeal. "She said she drove out in the country someplace to buy a bushel basket of peaches because she wanted to make more compote. I don't even know what compote is, much less care that she can't buy decent peaches at the store and—"

"Is she home now?"

"Her car broke down. She tried to find a garage, but they were all closed because it's Sunday, so she wants you to come get her. I wrote down the name of the town and the directions. There's some dorky café where she's waiting, but it closes at seven. After that, she'll be in her car about a mile down some crummy road."

"You were planning to tell me this before you left for Inez's house, weren't you?" I said sharply.

"Oh, Mother," she said as if I'd accused her of some heinous crime, "I said I Wrote It Down."

The teapot began to whistle, and by the time I'd turned off the burner, Caron was gone. I went into the living room and found the note, which indeed had all the pertinent information for Miss Parchester's rescue. Trying to convince myself Caron wouldn't have sailed away without telling me, I calculated how long it would take me to retrieve the peaches and Miss Parchester and arrive back home. At least two hours, I concluded, looking wistfully at my tea.

The café would close in half an hour. I picked up my purse, turned out the light, and went down the stairs to my car. I was heading for the highway when I had a sudden image of Caron in the kitchen doorway, her expression resplendent with self-pity. That was not remarkable. What was strange was that she was carrying a duffel bag. At least half of her ward-

robe resided in Inez's closet (the other half on her
own bedroom floor). All she usually took was a backpack with underwear and a toothbrush.

I had a fairly reasonable idea what was in the duffel
bag, but I couldn't leave Miss Parchester in the deep-
ening gloom along a country road.

When I returned home two hours later, would the
first call be from the animal shelter—or from the police station? And would Franklin Adamson take a
check?

NINE

The directions were pretty good, which is to say only a few vital turns were omitted. I prowled unpaved back roads for the better part of two hours, then found the highway and a gas station with a moderately articulate employee. He pulled out a map and, after much mumbling and clucking, showed me how to get to the tiny backwoods town. He described it as the Roadkill Capital of the World, but I dismissed that as hyperbole. Or wishful thinking.

By the time I found the sign that proclaimed a population of seven hundred fifty or so souls, all of them were in their homes behind drawn drapes. The only establishment resembling a café was closed for the night. A motel sign promised at least one V CAN Y; this was not surprising, since the town was hardly a hotbed of riotous nightlife. I stopped under a streetlight and studied the note, then took off down yet another unpaved road. It eventually led to a gate with a large padlock.

This never happened in mystery fiction, I thought irritably as I maneuvered to turn around in the narrow confines. There were no long, tedious passages in which a character drove around in the dark looking for one little old lady and a bushel basket of peaches. The fictional sleuths were much too busy stumbling over clues and corpses to waste time on irrelevant and noticeably ineffectual errands. At least the private eyes were; the amateurs baked cookies and talked to cats.

I returned to the main road. This time I saw a hand-painted sign advertising the proximity of a fruit stand down yet another dirt road. It seemed possible that peaches would be out of season before I rescued Miss Parchester, and she would have to turn her attention to making applesauce—or cranberry sauce. At last I spotted a small, shuttered structure and a boxy little car that looked as if it would be started with a crank. I pulled up behind it and waited for Miss Parchester to join me. She did not.

I approached the car and discovered it was uninhabited, then looked at the shadowy woods that were as dense and tangled as matted fur. If Miss Parchester had decided to take a shortcut to the nearest farmhouse, she might well have twisted her ankle or been beset by wildlife. I decided not to consider that as an alternative. She had not been walking down the road toward the highway. That left only one direction.

I got back in my car and drove slowly into the black tunnel. After what must have been a goodly chunk of eternity, I came around a curve and saw a squalid house. Lights shone through blinds crisscrossed with cracks. I parked behind a truck set on concrete blocks, walked across the weedy yard to the porch, and knocked hesitantly on the front door. The whiskery man who opened the door did not appear to relish the idea of company. He also did not appear to have bathed within months; unidentifiable matter clung to his beard and dotted his oily overalls.

"Good evening," I said. "I'm sorry to disturb you, but I'm looking for—"

"What happened to your head?" he growled.

"I bumped it," I said with a self-deprecatory laugh.

"I'm looking for a friend of mine, a white-haired lady of sixty-five years or so. Her car broke down about a mile away from here."

"What's wrong with it?"

I tried to peer over his shoulder in hopes of seeing Miss Parchester perched on a sofa with a nice cup of tea. "I don't know, and my friend seems to have wandered away. You haven't seen her, have you?"

"Nobody's got no business doing anything out this way. This is all my property, from the paved road down to the creek." He pulled out a stained handkerchief and noisily blew his nose, then stuffed it in his pocket. "This friend of yours is trespassing. So are you."

Trying to assure myself that he hadn't bound and gagged Miss Parchester, I said as calmly as I could, "I am very sorry about trespassing. My friend may have already found a ride home. Would it be possible for me to use your telephone to call her house?"

"Nope."

"I'll gladly pay for a long-distance call." I fumbled with my purse and pulled out my wallet. "What's it cost to call Farberville from here?"

"I reckon it costs a dollar," he said.

All I had was a five-dollar bill, but I wasn't going to demand change from this flea-bitten troglodyte. My hand shook as I took out the bill and gave it to him. He studied it for a long while, as if he suspected it were some exotic foreign currency, then put it in the same pocket as his handkerchief and stepped back. I stepped forward just as the door closed in my face.

"Hey!" I shouted. "What about the telephone call I just paid for?"

The door creaked open to a tiny slit long enough for him to say, "Ain't got a telephone." It closed before I could demand my money back.

"This doesn't happen in fiction, either," I said aloud

as I stomped back through the weeds. I sat in my car and glowered at the windows of the house, torn between breaking down his door or accepting another financial setback with as much grace as I could muster. But what if Miss Parchester had been ushered in and come to some dire fate best left undescribed?

I finally eased open the car door and took a circuitous route to a window on the side of the house. Barbed wire coiled around my bare ankles. Splintery boards squeaked menacingly, threatening my shapely calves. A tin can rattled across a stretch of rocks. However, I was not confronted with angry shouts or shotgun blasts, and I arrived at the window without undue damage.

I rose on my toes and peeked under a tattered blind. If he had a telephone, he kept it in another room. This one was almost devoid of furnishings except for a sofa that would have been rejected at the city dump, a couple of crude chairs, a lamp without a shade, and a large-screen television set. On the sofa lay an enormous white hog, its eyes locked on the television. As I stared, the man came into the room and picked up a clicker. The hog twitched excitedly.

It was all too bizarre for a mild-mannered bookseller. If Miss Parchester was in there, she would have to await the arrival of the National Guard to be rescued. I returned to my car and backed onto the road before turning on the headlights. When I arrived at her car, I quickly made sure she wasn't sitting in the front seat, grabbed a peach from a basket in the backseat, and continued back to the town.

There was a pay telephone outside the café. I found a dime and dialed Miss Parchester's number. She answered with a timorous, "Hello?"

"This is Claire. I received your message and came out to this town to fetch you. I was worried when I found your car abandoned on a dirt road."

"Oh, dear," she said with a sigh. "I'm so sorry about this, Claire. A gentleman stopped and picked me up as I was walking along the road. He was kind enough to bring me right to my doorstep. I called your apartment to tell you, but no one answered."

I waited until a truck rumbled by, then said, "At least you're safely at home. Be sure to keep your doors locked. There was another death on Willow Street."

"So Melanie was telling me just now. It seems you frightened her very badly, Claire. She's only a child who's trying to make her way—"

"Just now? Is she there with you?"

"Would you like to speak to her? It would be gracious of you to apologize for your behavior this afternoon."

I leaned against the wall of the café and tightened my grip on the receiver. "Melanie pointed a gun at me, Miss Parchester. She claimed she didn't shoot Jasmine Hadley, but she knocked me down and ran away. The police have been looking for her ever since."

"I'm sure she has a perfectly good explanation," Miss Parchester said reproachfully. "Papa always stressed the importance of the presumption of innocence. It's the cornerstone of our judicial system."

"It certainly is," I said, fighting not to giggle as the absurdity of the moment enveloped me like a cloud of gnats. I took a bite of the peach and let the juice dribble down my chin. "I think I'd better say good-bye now and drive back to Farberville. Let's do have tea sometime this week."

"Could I ask a tiny favor? I was hoping to start making compote in the morning, but the peaches are in the backseat of my car. Would it be too inconvenient for you to bring them with you?"

"No problem." I broke off the connection and found another dime. The dispatcher at the Farberville police

station informed me that Peter was not available, but
agreed to pass along my message concerning Melanie's
whereabouts. Feeling moderately self-righteous, I drove
back down the road to Miss Parchester's car.

The peaches were gone.

It was nearly eleven o'clock by the time I arrived
home. I thought about calling Inez's house to find out
if she and Caron were curled in front of the television,
but decided to hope for the best.

I was carrying a cup of tea into the living room
when the doorbell buzzed on the porch downstairs. A
myriad of terrifying images flashed through my mind
as I hurried down the steps. The sight of a uniformed
policeman did nothing to alleviate my escalating panic.
Policemen do not deliver pizzas, nor do they make
house calls out of boredom.

"What?" I demanded.

"Are you Claire Malloy?"

I nodded, then licked my lips and carefully said,
"Has something happened to my daughter?"

"All I know is that I'm supposed to take you to the
station. I'll give you a minute to get your keys so you
can lock the door."

I stumbled upstairs, found my purse in the kitchen,
and stumbled back down into the long arms of the
law. "Has there been an accident?" I asked as we
walked to his car.

"I don't know, ma'am." He gave me a puzzled look.
"You were over on Willow Street last night, weren't
you? I thought you said you lived there."

"I didn't say any such thing," I retorted, then
climbed into the passenger's seat (before he could suggest the backseat), folded my arms, and stared fiercely
at the bug-encrusted windshield. Surely no one would
fire a gun at a bear in the yard, I told myself. Surely
Melanie wouldn't harm Miss Parchester. Surely this

was a misunderstanding. Surely I wasn't going to degenerate into hysteria.

The officer escorted me inside the station, told me to sit on a bench, and disappeared down a hallway. The desk sergeant glanced up incuriously, then resumed typing on a vintage machine. Male voices and footsteps echoed from the back of the building.

I was trying to assure myself that I wouldn't have been kept waiting in an emergency when the young officer returned and said, "Follow me, ma'am."

"I'm not doing anything until I've been told what's going on."

"You're going to be booked for hindering apprehension. Soon as the paperwork's done, you can call your lawyer, but you'll have to remain in custody until the judge sets bail. That won't be until in the morning."

"Hindering whose apprehension?"

"Melanie Magruder's," Peter said as he came around a corner. He'd deteriorated quite a bit since I'd last seen him in Jasmine's front yard. His jacket was wrinkled, his necktie loosened, and his demeanor even less cordial. "If you'd told us where she was earlier in the evening, we might have been able to pick her up. By the time we got to Miss Parchester's house, Melanie had left for an unknown destination."

"I called you as soon as I found out she was there," I said icily.

"You were supposed to wait at your apartment in case we had more questions," he continued as if reading a subpoena. "Instead, you went to Harry Tillington's hotel room for a chat. Then you vanished for the next four hours. I suppose I ought to be impressed that you paused in your investigation long enough to call the station, but I'm not. Maybe a night in jail will convince you to stop this meddling."

I was so outraged that I came alarmingly close to

bursting into tears. Numerous retorts came to mind, but none of them seemed likely to improve the situation. When at last I could trust myself, I said, "If you're interested, I will explain where I've been and why. Let me make one thing clear, though—if I spend so much as one minute in a cell, you will not spend so much as one minute in my bed in the future."

This time the desk sergeant's glance was hardly incurious. The young officer behind Peter was fascinated; he looked as if he was struggling not to beg for details. Lots of details.

Peter seemed unprepared for my remark, and he sounded deeply disgruntled when he finally responded. "This is not the place to discuss personal matters. Would you be so kind as to accompany me into my office, Ms. Malloy? Perhaps your offer to illuminate me will forestall incarceration."

He'd been watching too many cop movies, I decided as I sailed past him. Once we were in his office, I said, "You certainly are leaping to a lot of conclusions these days. Harry Tillington has a legitimate interest in Zeno's problems, and all I did was tell him what I knew and advise him to go to the police station. As for my mysterious four-hour disappearance, I was on a mission of mercy." I proceeded to explain what had happened, concluding with the suggestion he contact the local law enforcement official in the little town to report the purloined peaches.

"Okay," Peter conceded, "I can understand why you did what you did. I made some assumptions based on your history, and I apologize."

"You do? Shall I call a press conference?"

"Don't press your luck, Claire. This has been one rough day thus far." He rocked back in his chair and regarded me across the desk. "We're not making much progress, either. Zeno insists that he was unaware Ruthanne was inside the house when the fire started, and he may be telling the truth. We'd like to interview Ms. Magruder, but she's a nimble young woman."

"So you haven't charged Zeno? What about the message he purportedly sent to the hotel?"

"He says he didn't."

"If he did, he might not remember," I said as I tried to rock back in my chair. For all intents, it was bolted to the floor. Interrogatees were not meant to relax, obviously, but instead to sit up straight and pay attention. "But wait a minute, Peter. Harry said he took Ruthanne straight to the hotel. Why would Zeno *send* a message instead of calling her on the telephone? It seems odd, unless Joshua misquoted her."

"I didn't realize you'd cross-examined him, too," Peter murmured. "Is there anyone you've missed?"

"After I discovered Jasmine's body, I asked him to call 911," I said levelly. "While we were waiting on his porch, he told me that Ruthanne said Zeno had sent a message. Someone's lying."

"That occurred to us, so we went by the hotel and made inquiries. Someone with a muffled voice called the desk and left a message. The bellman was a bit surprised when Ruthanne answered the door, but he gave her the note. The gist of it was that she needed to come back to Willow Street if she wanted her husband to cooperate."

"So it could have been anyone," I said.

"Anyone who knew where she was staying."

I couldn't remember if she or Harry had announced it during the two unpleasant scenes on the sidewalk. It was likely that Anthony Leach had known, or even recommended the Drakestone Hotel during his call to Houston. He could have passed the information to Joshua Dwain. And I couldn't rule out Jasmine Hadley, who might have heard the same from Leach and disguised her voice. When she first arrived, Ruthanne had gone into the house with Zeno; once she'd realized it was a depository for junk, she might have told Zeno where she intended to stay. He might have told Melanie. I'd eliminated no one.

Peter was grinning at me. "Does the shrewd amateur sleuth have any brilliant deductions to share with the bumbling British chief inspector?"

"Only that Jorgeson has a good memory for trivial remarks." I wasn't sure why he was being so amiable, but I was willing to play along. "Have you received a preliminary autopsy report on Jasmine Hadley? Could it have been suicide?"

"There were no powder burns surrounding the entry wound, and no suicide note, either handwritten or contained in her computer files. We're treating it as a homicide."

"How long had she been dead?"

"Several hours."

"Does that clear Melanie? If she shot Jasmine, she wouldn't have hung around half the afternoon waiting for witnesses to pop in and admire her handiwork."

"It doesn't clear anyone, including you. We have no idea what Melanie did before her arrival at Miss Parchester's house. Maybe she remembered she'd dropped the gun in Jasmine's apartment and went back to retrieve it. It's unfortunate for Zeno that we'd allowed him to go get cleaned up and try to find Tillington. Leach spoke with Joshua Dwain at the hospital and then went to his office to work. No calls, no visitors. Dwain says he went home to rest. If Miss Parchester is telling the truth, she was off buying peaches, but she could have shot Jasmine on her way out of town. Tracy Dwain's the only one of them with an alibi."

"Miss Parchester has no motive, nor do I," I said with admirable dignity. "One of the others might, if

Jasmine saw something significant out her office window just before the fire. Did she?"

"She said she saw Joshua and Ruthanne out in front of the house. She went to the kitchen to get a pack of cigarettes, and when she returned, they were gone. She had resumed working when the fire broke out." He waited expectantly for me to blurt out more questions, but when I merely yawned, he said, "No one in the neighborhood knew much about her, other than that she claimed to be a writer. We searched the apartment and found very little in the way of personal effects such as an address book or correspondence from family and friends. We tried her agent's telephone number but got a message on the answering machine that said he was out of town. We're hoping he'll be able to help us when he gets back."

"Did she really write mysteries?"

"That's for you to find out, Ms. Marple. We're a tad more interested in her untimely death." He stood up and came around the desk to open his office door. "I'm going home to get some sleep. You'd better take some aspirin before you go to bed, Claire. That bump on your forehead may start aching in the middle of the night."

There was solicitude in his voice, as well as in his expression. He had apologized. He hadn't grumbled at me in well over fifteen minutes, and he'd offered tidbits of information like canapés on a silver platter. I wasn't sure of his motives, but I decided to take the magnanimous course and paused in the doorway.

"I'm sorry about my comment on the bench," I said. "It hasn't been much of a day for me, either."

His milky brown eyes met mine. "It could end on a high note, you know."

Willow Street was not mentioned again. At dawn, Peter dragged out of bed to go home, shave, and head for the police station. I lay in bed for most of an hour, trying to define my emotions and place them in orderly pigeonholes. A few curly black hairs remained on the adjacent pillow; I picked one up and twirled it between my fingers, wondering how I'd feel if I did so every morning. The problem was that we were a classic case of stereotypic roles, but they were reversed. I was supposed to be the one who demanded security and stability; he was supposed to be leery of commitment. Maybe we'd both paid too much attention to the women's movement in the seventies.

I was still musing as I made a cup of tea, went into the living room, and switched on the television. The local news, interspersed between lengthy segments in which carefully coiffed people laughed merrily, failed to mention Jasmine's murder. To my heartfelt relief, there were no reports of gorillas or bears roaming the alleys of Farberville. I made a mental note to remind Caron of potential consequences of getting caught in such undignified circumstances. At the least, Rhonda Maguire would rejoice in the subsequent ignominy.

It occurred to me that Miss Parchester was expecting to have her peaches delivered. After I'd explained where they were likely to be, I could ask her if she'd seen Ruthanne arrive in a taxi as Joshua had said. She was the only remaining witness now that Jasmine had been killed. I was also curious to find out when Melanie had dropped by—and what she'd said.

I glanced at Anthony Leach's well-tended yard as I parked across the street. As I'd recalled, there was NO FOR SALE sign prominently displayed to attract the attention of potential buyers. He'd made it clear that he was desperate to sell the house and Zeno's nonsense had soured a promising deal. Could he have witnessed Ruthanne's encounter with Joshua, waited until the latter left, and then either had words with her or followed her inside the house? He had an obvious motive for the arson, but it was hard to assign him one for her death. Why not simply wait until she left?

Miss Parchester came out onto her porch. "How nice of you to come so promptly, Claire. I like to allow the compote to simmer all day to bring out the flavor. My goodness, what happened to your forehead?"

I followed her into the living room and told her my theory concerning the present location of her peaches. She shuffled into the kitchen and returned with two cups of tea, then sat across from me and said, "They were very juicy peaches. I do hope that man and his pet enjoy them."

I did not comment on her innocent assumption about the relationship. "Tell me about Melanie's visit."

"When I came home last night, I found her hiding in the garage. She was extremely frightened and begged me not to call the police. I agreed to listen to her story before deciding." Miss Parchester took a sip of tea and twinkled at me over the rim of the cracked porcelain cup. "It's very important to have all the facts. Papa used to—"

"Why did Melanie go to Jasmine's apartment?" I asked hastily.

"I'm not quite clear about that, but I believe she wanted to find out if Jasmine had been looking out the window just before the fire. She'd been there only a moment when she heard someone coming up the stairs. She picked up the gun out of fear, then realized she'd put herself in a very sticky situation and decided her only hope was to flee."

"And she fled to your house," I said. "How convenient for her that you were away."

"I was not unsympathetic, since I myself have found the need to avoid the police on occasion. They can be narrow-minded in the midst of an investigation."

I couldn't argue with that. "Did you get any hint of what Melanie thought Jasmine might have seen?"

"I would think she saw what I saw," Miss Parchester answered in a tone that implied my question was uninspired. "Her window looks out on the front of Zeno's house."

"What did you see?"

"I believe I was telling you on the telephone about Joshua's immature display when I heard a second voice. I wasn't sure, since Nick and Nora were barking ever so loudly and I was concerned about them. I did go out onto my front porch and observe a most unmannerly exchange between Joshua and Ruthanne. She went so far as to slap him. I do not believe that physical violence can resolve a conflict of that nature. It only serves to heighten an already volatile situation. I was about to go out into my yard and tell her so, but the dogs once again started barking as if the bears had returned. Did I mention that there were bears in the backyard earlier in the evening?"

"I think you did," I said, not sure if I ought to blurt out the truth. Unlike the resident on Washington Avenue who'd called the animal-control officer, she did not seem particularly upset at the idea of ursine prowlers. "So Ruthanne slapped him? He gave me the impression she'd threatened to call the police, and this was enough to send him slinking home. Are you positive he had a gun?"

"Oh, yes."

"You seem to be the only person who saw it."

"Ruthanne Gorgias certainly saw it. She said some very cruel things about his lack of courage to use it should Zeno present himself as a target. Joshua protested, which is when she slapped him. She then snatched the gun out of his hand and left him on the sidewalk. It must have been very humiliating for him."

"So Ruthanne took the gun away from him," I said slowly. "He's such a pompous little thing with old-fashioned ideas about male superiority that it truly must have been humiliating. He lied about it to the police, but he may have thought the gun was destroyed in the fire, along with the only person who knew he'd had it." I looked at Miss Parchester, who appeared to be fascinated by the configuration of her tea leaves. "Did you tell the police about this?"

"The only time I've spoken with them was last night when they came banging on the door. They were so rude about Melanie's visit that I merely answered their questions and sent them away."

"Did they ask you if Melanie still had the gun she picked up in Jasmine's apartment?"

"I told them she did not."

I leaned forward. "How did you know that, Miss Parchester?"

"At some point yesterday she acquired a backpack and a few articles of clothing. After your call, I asked her to make a fresh pot of tea, and I took the opportunity to search through her things. I took the gun out of her backpack and hid it in one of my dresser drawers. I hope she won't be too angry when she discovers that it's missing, but I felt I had no choice." She refilled my cup while I sat and blinked at her, then added, "Unfortunately, the gun is a .357 Magnum."

"Unfortunately?"

"If it had been a revolver, Melanie could have cleared herself by submitting to a paraffin test."

"And you didn't mention any of this to the police," I said as I sank back.

"Melanie is in enough trouble by now, and as we both know, it's against the law to carry a concealed weapon. That is in no way protected by the Second Amendment."

I wondered what Papa would have said.

TEN

As soon as I arrived at the bookstore, I called Peter and told him the purported location of the elusive weapon. He did not sound especially grateful for my civic-minded assistance, but I wrote it off to his lack of sleep. I made coffee, poured myself a mug, and settled down with the morning newspaper to see what was to be gleaned like golden nuggets of wheat (or whatever wheat comes in, anyway) from within its inky confines.

There was a large photograph of the burning house and a smaller one of Zeno, who had ignored the reporter's questions in order to elaborate on the significance of interactive environmental art. The police had refused to comment on the ongoing investigation into the fire and the discovery of Ruthanne's body.

Jasmine's death had not merited the front page. The article buried toward the back related only the bare bones—that she had been found in her apartment by an unnamed friend. The police again had refused to comment.

Somebody needed to comment about all sorts of things, I thought as I sipped coffee. Melanie would be my witness of choice, but she was unavailable until the police nabbed her or she chose to resurface. Her track record was such that I'd put my money on the latter.

I finished the newspaper without finding any reports of unconventional backyard pillagers. After I'd done the crossword puzzle, I flipped to the real-estate section and scanned the agency ads for a reference to Anthony Leach's house. When that proved futile, I dialed the number of the largest agency.

"I'm only interested in the historic district," I said once I'd been transferred to an agent. "Do you have any listings on Willow Street?"

"No," the woman said brightly, "but just this morning we listed a fantastic old house on Washington Avenue. It has four bedrooms, two—"

"Nothing on Willow Street?"

"There have been some problems in that area. Why don't we run by this house on Washington so you can appreciate what a bargain it is? All it needs is a little bit of remodeling and—"

"I understand bears have been reported in the area," I said, murmured a polite farewell in the ensuing silence, and moved on to the next agency. By the time I called the last of them, I'd pretty much figured out that Leach's house was not listed in the customary fashion. I squinted at the row of FOR SALE BY OWNER ads, eliminated as many of them as I could based on the terse descriptions, and then dialed the number of the first of the remaining ones. It was located near the campus. The second was a mobile home, the third in a swanky new subdivision. My next several calls went unanswered.

I was beginning to question the brilliance of my scheme as I dialed yet another number.

"Anthony Leach and Associates," said a woman in a transparently contrived British accent.

I mentally patted myself on the back. "I'm calling

in response to an ad in the newspaper concerning a house for sale."

"I'll put you through to Mr. Leach."

Panic replaced smugness, and I considered hanging up before Leach came on the line and recognized my dulcet tones. However, I wasn't going to get any answers if I didn't ask any questions, so I clamped my nose between my thumb and index finger and hoped for the best.

"Good morning!" Leach said with excessive enthusiasm. "I understand you're interested in the ad in the paper. I don't believe my receptionist caught your name, Mrs.... ?"

"No, I don't believe she did. Can you tell me about your house and neighborhood?"

He described it all in glowing terms, stressing the charm of the setting, the venerable maple trees, the spectacular azaleas and rhododendrons, the convenience of the library, and so forth. "The price is already more than fair," he went on, "but I am willing to accept a sum substantially below the appraised value if you're flexible."

"Flexible?" I squeezed my nose more tightly. "What do you mean?"

"I would require a certain amount of cash up front as a sort of—well, deposit on the offer. The price of the house would be lowered accordingly."

"Is that legal?"

"As an attorney, I am well versed in the laws governing property transactions. Shall we make an appointment for you to see the house?"

"I still don't understand about this deposit," I said mulishly, presuming mules said things in an adenoidal whine. "If I give you a thousand dollars, then the overall price of the house will be a thousand dollars less?"

Leach harrumphed. "I was thinking of something

more in the range of twenty-five or thirty thousand dollars. Could you be so kind as to identify yourself, madam?"

"Dian Fossey," I said, then hung up and sat back with a smile. Leach might have been well versed in the pertinent laws, but I suspected he was more than willing to break a few of them in order to cheat his wife out of her share of the proceeds from the sale of the house. And he needed to do so before she returned and discovered he'd sold the shag carpet from under her feet. To my regret, that did not imply he would commit a murder to do so.

Toward the middle of the morning I called the Drakestone Hotel and asked for Harry's room. He answered with a groggy, "Yeah?"

"I apologize if I woke you," I said, "but I was wondering what happened to Zeno. Was he charged?"

"Not yet, but he can't leave town."

"Do you know where he is at the moment?"

"Yeah, he's right across the hall. We didn't leave the station until midnight, and then we went out to get a sandwich and something to drink. Long about the second drink, he got this grand idea that he was going to use all his money to buy property in the mountains and open a retreat for malnourished, under-appreciated young artists. He told me all about it until dawn."

"And the Dwains?"

"Sometimes Zeno has the attention span of a minnow." He yawned so broadly I heard his jaw creak. "I guess I'd better get off now and start trying to track down the insurance policy that covered the canvases destroyed in the fire. I may have to fly down to Houston later today or in the morning and go through Ruthanne's files. Keep in touch, Claire."

For the next half hour I tried to engross myself in invoices, but my mind kept drifting back to the spate of crimes on beleaguered Willow Street. I found a piece of paper and amused myself drawing a map of the relevant houses. The result would not have excited browsers in a San Francisco art galley, much less those in Paris, but it had a certain primitive charm. I added a small stick figure in front of Zeno's house and then added another to represent Ruthanne. Jasmine would have had a clear view of the two while they were on the sidewalk, but I wasn't sure if the roof of the porch might have blocked her view of the front door—and whoever opened it.

It was not an architectural riddle that could be easily resolved, in that the porch no longer existed and Jasmine's apartment was hardly on any guided tours. But she must have seen something, I told myself as I drew zinnias in Miss Parchester's front yard and basset hounds in the back. And someone had killed her to keep her from telling it to the police.

I was attempting to draw two cavorting gorillas when the front door opened and the ex-anthropoids themselves came trudging inside. "What did you do last night?" I asked.

"Nothing." Caron slumped against the nearest rack and flipped a trickle of sweat off her face. "It is so incredibly hot outside. I mean, even with the fan on, it was all I could do not to drown in my own bodily fluids. Why do I have to live in the only apartment in the entire country without central air-conditioning?"

"We just have window units," Inez began, then realized the enormity of her blunder and glided out of sight.

"Life's tough," I said.

"Life," Caron replied as she slithered toward the floor, "Is Unbearable."

I was not impressed. "Why is that, dear?"

"Rhonda Maguire is having a pool party tomorrow night," Inez said from the vicinity of the cookbooks.

"She said she wanted to invite us, but her mother will only let her have a total of five couples. She said she felt terrible about it, but if she really felt that way, she was hiding it well. It's not like we wanted to hear all the details about who the honorees are and what she's serving and how she's putting up balloons and streamers."

"Like we care," said Caron.

I had a hunch it was not the time for mature observations about the darker side of human nature. "Why don't you call some of your other friends and make plans to go to the mall? You can shop, get a pizza, and then go to a movie."

"And be totally humiliated if anyone saw us?"

"I fail to see why that would be humiliating. There are at least two hundred kids in your class. Ten of them will be at Rhonda's pool, which means a hundred and—"

"I Don't Do Math in the summer," Caron said as she stood up and brushed off her derriere. "Anyway, Rhonda is nothing but a virus that's mutated to the point she can't be cured with penicillin. She ought to be locked up in a lab so scientists can poke her with needles and drip chemicals into all her orifices."

"Acid," Inez contributed loyally.

I watched Caron as she headed for the textbooks, no doubt in search of the perfect compound to pour into a swimming pool. Suddenly it seemed like an ideal time to continue sleuthing—elsewhere. "Listen, dear," I said, "I need to run a few errands. If you'll mind the store, I'll pick up hamburgers and milk shakes on the way back, and you two can go have a picnic under a shady tree on the campus."

This was deemed quite as humiliating as being seen at the mall, but, after a tedious argument, I went out to my car. It occurred to me that I lacked a purpose, which meant I lacked a destination. The only person apt to be at home on Willow Street was Miss Parchester—unless she'd been hauled away to jail for impeding an investigation. I had no desire to pop into Anthony Leach's office to discuss illegal real-estate transactions. After such a lengthy session at the police department, Harry and Zeno deserved to be left in peace, albeit temporarily.

I finally decided to track down Joshua Dwain. He'd been evasive before, but he might be more forthcoming if I confronted him with what I'd learned and offered him a chance to explain. Five minutes later I determined I could do neither at his house, since his car was not parked in the driveway. Resisting the urge to engage in a bit of breaking and entering (I did so out of prudence rather than principle—a woman was sweeping her sidewalk near the corner and a bicyclist was coming up the street), I drove to the most likely place.

The Bible Academy was housed in a two-story structure with all the visual frivolity of an army barracks. In a former life, it had been the site of a private business college that had gone out of business once the federal government noticed that an unacceptably low percentage of the graduates were repaying their student loans—mostly because they were unable to find employment.

The parking lot was filled with shabby cars and bicycles. I parked on the street, opened the car door, and then hesitated, unsure how to comport myself in an environment fraught with future missionaries. Cursing was obviously out, as well as jocular references to their particular graven images. But what if they were to sense my lack of religious conviction? Would I be dragged away to a baptismal font to be saved from damnation? Would they hold me hostage and pray over me until I agreed to attend their Sunday school potluck suppers?

Perspiring only a bit, I went up a short flight of concrete steps and into a well-lit hallway. A few men and women moved about purposefully; none of them had the fervent gaze of an evangelist intent on saving a soul before lunch. In fact, I noted with a flicker of disappointment, they looked more like the staff of a large insurance office.

A sign near the entrance welcomed me and requested that I go directly to the office. I wasn't pleased at the idea of announcing myself, much less explaining the reason for my visit. However, there were at least a dozen doors on each side of the hallway and likely to be an equal number on the second floor. It was hard to envision myself opening every one of them in search of my prey.

A young woman in a white blouse, dark skirt, and unflattering wire-rimmed glasses approached me. Her complexion was as pasty as that of both Dwains; it seemed that fundamentalism was an indoor sport.

"May I help you?" she said.

"I'm looking for Joshua Dwain. I believe he's a student here."

"He just got out of a seminar. You may be able to catch him in the student lounge at the far end of the hall upstairs if he didn't already leave. The building's locked from noon till one."

I thanked her and went up the nearby staircase, wondering if I would regret this transgression into the inner sanctum. The hallway was uninhabited and significantly darker. Doors were closed, but there were no sounds from within to indicate classes (or masses) were in session. Downstairs, footsteps and voices faded as the students and faculty departed for lunch.

Peeling letters proclaimed the last door on the left to be the STUDEN L UNGE. I reminded myself I was in the middle of sunny Farberville, squared my shoulders to maintain the illusion I wasn't intimidated, and went inside.

The sofa was shabby, the table and chairs scratched, the soda machine of antique vintage, the carpet worn from years of accumulated abuse. A bare bulb in the ceiling cast an anemic light. No great flash of perspicacity was needed to understand why no one was lounging. Or lunging.

I was about to leave, when a door in the corner opened and Joshua Dwain emerged, accompanied by the sound of a flushing toilet. He jerked to a stop when he saw me and then said, "What are you doing here?"

"I came to talk to you."

"I have nothing to say to you. I've already told the police everything I know."

I shook my head. "No, you didn't, Joshua. You lied to them about having a gun the night of the fire. That constitutes impeding an investigation—especially when your gun may have been used in a second homicide."

"I didn't have a gun," he insisted, retreating as I advanced on him.

"The police now have the gun Melanie took from Jasmine Hadley's apartment after the shooting. It's a matter of time before they trace it back to you. They are notoriously unamused when they discover a witness has lied to them."

"They can't trace it back to me. I bought it from—" He stopped, but we both knew it was Too Late (as Caron would say).

"From a pawnshop?" I suggested.

"The shop was bulldozed out of existence years ago," he said with a shrug. "What business is it of yours, Mrs. Malloy? Hasn't there been enough tragedy already?"

I sat down on an arm of the sofa and considered his questions. "It's hard to explain, but at some obscure level, I guess I agree with Miss Parchester that an individual has the freedom to express himself as he sees fit, as long as he doesn't do actual harm. Shouting 'fire' in a crowded theater is one thing; putting a bunch of junk in your front yard is another."

"Are you saying no harm was done?" His eyes began to burn with the fervor I'd ascribed to evangelists. His voice grew louder until he was almost shouting at me. "Zeno's hands are covered with my wife's blood! 'Whoso sheddeth man's blood, by man shall his blood be shed: for in the image of God made he man.' Zeno deserved to have been inside the house when it burned to the ground! It would have been his first taste of eternal hell!"

I rather wished someone would come wandering into the lounge to use the soda machine. I would have warmly greeted a janitor, an officious secretary, or even the girl with the wire-rimmed glasses. As it was, I was intently aware that Joshua and I were the only two people in the building, and I doubted I could protect myself with a limp throw pillow or a handful of pamphlets expounding on the euphoria of chaining oneself to the door of an abortion clinic. It seemed wise to drop the topic of Zeno's guilt and return to a less emotional one. "I wasn't kidding when I said the police have the gun in their possession."

Some of the intensity faded from his face. "Okay, I had a gun when I was in front of Zeno's house that night. I wanted to scare him into realizing the magnitude of what he'd done. If he'd come outside, I . . . I don't know."

"But Ruthanne arrived," I said encouragingly.

"She didn't care about what happened to Tracy; all she wanted was to write a check to absolve herself and her husband of any responsibility."

"She took the gun away from you, didn't she?"

He sat down at the table and stared at his clasped

hands. "I wasn't man enough to take it back and slap the sneer off her painted face. Instead, I allowed her to make a mockery of me right there on the sidewalk. I turned around and went home like a whipped dog."

"So Ruthanne had the gun when she went up to Zeno's porch. Did you see who opened the front door?"

"The only other person I saw was Mrs. Hadley. She was standing at the window, watching us. I'm sure she enjoyed the scene as much as she enjoyed taunting Tracy for her beliefs."

"You didn't glance back? You didn't hear anything when Ruthanne went inside the house?"

He closed his eyes and pursed his lips. I wasn't sure if he was offering a prayer before he attacked me or merely recalling the events. It proved to be the latter when he said, "I think I heard a male voice say, 'Come on,' or something like that. It could have been, 'Come in,' I suppose."

"Was it Zeno's voice?"

"I don't know, Mrs. Malloy. It barely registered at the time, and I didn't look back. After I calmed down, I went to the hospital."

"What time was that?"

"I sat in the hospital chapel for more than an hour, and I got to intensive care at eleven." He looked at his watch, then picked up a briefcase from a chair and said, "I need to go to the hospital now so I can make it back for my next class."

I remained where I was as he walked out the door. What he'd admitted wasn't very helpful, I decided with a frown, and it did nothing to exonerate him. Miss Parchester had seen him walk away from the angry exchange, but he could have returned shortly thereafter, gone into the house, taken his gun back from Ruthanne and used it to hit her, then set the fire. His claim to have arrived at the hospital before ten could be a calculated lie.

But there might have been a witness in the hospital lobby. Surely Harry would have noticed Joshua's arrival. With any luck, he also might have noticed the time and be able to confirm or demolish Joshua's alibi.

Downstairs, a door banged loudly as Joshua left. I was alone in the Bible Academy, not a place I'd ever imagined myself inside, much less as the sole inhabitant and sovereign of the realm (until one o'clock). I could sing ribald barroom ballads, draw pentagrams on the classroom floors, and scrawl ominous messages about satanic rituals on the chalkboards.

However, Joshua would finger me and I'd find myself tied to a stake while he and his colleagues gathered firewood. In terms of interactive environmental art, it would eclipse anything Zeno could produce. Caron could sell enough tickets to buy a convertible (and Louis Wilderberry's attention, if not his devotion).

Telling myself to have a discussion with her about the incontrovertible flaws of the male psyche, I availed myself of the facilities in the rest room, wryly noting the coarse toilet paper (akin to a hair shirt, I supposed), and then came into the lounge in time to hear stealthy footsteps in the hallway. I slipped back into the bathroom and locked the door.

The footsteps continued into the lounge and across the room. Students and staff members would have no reason to creep around the building, even during the lunch hour. An unauthorized prowler would assume no one else was there to hear him or her and go stomping about. If Joshua had returned, he would know I was in the lounge. Sneaking up on me would serve no purpose.

I held my breath, which was just as well in the stifling confines of the tiny room. Surely the oxygen would not be depleted before the unknown person grew tired of the tacky decor and withdrew. The footsteps were replaced by other minute noises, impossible to identify. They, along with the dubious ventilation and darkness, were having a very poor effect on my usually impeccable composure. And the entire scene was annoying, not to mention ridiculous. I was not a dithery heroine who'd ascended one too many staircases in the middle of the night. I was nearly forty, not barely twenty-one. I owned a business, changed flat tires, and never whimpered when having my teeth cleaned. If I wished, I could purchase the appropriate equipment and climb mountains, kayak down churning rapids, blow up all the bridges in Madison County— or take up duplicate bridge.

I was about to burst out of the restroom and take my chances when I realized the noises had stopped. I opened the door and ascertained that the room was empty, then came out from my prison. No one had left a stack of pamphlets or a bucket of dirty water and a mop. There were no chalky pentagrams on the floor.

The prowler had been busy, though. Convinced I was the only person in the building, I'd not bothered to take my purse into the restroom. Now its contents had been dumped on the sofa and scattered on the floor. My wallet was wedged between cushions. I snatched it up and discovered that my last twenty-dollar bill was gone, but not my few credit cards and a dog-eared library card. Exasperated, I began to gather up the various treasures.

It took me a while before I determined that my car keys had not fallen beneath a cushion or been kicked under the table. Muttering a few words heretofore unheard in the hallowed halls of the Bible Academy, I crammed everything back into my purse and went out to the hallway in hopes that the petty thief had tripped and broken several bones in a mad sprawl over the doorsill. It was a particularly uncharitable thought, considering my locale, but I nourished it into full bloom as I stalked down the stairs and out the front door. My car was no longer parked across the street.

As soon as the door clicked behind me, I realized I'd locked myself out of the building at a time when I had no transportation. No one would return for another half hour. Even if I had access to a telephone, I wasn't sure whom to call or how to explain what had happened without exposing myself as an easily terrified idiot who could fantasize about climbing mountains but was unwilling to prevent her car from being stolen.

I was about to take a hike when I saw a pink bicycle partially hidden behind a bush. It was the old-fashioned kind, which meant it lacked elaborate gears and the sort of seat that sends many a proctologist's child through college. Caron had been outraged when she'd received a similar model for her twelfth birthday; her reaction had been the first hint of what had now become a full-scale hormonal cascade.

I pulled the bicycle out to the sidewalk and examined it. The tires were not flat, nor did there appear to be any damage to the frame. There were a few cobwebs in the spokes and a goodly amount of dust, but I surmised it was in reasonable working order.

I moved along to the moral perplexities. Of course, I would return it as soon as I could arrange other transportation, but taking it would constitute theft. The horrified owner might question her most cherished beliefs concerning the inherent goodness of her fellow students. Then again, the temperature was well over ninety and the store was at least two miles away. The owner hadn't pedaled away for lunch; it was possible she'd driven away in a stolen car.

The last hypothetical clinched my decision. I took

a deposit slip from my checkbook, scribbled a note of apology and the telephone number at the store, and stuck it on a branch of the bush where it was easily visible.

Then, gripped with the terror that had eluded me earlier, I climbed on the seat and grasped the handlebars. I'd last ridden a bicycle in college, but in theory, one never lost the ability.

"In theory," I croaked as I went weaving and wobbling down the street toward the Book Depot, where Caron and Inez impatiently waited to be relieved of their onerous responsibility. They might not care that my car and last twenty dollars had been stolen, that I'd committed a crime, or that I'd been forced to jeopardize my life to return. What was truly going to upset them was that I hadn't brought back lunch.

ELEVEN

By the time I rattled over the railroad tracks beside the Book Depot, my curls were plastered to my head like dead worms, my jaw ached, my neck tingled from a sunburn, and I needed windshield wipers to combat the sweat streaming into my eyes. I leaned the bicycle against the wall, made sure my legs were steady enough to carry me, and staggered inside the bookstore.

Caron and Inez were too horrified to do more than gape at me as I continued into the office, dampened a paper towel, and sprawled in the chair behind the desk to blot my dripping face. Whoever had stolen my car deserved something slightly more excruciating than being drawn and quartered, I decided as I reached for the telephone to report the crime.

"What On Earth have you been doing?" said Caron from the doorway. Inez nervously peered over her shoulder, her mouth round with wonder.

"Just listen," I said, then dialed the telephone number of the police department and asked to speak to Peter. He was unavailable, so I settled for Jorgeson. I was in the midst of my recitation when a realization thundered into my mind with the subtlety of a two-thousand-pound bison. Caron and Inez seemed to interpret my expression as symptomatic of an impending heart attack and silently disappeared, either to seek medical help or to avoid having to deal with icky symptoms.

"Ms. Malloy?" said Jorgeson. "Are you okay?"

"There's something strange about this," I said as I envisioned the parking lot and street next to the Bible Academy. "This was no casual thief who found my purse and took advantage of it. The perpetrator has to be someone who knows me—or at least knows my car."

"Now you just said your purse was in plain sight on the sofa and you were hiding in the rest room. It was likely to be a dope addict who waited in an empty classroom and, after everybody left for lunch, went looking for something to steal." He paused, then said tactfully, "You pedaled a long way, Ms. Malloy, and it's hot enough to raise blisters on the pavement. You probably ought to drink plenty of water and stay in bed the rest of the day. I'll get your license plate number from the DMV, file the report, and have the patrol officers keep an eye out for your car."

"If my car had been the only one in the parking lot, the thief could have assumed it was mine. But the lot was filled when I arrived, so I parked across the street. Whoever took the keys was able to recognize my car."

Jorgeson did not sound impressed. "Or got lucky."

"There were a dozen cars closer than mine. Do you honestly believe this thief went from car to car, testing the key? Wouldn't this look a little suspicious?"

"Then who was it?"

I tried to keep the frustration out of my voice, but I didn't have much success. "If I knew who it was, I'd already have told you, Jorgeson."

"I think it's going to turn out to be some addict, but I'll make a note of your theory in the report and have a word with the lieutenant when he gets back."

"Where is he?"

"Willow Street. I'm not supposed to tell you anything, but it looks like they found the blunt object used on Ms. Gorgias. The lab will have to confirm it, naturally."

I felt as if I were pedaling uphill and gulping lungfuls of carbon monoxide. "What is it, Jorgeson?"

"An empty ouzo bottle. The lieutenant's convinced Zeno's fingerprints will be on it. It just confirms our theory that Zeno left the message asking his wife to return to the house, let her inside, and then lost his temper and bashed her."

"He wouldn't burn down his house," I said. "He was very attached to it for sentimental reasons—Uncle Stenopolis and all that."

"So maybe someone else did it for him. We're still looking for Melanie Magruder." He repeated his suggestion that I drink water and take it easy, then hung up before I could ask any more questions.

I sat back and tried to imagine a desperate addict stumbling from car to car. Jorgeson's imagination obviously was better than mine. I filled a coffee cup with water and went into the front room, thinking fondly of my battered hatchback and the years (and years) it had served me loyally. It was not so much the loss of an old friend that unsettled me as the sense of impotence. I could not dash up to Miss Parchester's house for tea or to the grocery store for a carton of milk and a box of cookies. I could walk to and from the bookstore, of course, but I was confined to the area unless I were willing to pedal about town like a politically correct environmentalist. Which I was not.

"Weird," Caron said as she came back inside the bookstore. "That's my bicycle, you know."

"It is?"

"I scratched my initials on the frame one day when I was bored and everybody else was away at summer camp. I did it to bolster my low self-esteem. You may not have realized how demeaning it was to be the only sixth grader who did not—"

"Are you sure it's your bicycle?" I asked. "How could it be? I saw it in the garage a couple of days ago."

She gave me a pitying smile. "I am capable of recognizing My Own Bicycle, Mother. I was the only one of my friends who did not have a ten-speed, and I spent a lot of time debating whether or not to take a wrench and reduce it to nuts, bolts, and spokes. And that ghastly color! I was so mortified it's a miracle I didn't run away from home and join a—"

"When's the last time you saw it?"

"How would I know? It's been mildewing in the garage forever. Inez is waiting for me. I suppose we're going to her house to lay out. At least my obituary can say I had a good tan."

I was still struggling with her pronouncement. "Was your bicycle in the garage this morning?"

"I wasn't in the garage this morning. I spent the night at Inez's—remember? I guess short-term memory is the first to go."

She left before I could come up with an adequately scathing retort. I went outside and studied the bicycle. The scratches were too numerous to be deciphered, but the cobwebs and rust suggested it might have spent many idle years in a garage such as ours.

"Curiouser and curiouser," I murmured as I tried to figure out how it had made its way from my garage to the Bible Academy on the far side of the campus. It was not some uproarious cosmic coincidence. Someone had stolen the bicycle and later abandoned it for my car. Anthony Leach and Joshua Dwain had perfectly adequate cars of their own. Zeno had been driving his truck the previous day. Presumably, Harry was still using the rented Cadillac. Miss Parchester was not a plausible suspect.

But dear little Melanie Magruder had no transportation other than her fleet feet—and no misgivings when it came to matters of petty pilfering. Mentally adding grand theft auto to her rap sheet, I wasted most of an hour speculating about her present whereabouts. If my theory was correct, she had not left town after her cozy chat with Miss Parchester but instead had found a place to spend the night (my garage?) and expended a great deal of energy following me all over town.

Perhaps she was still determined to talk to Zeno, I thought as I refilled my coffee mug with water and scanned my notes. If she knew that Harry was staying at the Drakestone Hotel, then she might conclude Zeno was there, too.

It wasn't much to act on, but it was better than brooding all afternoon. I wheeled the bicycle inside, stuck the CLOSED sign on the door, turned off the lights, and was locking the back door, when I realized I couldn't jump in my car and drive to the hotel. My earlier sense of simmering impotence now boiled over like an untended cauldron brimming with eye of newt, toe of frog, wool of bat, and tongue of dog. And those were the prosaic ingredients.

Farberville lacked a mass transit system, and taxis did not rove the streets like lustrous yellow predators. The hotel was on the old square, where faltering department stores battled the evil forces of the mall with sidewalk sales, Christmas lights, and free parking—for those who possessed cars.

If I went back inside and spent the rest of the afternoon minding my own business (which had become a popular theme), I might find myself on foot for a very long time. It seemed likely that Zeno would be taken back into custody and charged as soon as the lab confirmed that his fingerprints were on the purported

weapon. Melanie would realize she had no hope of
talking to him and decide to see how far she could
get on whatever remained in the gas tank and a scant
fistful of dollars. Kalamazoo might be out of range,
but there were numerous potential havens along the
route.

This time my curses were more than vivid as I
climbed onto Caron's bicycle, settled sunglasses on my
nose, and wobbled away once more. I didn't bring the
traffic on Thurber Street to a halt, but I did earn a few
startled looks and crude catcalls. No one suggested I
might qualify to participate in the Tour de France.

The desk clerk at the Drakestone Hotel appeared
to doubt that I was of sufficient refinement to darken
the lobby of his establishment. Although he was well
under thirty, he managed to exude the pomposity of
a butler confronting an uninvited member of the bour-
geoisie. "May I assist you?" he said in a tone that
implied the premise was preposterous.

"I don't see how," I said as I stopped in front of
the elevator and tried to remember Harry's room
number, or even which floor it was on. It was not a
moment I would later share with Caron.

The desk clerk failed to appreciate my candor. "Are
you a registered guest?"

I turned around and stared at him, doing my best
to pretend I wasn't sweating copiously and likely to
pass out before I could punch an elevator button. "I
am here to visit a registered guest. You do have visita-
tion hours, don't you?"

"Please allow me to call this guest on our house phone
and inform him or her of your imminent arrival."

I was in a foul enough temper to say, "Then snap to
it. I haven't got all day to stand around and exchange
banalities with the hired help. The guest's name is
Harry Tillington."

The clerk kept his eyes on me as he made the call,

and his disappointment was evident as he murmured
into the receiver, told me the room number, and gestured at the elevator. "Mr. Tillington is expecting
you," he added, managing to make that sound even
more preposterous.

He was wrong. As I emerged from the elevator,
Harry came out into the hallway, hastily buttoning his
shirt. There were daubs of shaving cream on his damp
face and a towel draped around his neck. "Is something wrong?" he demanded loudly, then lowered his
voice to a whisper. "Is Zeno about to be charged?"

"It's likely. Where is he now?"

Harry pointed at the door across from us, then
pulled me into his room and shut the door. "I was
shaving," he said, in case I was unable to make the
leap for myself. "I'm supposed to catch a late-after-
noon flight to Houston. Maybe I'd better change my
plans. Zeno's been in trouble before, but never anything like this. Should I call the lawyer?"

"Calm down," I said, pushing him down on the corner of the bed. "As far as I know, the posse's not on
its way at the moment. Would you mind if I helped
myself to a glass of water?"

For the first time, he seemed to notice I was a bit
disheveled and that my winsome face was redder than
a winesap apple. "Let me get some ice, Claire. I'll just
be a minute."

He grabbed the ice bucket and disappeared down
the hall. I was about to sit down when I noticed a
door that was slightly ajar. Exertion may have dimmed
my innate curiosity, but it had not entirely diminished
it. I took a quick look into what proved to be an
adjoining room, and was perched on the sofa with my
ankles primly crossed when Harry returned.

"Have you talked to the police?" he asked as he
dropped ice cubes into a glass, filled it with water, and
gave it to me. His hand was shaking so badly that

water splashed on my knees, but I was too tactful—
and grateful—to mention it. His voice wasn't much
steadier as he continued. "Last night the police
seemed satisfied with Zeno's story, or at least acted
as though they were. They wouldn't have allowed him
to leave if they weren't, would they? Why are they
going to arrest him now?"

"They found the murder weapon—an ouzo bottle
covered with his fingerprints. That may be all they
need to charge him."

"What did they expect to find on an ouzo bottle
in that house—the Greek ambassador's footprints? It
doesn't mean anything. Sure, Zeno was angry at Ruthanne and worried that she actually might be able to
have him packed off to be evaluated." He went to the
desk and poured himself several inches of scotch, then
put down the glass and looked at me with a dazed
expression. "Hell, maybe he did it and just doesn't
remember. He's got to be the loosest cannon I've ever
met. I should have stayed in the car business with my
brother-in-law, even if he is a jerk. I could have ended
up owning the biggest Ford dealership in the Southwest and be taking free trips to Hawaii every year to
play golf and drink piña coladas by the pool."

Unable to contradict him, I said, "There may be
other fingerprints on the weapon, and as you said, his
would be there in any case. Is he still asleep?"

"Yeah, I guess so. I left a message for him at the
desk that I'll be back tomorrow evening. Before he
went to bed, he promised not to leave the hotel unless
he first checks with his lawyer. I wish I could trust
him." Harry sat down next to me and squeezed my
hand. "I don't suppose you'd agree to babysit until I
get back? If you just stay in my room with the door
open, you can stop him if he tries to leave. I'll be
back before you know it."

"Sorry," I said, "but I'm in too much trouble with

the police already. I have no way of preventing Zeno from doing whatever he chooses, and I don't want the responsibility if his choice is to board the next transatlantic flight."

"It was just a thought," he said sadly. "There's not much I can do for Zeno if he is charged, so I might as well try to find the insurance policies. I'd better pack and head for the airport if I want to make my flight."

"Let me ask you something, Harry. While you were in the hospital lobby watching for Zeno, did you see Joshua Dwain arrive shortly before ten o'clock?"

"I'm not sure about the exact time, but he showed up around then. He didn't see me, though. As soon as I spotted him coming across the parking lot, I scooted around the corner by the gift shop. I admit it was cowardly on my part, but the last thing I wanted was for him to start screaming at me. Excuse me for a minute while I finish shaving and pack my tooth-brush." He went into the bathroom and closed the door.

I glanced at the door that led to the adjoining room. Babysitting was not my style, but searching Ruthanne's hotel room certainly was. I rapped on the bathroom door and, over the sound of gushing water, said, "I'll let myself out, Harry. Call me when you get back from Houston."

Without waiting for a response, I hurried into the next room, eased the second door shut, and waited to hear indications of his departure. It would have been nice if he'd stopped to make an incriminating call, but he did nothing more diabolical than blow his nose before slamming the door to the hallway.

The room was identical to Harry's, except for the collection of luggage aligned against the wall and the designer outfits visible in the closet. The bed was made and the surfaces devoid of dust; in the bathroom, fresh bars of soap and tiny bottles of shampoo were aligned next to a daunting assortment of makeup accessories, barrettes and hairpins, jars of facial cream, and plastic vials of prescription medicines. As long as Harry kept the account open, the hotel seemed willing to pretend it had a guest who was not biologically dysfunctional.

I had no idea what I hoped to find. If there were fingerprints indicating that anyone other than Ruthanne, the police, and hotel maids had been in the room, I wouldn't be the one to chance upon them with a gurgle of glee. The police would have done a cursory search of the luggage, desk and dresser drawers, coat pockets, and other obvious spots. Surely Ruthanne had taken her purse with her when she went to Zeno's house. The wastebasket was empty. The pad beside the telephone was blank.

Sinking down on the corner of the bed, I waited for a burst of inspiration. My eyes drifted around the room and finally settled on a hand-tooled leather briefcase tucked behind a suitcase. The police had already pawed through it, no doubt, but they'd been in search of something concrete to further implicate Zeno. I wanted to find something to do the opposite.

The briefcase was unlocked. I released the clip and sighed at the skimpy contents: a packet from an airline, a piece of paper with Leach's name and a telephone number, a calculator, and an unsullied legal pad. Beneath the pad were a dozen unopened envelopes. In that ripping them open (or even discretely streaming them open) would constitute a federal offense, I merely read their return addresses. One was from a gallery in New York, another from one in Dallas. A third informed Ruthanne that she had qualified for a platinum credit card. Beneath that were several utility bills, bank statements, and letters from what sounded like brokerage firms.

The last in the stack was from the Internal Revenue

Service. Unlike the others, it had been neatly slit open. I pulled out the single page and read a superficially amiable message that did little to disguise a most unwelcome invitation. I'd received such a missive once upon a time. The subsequent audit had left me with a bout of gastritis and my accountant with a tic in his right eyelid and, so he claimed, a debilitating fear of small rooms.

From what Zeno and Harry had said about Ruthanne, I suspected she would have been more than prepared to take on the IRS. Unlike others of us, her files were apt to be orderly and inclusive, her bank statements effortlessly available, her portfolio as pleasurable to read as an illustrated Italian cookbook.

I shuffled through the envelopes once again and was about to replace them, when I realized I'd seen something peculiar on one of the bank statements. I retrieved it and looked more closely. It was addressed to Ruthanne H. Adair. The post-office box was not the same as that on the other envelopes, including the one from the IRS. After a moment of further shuffling, I found another from a brokerage firm addressed to R. H. Adair at the second post-office box.

So Ruthanne had two names, and post-office boxes to go along with them, I thought as I replaced the envelopes and closed the briefcase. If Adair was her maiden name and she'd taken the feminist approach of retaining it, she had not insisted on using it in all instances. The IRS might not have sent a wedding present, but it was aware of her married status; the letter was addressed to Zeno and Ruthanne Gorgias. The utility companies were not confused by any dual identities.

Wondering what it meant, I set the briefcase where I'd found it, took one final look around the room, and attempted to reenter Harry's hotel room through the adjoining door. Any idle dream I had of searching it evaporated when I discovered it was locked from his side. However, I'd discovered something of interest, and I was feeling rather proud of myself as I let myself out of Ruthanne's room.

Zeno's door was closed. I pressed my ear against it and heard a series of erumpent snorts and smacks that suggested he was asleep. I hesitated, unwilling to bother him but eager to find out if he'd heard from Melanie. It was conceivable that she was in bed with him, exhausted by her bicycle tour, exploration of the Bible Academy, and theft of a car.

I looked both ways and then tried the doorknob. Unsurprisingly, it was locked. I could have called him from either Harry's or Ruthanne's room, but I'd locked myself out of them as adroitly as I'd locked myself out of the Bible Academy. The desk clerk might become suspicious if I returned to the lobby to use the house phone, and he had the weasellike chin of someone willing to tattle to the police.

As I stood there, a housekeeping cart came squeaking around a corner. It was propelled by a figure in an ill-fitting uniform, bare legs, and sneakers. The bandanna around her head was not adequate to hide the thatched-cottage hair.

"I've been looking for you," I said coldly.

Melanie hunched her shoulders and feigned great interest in the collection of cleaning supplies. "Yes, ma'am," she mumbled. "I'll get to your room just as fast as I can. Please don't report me—it's my first day on the job and I'm still learning the routine. Sorry about the delay." She turned the cart and shoved it in the opposite direction.

I hurried after her and grabbed her arm before she could make it to the stairwell. "You can either stop and talk to me, or see how far you can get in the time it takes me to call the police and tell them where you are. I'm not saying they'll bring in a SWAT team and bloodhounds, but yesterday they described you as 'armed and dangerous.' "

"Well, that was yesterday. I don't know what happened to the gun, but it's not in my backpack anymore. I was annoyed because I was thinking I could pawn it."

"The police have it," I said. "Now, where can we talk?"

"How'd they get it?" she asked, startled.

"After you answer my questions, I'll answer yours. I assume that this new career of yours allows you access to all these rooms. Harry's is vacant at the moment."

"You sure seem to know things," she said as I dragged her down the hall. "And I'm beginning to wonder if you're following me. Every time I turn around, there you are. It's starting to get on my nerves. Don't I have the right to some privacy?"

"Yes, you do. You also have the right to remain silent because anything you say can and will be used in a court of law. You have the right to an attorney, and—"

"What is this—a comedy club?"

I unclipped the key chain from her belt and unlocked the door of Harry's room. "Yeah," I said grimly, "and I'm Whoopi Goldberg."

TWELVE

I led her to the sofa, glared until she sat down, then crossed my arms and said, "Where is my car?"

"Did you forget where you parked it? My aunt lost hers once in a mall parking lot. She couldn't find it until all the stores closed and everybody else left, and then she had to drive around town for a couple of hours before she remembered where she lived. She wasn't much older than you when they finally had to institutionalize her. It was real pitiful."

"I know precisely where I last parked my car—and so do you. What I don't know is where you parked it earlier this afternoon. I suggest you tell me right this minute."

"What makes you think I took your car?"

"What makes you think I won't put you in a closet and call the police?"

She sank back and shrugged. "It's out in the alley behind the hotel, but that doesn't mean I stole it. What happened was I got worried about you when Joshua Dwain came banging out of that Bible building like he'd just finished hacking up one person and was looking for his next victim. His expression was something to behold. You ever see that movie with Charlton Heston where he's Moses and he comes down

from the mountain with the stone tablets and finds
everybody in the middle of an orgy?"

I went to the desk and reached for the telephone.
"I don't need to look up the number, Melanie. Even
in my advanced stage of senility, I can remember
three digits."

"I was trying to liven up my story," she said huffily.
"Anyway, I was right there behind a bush, so I slipped
through the door before it could lock to make sure
you were okay. I looked around, then went upstairs
and tried all the rooms until I got to the lounge. Your
purse was right there, but you'd disappeared. I figured
Joshua had put your body in a storeroom and would
be back any minute to dispose of it. I was too scared
to stay there one more second. I picked up your purse
to take care of it for you, but then everything fell out
and I panicked and ran away."

"You overlooked a few elements in this enchanting
narrative. Everything may have fallen out of my purse,
but my money did not fall out of my wallet."

She had the grace to squirm. "I thought I'd better
have a little cash in case I needed to hide out until
the police arrested him. Like I said, I was too scared
to call the police from there, but then I saw your car
keys and realized I could drive straight to the station
instead of wasting precious time trying to find a pay
phone."

"But a funny thing happened on the way to the
police station?"

"You could say that." She gave me a companion-
able smile, but let it fade when she realized I was
not reciprocating. "I started thinking I was being silly.
Joshua wasn't covered in blood or carrying a weapon,
and if he'd killed you, he wouldn't have left your
purse right there where the next person couldn't help
but spot it. I still needed to find Zeno, so I decided
to come here and call you to make sure you were still

alive. I guess I forgot I had your car. The keys are in my backpack in the cart outside. Do you want me to get 'em for you?"

"Don't even think about it," I said. "When did you take the bicycle from my garage?"

"What bicycle would that be?"

"The bicycle that I found near the door of the Bible Academy and identified as my daughter's. You took it and followed me. I have a vague suspicion you were more interested in my assets than in my companionship. Whenever we have an opportunity to spend some quality time together, you take off."

She estimated the distance to the door, caught my expression, and sighed. "It's this murder thing that's got me all confused. The police asked me so many questions I couldn't think straight. Then I find this body and this gun, and you attack me, so—"

"I attacked you?" I said, more mystified than insulted. "I seem to recall being shoved into Jasmine's office. I've got a bruise to prove it. You're beginning to sound a tad pathological, my dear."

"It's been a hard week."

I sat down on the bed and stared at her. "It certainly has been. How did you end up in that uniform? Is there a stout, naked woman in the stairwell?"

"Of course not! She's in a very nice little supply room at the end of the hall, resting her feet and having herself a cigarette. I wasn't sure if the police would be watching Zeno's room, so I thought I'd better check it out before I went banging on his door."

"Do you know which room he's in?"

"No, but I found out Harry Tillington's room is on this floor. If Zeno's here, he's bound to be where Harry can watch him. I don't suppose you know which is his room, do you? I really need to talk to him and it's getting kind of sticky."

"I would say it's getting very sticky, Melanie.

You're a fugitive as well as a suspect in two homicides. As I mentioned earlier, the police consider you to be armed and dangerous. A high-strung rookie might shoot you on sight. Your best chance is to tell me what it is that's worrying you. If I agree that you need to talk to Zeno, I'll tell you his room number and you can have a few minutes with him. But then you absolutely must call Lieutenant Rosen and wait for him."

"Can we have a drink first? I sure could use one after all the bicycling I did today. I almost lost you so many times I couldn't count 'em, but then I'd go around the corner and you'd be at a stoplight. I'm sure good old Harry wouldn't mind if we helped ourselves just this one time."

"You may have a drink after you've called Lieutenant Rosen. Talk to me, Melanie."

"Oh, all right," she said. "After Zeno and I had our argument, I went upstairs like I said. I was thinking about packing my stuff and heading for the bus station, but then I decided to wait until morning in case Zeno wanted to apologize. When that guy started yelling out on the sidewalk, I went into the front room so I could see what the hell was going on. He sounded so crazy that I got worried he might break into the house and come after me, too, so I went downstairs and locked the front door."

I held up my hand. "Wait a minute, Melanie. You and Zeno both told me there were no keys to any of the doors."

"There's one of those little chain things like the one on that door right over there. It was so rusty I wasn't sure it would do any good if he tried to kick down the door, but it was better than nothing. Then I went back to the bedroom and wedged a chair under the doorknob."

I considered the implications of what she'd said. Un

less Ruthanne was a great deal stronger than she'd
appeared, she had not kicked down the front door.
Someone had undone the chain and admitted her.
Joshua Dwain had heard a male voice as he walked
across the street. It did not require much mental effort
to come up with an obvious suspect—and it wasn't
one of Miss Parchester's basset hounds.

"You have to tell this to the police," I said to Melanie. "I realize it won't help Zeno's case, but you have
to tell them anyway."

She pulled off the bandanna and ran her fingers
through her hair. Once it was ruffled to her satisfaction, she said, "I'm not talking to them until I hear
what Zeno has to say. I haven't seen him since yesterday morning when the police came and hauled us off
to the station. I hadn't asked him if he undid the
chain, because it didn't matter until the police told me
about Ruthanne's body. Up until then, I didn't even
know she set foot in the house, much less went and
got herself killed."

"You and Zeno were the only two people in the
house. One of you must have let her inside. If you're
telling the truth, you didn't. That doesn't leave a lot
of other choices."

Melanie's eyes filled with tears. Snatching up the
bandanna, she went into the bathroom and slammed
the door. I should have taken the opportunity to call
Peter, but I myself wanted to hear what Zeno had to
say. I was once again teetering at the brink of some
very hot water. She was more than capable of dashing
down the stairwell, leaving me in an even more awk-
ward position. But I'd pretty much promised her that
she could have a moment with Zeno before she meekly
turned herself in. I would have felt a good deal less
apprehensive if I had been handcuffed to her, but that
was not an option until my Junior G-Man kit came in
the mail.

When Melanie emerged, her eyes were red but her cheeks were dry. "I want to talk to Zeno," she said, her hands on her hips.

"Let's go get my car keys and the money you took from my wallet, and then I'll take you to Zeno's room," I said, aware that I was in danger of a swan dive into the hot water—and that the swan dive was apt to be a swan song, as far as Peter was concerned. "Please promise that you won't run away this time, Melanie. I was almost arrested last night because the police thought I'd stashed you at Miss Parchester's house. I do not care to go through that again."

"Did that old lady take the gun out of my backpack?"

"She was worried that you might get into more trouble for carrying a concealed weapon."

"I don't see how I could get myself in any more trouble than I'm already in," she said, grinning. "So I'm armed and dangerous, huh? Do you think I'll make the most-wanted list and have my picture on the wall at all the post offices in the country? That'd really impress folks back home. We've never had a local celebrity."

I bit back a laugh as she practiced her front and profile poses in the dresser mirror. "Anything's possible."

"Not anything. For instance, I can't give you back your twenty dollars. I had to give it to the maid to convince her to loan me her uniform and the cart."

My momentary amusement dried up. "Melanie, you have got to stop bribing people with my money. I didn't mind buying you lunch, but I am not at all pleased to be funding these dubious activities of yours. Go get your backpack and give me back my keys before you get the impulse to trade my car for a movie ticket and a bucket of popcorn."

"I was going to bring your car to you later today,"

she said as she marched past me and out the door.
"When I first met you, I thought you were a nice
person, but all you've been doing lately is accusing
me of things. I may have to reconsider my opinion
of you."

I had no reservations about my opinion of her: in-
corrigible. I followed her down the hall and waited
until she took her backpack from under a pile of wet
towels. Once I had the keys in my pocket, I said,
"Zeno's in the room across from Harry's, or he was
when I saw you coming around the corner. Let's find
out if he's still there, shall we?"

She had no difficulty seeing through my artful ploy.
"I don't recall inviting you, honey."

"I am not letting you out of my sight," I said, "and
the meter's running. If you want to stand here and
argue, it's fine with me, but in exactly five minutes
one or the other of us is going to be on the telephone
with Lieutenant Rosen."

"I wish you'd get off this thing about him. He was
polite enough, but he sure did a lot of sitting across
the table like a bullfrog, not even blinking. I was beginning to feel like a juicy dragonfly by the time he
let me leave."

"Four minutes and counting," I said.

"Come on, then." She went to Zeno's door and
pounded on it with her fist. "Zeno! Open this door!"

After a moment in which at least one of us was
holding her breath, Zeno obliged. He was wearing
only skimpy briefs, but this did not deter him from
bounding into the hall to throw his arms around Melanie. "My dear! I have been so deeply worried about
you. The police kept badgering me with questions
about where you might be. And this terrible shooting
across the street! They seem to think you're involved,
but I assured them that you would not do such a
thing."

"Let me go," Melanie said, struggling to free herself. "We've got to talk—right now."

Zeno obediently dropped his arms and looked at me. "Do the police know she's here?"

"Not yet," I said as I herded them into the room, closed the door, and leaned against it, trying to look as stony as an Easter Island monolith. "But Melanie's going to turn herself in as soon as she's asked you something."

He flopped across the bed and gazed mournfully at the ceiling. "Why must they hound us like this? All I want to do is make my art so—"

"Cut the crap," snapped Melanie. "Listen up, Zeno. Did you unhook the chain right before the fire?"

"What chain?"

"The chain on the front door. I hooked it when that religious weirdo started yelling threats."

Zeno lifted his head to look at her. Despite his wounded expression, there was an undertone of sharpness in his voice. "I told the police many times that I remained in the back of the house, where I heard no one at all. I did not hear Joshua's threats, nor did I hear Ruthanne when she came inside the house."

I couldn't decide if he was lying. I heartily agreed with Harry's estimation of Zeno as a loose cannon. His self-absorption was unparalleled in its constancy and dedication. And he was far from witless. "Melanie swears she didn't unhook the chain. If you didn't, who did?" I asked.

He rolled out of bed and began to pace as best he could in the confined space, his face creased in thought, his hands cutting through the air. I prudently retreated to the sofa and watched him with the awed fascination of a child at a zoo. A near-collision motivated Melanie to take sanctuary in the middle of the bed, her feet tucked under her.

"I have it!" he said abruptly as he barely averted a

close encounter with the edge of the desk. "The two actresses who were to symbolize the impingement of nineteenth-century science on traditional religious mythology—they could have hidden somewhere in the house. Perhaps they locked the door to the storage room and waited there until they thought we were upstairs. They came out and unhooked the chain in case they needed to escape through the front door. But in came Ruthanne—with a gun!" He widened his eyes and bared his teeth in facetious terror. "They panicked, hit her on the head, and then set the fire to cover up their crime. We must find out who they are and tell the police at once!"

"The two so-called actresses didn't have anything to do with it," I said. "When the commotion started out in front, they climbed through the kitchen window. They were at their respective homes well before Ruthanne arrived."

"Are you sure?"

"Very sure," I said firmly. I was debating whether to elaborate when there was a knock on the door.

Melanie gulped. "I don't suppose you ordered room service?"

"No," Zeno said, "but it could be Harry. Yesterday while I was being questioned, he went out and bought me some clothes, but they did not please me. An artist does not wear boxers and a banker's suit. Maybe he's bringing me some new things."

"Or it could be the maid," I suggested in a thin voice.

It proved to be none of the above, alas, but instead a quartet of uniformed officers, which is why I did not pull into my garage until nearly three hours later. This is not to imply I wasn't delighted at the idea of sleeping in my own bed rather than on a cot in an odoriferous cell. Melanie and Zeno did not share my fortuity;

he'd been charged with first-degree murder and she with conspiracy.

Peter had been livid, or so I assumed based on the one quick glimpse of him I'd seen on my way to the interview room. He had not entered the room or asked to speak to me when Jorgeson finally sent me away. The young officer who'd driven me back to the hotel had exercised his right to remain silent, and so had I.

My car was in the alley, parked under a sign that warned a tow truck would be summoned. The officer grunted but did not start writing a citation on the spot. One of his colleagues had already done so. I added the twenty-five-dollar charge to Melanie's account.

But I was free, although Jorgeson had made no promises that I would remain so after Peter finished with Zeno and Melanie and could consider my involvement (he would use another word). It was too late in the afternoon to bother reopening the bookstore; I would wait until the morning to make a million dollars, retire, and move to a little-known Caribbean island where the only corpses would be those of flattened mosquitoes.

I was not surprised when I determined that Caron's bicycle was no longer leaning against a wall in the garage. A pallet of old blankets in one corner confirmed my theory that Melanie had availed herself of my unsuspecting hospitality. Wondering if I might as well openly adopt her and add her name to the checking account, I trudged upstairs.

She had never gotten her drink, I thought as I poured myself one and wandered into the living room. It was likely she wouldn't get much in the way of her choice of liquid refreshment for a long while, although I was not at all convinced she was responsible for either death. I tended to believe her story about hooking the chain, since it only served to make one of the two occupants look all the more guilty.

Unless she was trying to heap more suspicion on Zeno, of course. But why bother, when it would have been so much easier to fade into the sunset, never again to darken the sidewalks (and bookstores) of Farberville? I'd thwarted her once, but she'd had abundant chances over the last twenty-four hours. And a variety of modes of transportation, courtesy of a meddlesome bookseller.

In any case, I resolved to resign from my role as Oracle of Willow Street. Peter would have to tunnel his way to the truth without the benefit of my well-intentioned contributions. Zeno had the services of an experienced criminal lawyer and the financial resources to keep him captivated. Melanie would end up with a public defender, but there was nothing I could do about that.

On that cheery note, I changed into my robe, fixed a sandwich, switched on a fan, and settled in to do some fictional sleuthing. At some point, Caron called to say she and Inez were sleeping at the latter's house because it was Not An Inferno. I told her to call in the morning.

I was trying to pin the crime on the donkey (okay, the vicar's second wife's ne'er-do-well brother) when the telephone rang again. Praying it wasn't Peter, I picked up the receiver and made a tentative noise.

"Oh, Claire, the most dreadful thing has happened," Miss Parchester said, her voice ascending into a plaintive wail. "I don't know what to do!"

THIRTEEN

W hat is it, Miss Parchester?" I demanded as visions of bodies danced in my head.

"It's Nora. She's deathly ill. Her belly is so bloated that I'm terrified she has some sort of intestinal blockage. She's lying in the grass, her eyes closed and her tongue just—just lolling. Her breathing is laborious. I don't know what to do, Claire. Should I call an ambulance?"

"Don't call an ambulance," I said. "You need to take her to your vet. I'm sure there's an emergency after-hours number, and this definitely qualifies."

"My car is in the shop. A nice man towed it in earlier today, but he's not going to have it ready for me until tomorrow. I can't wait until then!"

"Call the vet and tell him we're coming. I'll be there in five minutes." I yanked on shorts and a T-shirt, grabbed my keys, and ran down the steps to my car. It had grown dark while I was reading, and I realized it was nearly nine o'clock. In that I wasn't overly fond of dogs, my concern was for Miss Parchester, who was more than overly fond of hers. Her recitation of Nora's symptoms did not forebode well for either of them.

I pulled into the driveway and left the engine running. Miss Parchester rushed me through the kitchen to the back porch. Nora was sprawled near the bottom step, covered by a blanket. Nick barked from somewhere in the yard.

"I reached the vet," said Miss Parchester. "He's going to meet us at his office. Can you lift her?"

"I'm going to try my best. Hold the back door for me." I knelt beside Nora and appraised the situation. The dog, to be blunt, was a chunk of lard; if she was more bloated than usual, I couldn't see the difference. While Miss Parchester twittered behind me, cautioning me to take care and remarking (rather offhandedly, in my opinion) that Nora might attempt to bite me, I slid my arms under the patient and somehow made it to my feet. Nora opened her eyes and rumbled menacingly, but subsided with only a rivulet of drool.

"How much does she weigh?" I gasped as I staggered through the kitchen, banging one hip against the counter and, seconds later, the other against the table. I would not have scored well in a ballroom dancing competition.

"Forty-three pounds. The vet was very unhappy with me for allowing her to get so chubby, but I cannot resist her when she looks up at me with those soft, brown eyes. She does so love her little doggie treats."

"And T-bone steaks."

Miss Parchester opened the front door. "My pension doesn't allow that luxury even for myself. No, every week when I shop, I buy a box of Choco-Bones for her and Meatie Treaties for Nick. He's not as partial to sweets."

My arms were screaming by the time I deposited Nora in the backseat of my car, but I managed to do so without dropping her or losing any of my own flesh. Miss Parchester arranged the blanket and then hurried around to the passenger's side.

After I'd elicited the address of the vet's office, I backed out of the driveway and squealed around the corner onto Thurber Street as if we'd just knocked off a bank. "Has Nora been acting peculiar lately?" I asked.

"Why, yes, both she and Nick have been in a state of agitation for days, barking at odd hours and refusing to finish their meals. I'd hoped that once things quieted down next door, they would revert to their happy selves, but they've gotten worse. Sunday night they began barking at dark and never completely settled down, but the police insisted on searching the yard and then lingered until dawn in case Melanie returned. Tonight they started up again and refused to quiet down. Colonel Culworthy must be furious with me over my inability to control them, but I've tried everything I can think of, short of bringing them inside."

"Why not bring them inside?"

"Fleas," she said. "They wear flea collars and I bathe them every week, but nothing seems to work."

And Nora was in my backseat. Trying not to imagine Caron's reaction when a flea attacked her, I pulled into the parking lot in front of the vet's office. The vet appeared immediately, scooped Nora out of the car, and carried her inside. Miss Parchester scurried after him, describing symptoms and apologizing for the necessity of disturbing him at home.

I followed them through a dim waiting room to an examination room flooded with fluorescent light. The room appeared to be adequately equipped for everything short of a heart transplant, but it was not a milieu I frequented on even rare occasions. The vet was of Miss Parchester's generation, with bushy white eyebrows, a bald head dotted with freckles, and a weathered face. He laid Nora on a stainless-steel table and pulled back her eyelids.

Miss Parchester touched his shoulder. "What is it, Dr. Hassard?"

"I won't know until we get test results from the lab, but it looks like barbiturate poisoning. I'm going to give her an injection and pump her stomach. You ladies need to wait outside."

"Never," said Miss Parchester, her face alarmingly pale but her expression determined. "I've had some medical training. I rolled bandages during World War Two, and I watched *Doctor Kildare* very faithfully. I await your instructions."

I stayed in the doorway, although I fully intended to retreat when the unpleasantness began. "Barbiturates? How could she get hold of them?"

Dr. Hassard's scowl made it clear that he found me somewhat less intelligent than the majority of his patients. "Since Nora does not have easy access to a pharmacy, someone must have given them to her, perhaps in hamburger meat. There appear to be a few bits around her mouth. Put on an apron and rubber gloves, Emily. You're going to need them."

"I'm going back to your house, Miss Parchester," I said. "I'll search the backyard and make sure Nick is okay, then come back here."

"Yes, dear," Florence Nightingale said absently as she figuratively rolled up her sleeves.

Neither of them glanced up as I left the examination room. Miss Parchester had not yet grasped the implications of Dr. Hassard's response, but when she did, she might forget some of the particulars of her extensive medical training. Unless Nora had gobbled up all of the lethal meat, Nick was in equal danger.

I almost cried in relief when I heard him barking. Almost, that is. I ran through the house to the back porch. There was meager light from the bulb above my head, but I was too frantic to go back inside and rummage through the drawers for a flashlight.

"Nick?" I called in a good-doggie voice. It didn't sound very convincing to me, but I wasn't dealing with

a Rhodes scholar. Miss Parchester had once told me
how her darlings had been expelled from obedience
school because of inadequate socialization skills.

He was still in the back, where the shrubbery had
created a veritable jungle over the decades. Hoping
he wouldn't peg me as a prowler and come snarling
out of the undergrowth, I began to search the yard as
systematically as I could. Five minutes later I found a
white Styrofoam cup, its rim riddled with teeth marks
and its interior licked clean. Shortly thereafter, I found
a second in a similar condition.

"Did Nora make a pig of herself?" I asked Nick,
who'd finally ceased barking and crept out far enough
to watch me. If I'd believed in anthropomorphic descriptions, I would have characterized him as petulant.
"Is that your problem, buddy? She got yours, too?"

Nick failed to answer my questions as he came forward, his tail wagging timidly. I ignored his comradely
gesture and finished searching the yard. There was an
inky recess beneath the porch. I suppose I could have
crawled into it and felt around for another cup, but
as I tried to talk myself into voluntarily risking contact
with spiders and other grossities of nature, I felt a
cold, disgustingly wet nose touch my ankle. I went
back up on the porch and pointed my finger at him.
"I don't do fleas, so hold it right there. You'll have
to wait here until we get back. Stay out from under
the porch, don't talk to strangers, and beware of
Greeks bearing gifts, okay?"

I stopped in the living room long enough to find a
house key in a basket, then locked the door and was
on my way to my car when I realized what I'd said to
Nick. Was it possible Zeno had thrown the cups over
the fence? I could concoct no motive for him to have
done so, nor for anyone else—except a neighbor who
could no longer put up with the canine cacophony.
The retired military man who lived next door was a

dog fancier. I had no idea who lived across the alley behind her house.

Miss Parchester was in the waiting room when I returned. There were some stains on her housedress, but instead of inquiring into their source, I assured her that Nick was fine and asked about Nora.

"She's going to recover," she said, beaming. "Dr. Hassard wants to keep her overnight, so we can leave. I do appreciate your help, Claire. I've been such a nuisance since all this bother started. You've been so kind to put up with us, and so patient, too. While I was waiting for you, I decided to make you executrix of my estate. If I should predecease Nick and Nora, I can take comfort in knowing they'll be looked after with affection."

She continued to ramble as I escorted her to the car. I felt a prickle of guilt over her presumption that I shared her concern for her dogs, but I kept my mouth shut save an occasional modest protest that I was not yet ready to be assigned a feast day. Therefore, I was unprepared when she abruptly changed the subject.

"Who did this vile thing, Claire?"

"I gave it some thought on the way back to the vet's office, but I didn't come up with anyone," I admitted. "Colonel Culworthy would never do something like that. What about the people on the far side of the alley?"

"Directly behind me are two sisters, Charlotte and Barbara MacMert. They're a tiny bit crotchety, and they steadfastly refuse to pass out candy at Halloween or buy Girl Scout cookies. However, they have at least a dozen cats, and I'm certain they would never harm Nick and Nora." She paused to blot the corner of her eye with a tissue. "And they left last week for a cruise down the Nile—or was it up the Nile? Oh, dear, I can't recall."

"It doesn't matter," I said gently. "What about the other neighbors?"

"One of the houses next to theirs is vacant, and the other is occupied by students who play music so loudly they wouldn't hear a sonic boom directly overhead."

"Call the animal shelter in the morning and report this," I said as I pulled to the curb in front of her house and handed her the front door key. "Ask if anyone else has reported a similar problem in the last week or so. It may be the work of some twisted kid who hates dogs."

"Could it be related in some way to the bears I saw in my backyard?"

"I don't think so," I said. "Will you do something for me, Miss Parchester?"

"Of course! Shall I make you a rhubarb pie? Mama's recipe won honorable mention in a contest in a magazine. If you don't care for rhubarb, I could make a pineapple upside-down cake or perhaps a blueberry cobbler."

"I have something specific in mind. I'd like to have a list of the times when Nick and Nora barked for no apparent reason. Think it over in the morning and give me a call when you're done; I'll come by to pick it up after I close the store."

"Are you sure you wouldn't prefer a rhubarb pie?"

"Quite sure, Miss Parchester."

I waited until she was safely inside, then drove home and fell into bed. I wish I could say I slept like a sedated basset hound, but I couldn't stop trying to fit together what might be a lengthy string of unrelated incidents. I would have had better success analyzing my feelings for a certain cop.

The following morning my body felt as if it had been in the path of rogue elephants. Muscles I'd never heard from in the past made their presence known with a vengeance. My progress to the kitchen was turtlish. Lifting a cup of coffee was painful. Certainly I'd experienced more physical strain the previous day than I had in, say, the last ten years combined, but I was worried that this was indicative of my advancing years. It was obvious that I could no longer blithely abuse my body without suffering its retribution.

It was a sobering thought, and it haunted me as I opened the Book Depot, read the paper in hopes of finding an article about dogs and drugs, and, when I could think of no more excuses to procrastinate, called Peter.

"Yes?" he said in response to my greeting.

"I'm sorry about Melanie," I said despite an urge to hang up and crawl under the counter. "She swore she'd call you as soon as she talked to Zeno. I didn't think an extra five minutes would matter. She did tell me something she hadn't told you earlier."

"Did she?"

I scrupulously repeated what she'd said about the chain on the front door. "That just makes it look all the worse for Zeno, doesn't it?"

"Maybe."

At least we'd broken the monosyllabic word barrier. Encouraged, I said, "But yesterday afternoon he came up with a half-baked theory about how Caron and Inez could have been hiding in the storage room. Don't you think it's possible that"—I realized I was speaking to a dial tone—"someone else was in the house, Mr. Moto? Joshua Dwain could have cut through someone's yard and gone around to the back of the house. Anthony Leach and Jasmine Hadley could have done the same. What if one of those three killed Ruthanne? Why, you ask? I'll work on it and get back to you as soon as possible. In the meantime, have a really nice day. *Sayonara*, Mr. Moto."

I replaced the receiver and stalked into the office to make immature faces in the bathroom mirror.

When that palled, I returned to the front room. My map of Willow Street was still on the counter; I sat and stared at it until that also palled. I finally turned it over, wrote the names of the principal players across the top, and tried to place each of them during the significant times. Ruthanne Gorgias was the only one of them with an irrefutable alibi for Jasmine's murder on Sunday afternoon, I decided with a discouraged sigh. Zeno and Melanie had been allowed to leave the police station. I had no idea what Zeno had done prior to his visit to the bookstore. Melanie had definitely been in the neighborhood, as had Joshua. Harry had not burdened me with his whereabouts. Anthony Leach's car had not been in his driveway, but he might have preferred not to advertise his presence and returned on foot.

I did no better eliminating possible dog poisoners. If I could be sure the Styrofoam cups had been thrown over the fence shortly before Miss Parchester found Nora in obvious distress, I could cross off Zeno and Melanie, who'd been in custody, and Harry, who presumably was in Houston. This left Leach and Joshua. However, there was no way to guarantee that the cups had not lain unnoticed all day. Or that Nora had not stashed them under the porch to lick at her leisure.

Or that this last dastardly crime had not been committed by someone who had received a poor grade in a journalism class ten years ago and had carried a grudge ever since.

I might be able to eliminate one suspect. A call to directory information in Houston produced Zeno's telephone number. (Picasso most likely had an unlisted number, along with Michelangelo and those guys.) Harry could have found the papers and been on his way back to Farberville, but it was not yet noon and he'd implied he would be back in the evening.

He answered the phone immediately. "Has Zeno

been charged?" he asked as soon as I'd identified myself.

"With first-degree murder," I said. "Melanie was charged with conspiracy."

"Where did they find her?"

"She was in the hotel room when the police came to pick up Zeno." I was considering whether to mention the third occupant when a question came to mind. "Harry, did you speak to Melanie at any time in the last two days?"

After a pause, he said, "No, the only time I actually laid eyes on her was Friday evening when Ruthanne and I had just arrived in town and she fell out of that tree. Last night Zeno was really worried about Melanie, but he claimed not to know where she was. How did she end up at the hotel?"

"Zeno must have told her that you and Ruthanne were staying there, and she figured out that you arranged for a room for him after the fire. What's odd is that she knew which floor you were on and was prowling around in hopes of finding him. The desk clerk is not an accommodating sort who would volunteer the information."

"Gee, I don't know," Harry said slowly. "Could she have called the hotel and talked to Zeno?"

"She didn't know which room he was in. All she knew was that you were on the fourth floor."

"I can't help you there. Thanks for calling to tell me about Zeno. I've already found the insurance policies. As soon as I've replaced all these folders, I'll go out to the airport and see if I can catch an earlier flight."

I realized he was sitting at Ruthanne's desk and that her filing cabinets were near—if not at—his fingertips. "Wait a minute, Harry. Did you know that Ruthanne was using the name Adair in some of her business transactions? She has at least one bank account in that name, as well as a letter from a brokerage firm."

"How do you know that?"

I could think of no remotely credible lie, so I told him the truth. "I didn't open the letters," I added virtuously, as if this negated the minor crime of searching her room. "Did she ever say anything to you that might explain it?"

"No, but she may have kept the savings account she had before her marriage, and she hadn't gotten around to informing her stockbroker of her new status. When I was married, my wife and I had separate accounts. Frankly, I don't think it means much."

"Maybe not," I conceded, "but as long as you're there, why don't you look through the files and see if you can find out what kind of accounts they are and how much is in them? If they're what you said, there should be only small sums. I heard Ruthanne say she'd been a clerk in a department store. I wouldn't think her salary would leave her with a lot of money to save—or to invest."

"I don't know if I should," Harry said, quite as virtuous as I'd been earlier. "Some of the drawers are locked."

"Then by all means start with those. The key's likely to be in a desk drawer. You're Zeno's agent, so you're acting on his behalf. The files are his property now."

Harry agreed and hung up. I was complimenting myself on my brilliant idea when a shadow fell across the floor.

Lieutenant Peter Rosen stood in the doorway.

FOURTEEN

Peter entered the store with all the enthusiasm of an acrophobic bungee jumper. His eyes were definitely not twinkling playfully, and no one but the most incurable romantic would accuse him of fighting to suppress any amorous impulses. The aura of antagonism that accompanied him was enough to singe my eyebrows.

"We have to talk," he said stiffly.

"Are you sure you wouldn't prefer to skip the preliminaries and go straight to the Miranda? It would save both of us some time, and, in all honesty, I'm not up to waltzing, verbally or otherwise."

"All I said is we have to talk."

I crossed my arms with only a tiny wince. "Go ahead, make your day. I'm guilty of everything you think I am, and a great deal more that you haven't discovered yet. This is not to imply I'm going to break down and offer a litany of my sins. I believe that's covered by the Fifth Amendment, but I may be wrong. Perhaps I should call Miss Parchester. Dear Papa must have written an opinion at some point."

"Don't be like this," said Peter, his expression easing fractionally (although said fraction was nowhere in the range of one half; my best estimate was one zillionth). "I spent the morning on the carpet with the chief, who's taking more than a cursory interest in the case. Your name shows up in the reports more frequently than our suspects'. The chief seems to think I'm in some way responsible for your continued involvement. He hinted that if I didn't put a stop to it, I might find myself in charge of security at high-school football games."

"How cheeky of him to assume you have any control over my actions. I hope you told him that I am a liberated woman who does exactly as she pleases."

"I may have mentioned that," he said with a rueful laugh.

He was trying to win me over—or at least partially disarm me—with his boyish demeanor, but I wasn't buying it. "Please note," I said, "that I am here at the bookstore, diligently doing whatever it is everyone keeps insisting I should be doing. Since I was permitted to leave the police department late yesterday afternoon, the only contact I've had with any of the Willow Street residents took place last night when I drove Miss Parchester and Nora to the vet's office. Do try to appreciate the fact that I have not asked you to drop the homicide investigation in order to devote all your energies to finding out who attempted to poison the dogs. Unlike your chief, I am not cheeky."

"Poison the dogs?"

"Someone threw cups of doctored meat into Miss Parchester's backyard. I suppose if each dog had eaten its share, neither would have been in much danger. As it was, Nora out-foxed Nick and ate both." I held up my hands in the traditional conciliatory gesture. Since I couldn't cross my fingers to absolve the impending fib, I did the best I could with my toes. "I suggested that Miss Parchester call the animal shelter this morning to find out if other cases had been reported. That was the end of my involvement."

"Poison them with what?" persisted Peter, who clearly was not grasping the essence of my speech, which was my very commendable (and equally fraudulent) withdrawal from the investigation.

I told him the details and then added, "*Sedate* is a more accurate term. I have no theories why anyone would do this, although Miss Parchester did admit that the dogs have been barking more than usual these last few days. She doesn't think any of her neighbors did it, though."

"I'll look into it—if you'll promise me one thing."

I crossed my toes harder and gave him my saintliest look. "Anything, Peter."

"I want you to promise to stay away from the Drakestone Hotel. We're keeping it under surveillance, and if word gets back to the captain that you were seen there, I'll spend the next four months busting potheads under the bleachers."

"Why would I want to go back to the Drakestone Hotel? I was not made to feel welcome there, and the desk clerk was smirking so hard when I was escorted through the lobby that I was worried his lips might implode. Well, I suppose I wasn't exactly worried."

"Zeno was arraigned this morning and is free on bail. He agreed to inform us of any change of address."

"I told you that I'm no longer concerned with the case. However, I do think it's considerate of you to keep an eye on Zeno until Harry gets back from Houston. I just hope the taxpayers don't find out that their hard-earned dollars are being spent on babysitting."

"We're predicting that Melanie Magruder may show up at the hotel again."

I dropped my pose and stared at him. "Melanie Magruder? How could she show up at the hotel ...

unless she's no longer in custody? Did she make bail and then disappear?"

"She escaped early this morning," he said, blushing like a schoolgirl. It was quite adorable, although I did not say so and instead arched my eyebrows and mutely waited for him to elaborate. He did so unhappily. "Just before dawn she started writhing on the floor of her cell and moaning about her appendix. The matron fell for it, called an ambulance, and was filling out the necessary paperwork to transfer her when Melanie bolted out the door. Half the staff has been suspended and heads will roll like balls in a bowling alley, but that doesn't do much in the way of getting Melanie back in custody."

"I tried to tell you she was slippery," I said, "but you wouldn't listen to me."

Peter ignored this opportunity to apologize. "Just stay away from the Drakestone Hotel—and away from Zeno. We have more than a circumstantial case against him. He's admitted he was at the scene, and his fingerprints are on the murder weapon. He's hot-headed, especially when he's been drinking. It's a straightforward case of domestic violence. We see way too much of it these days."

"What about Jasmine Hadley?" I demanded. "That was hardly domestic violence."

Peter approached the counter, although he maintained a judicious distance. "She must have seen Zeno open the door. We don't know why she didn't tell us the next morning, but perhaps she thought she could blackmail him, or she had a crush on him and was protecting him. It seems to be a common affliction. A lot of women have fallen for his dubious charms."

It was an exceedingly tactless remark. I gave myself a moment to compose myself, then said, "Zeno feels a moral imperative to make passes at women. Besides, being flattered is not unpleasant."

"Is flattery what you want?"

"No," I said crossly, not caring for this shift in the conversation. "I just don't believe Zeno killed Ruthanne. Have you taken a hard look at Joshua Dwain? He's more than capable of appointing himself an avenging angel of death. I was very uncomfortable yesterday when he was frothing at me. He actually said that Zeno should have died in the fire, and no doubt Melanie, too."

"He has an alibi for the time when the fire started. From witnesses' reports"—he eyed me narrowly but managed to keep any serious undertone of accusation from his voice—"the fire spread very quickly. Joshua Dwain was already at the hospital."

"Harry told me he saw Joshua in the lobby, but he wasn't definite about the time. Maybe Joshua arrived a few minutes after ten o'clock. That would have given him ample time to drop a few matches and drive across town."

"The shift changes at eleven. One of the orderlies who was keenly aware of the time saw Joshua walking in the direction of the chapel before ten o'clock. That concurs with Harry Tillington's account."

"What about Anthony Leach? He's desperate to sell his house while his wife is gone. Zeno's antics had already soured one deal. Late Friday afternoon Leach said something about another potential buyer. That's why he was so frantic to file the class-action suit and get a temporary restraining order."

"Both of which are within the realm of proper legal procedure," Peter said. "Murder and arson are not."

"Thank you for sharing that tidbit of legal trivia with me. Up until now, I'd assumed they were suitable pastimes for members of the bar. Does Leach have an alibi for Saturday night before the fire started?"

"He says he was at his office."

"Flimsy."

"The officers at the scene said you could have set the fire, raced down the alley, and then come strolling up Willow Street to establish your alibi. I tried to tell them that you do not race down alleys, but they looked unconvinced when they left my office. One of them begged me to stake out the Book Depot. I'm afraid we just don't have the manpower at the moment."

"Is there anything else you care to share with me before I resume my arduous duties as a dispenser of literary enlightenment?"

He looked at me for a long while, trying to unnerve me into breaking the silence. I refused to fall for his ruse by imagining him as Melanie had described him: an unblinking bullfrog. I'll admit I was beginning to feel the teeniest bit like a dragonfly when he finally said, "We have to make a decision about our relationship, Claire. You don't want to end up in another marriage as stifling as your first, and neither do I. You're everything my first wife wasn't, which is why I fell in love with you right after I accused you of murder."

"You disguised it well," I said primly.

"You were a very viable suspect, but I don't believe in long-distance relationships; in your case it might have been between Farberville and the women's detention facility three hundred miles away. However, I want you to know I'd already decided I would visit you every other Sunday for the duration of your sentence—despite the fact that you were rude to me."

"Did I accuse you of being a murderer? I think not."

"I was only doing my job," he said, covering my hand with his. "And I was only doing my job Sunday night when I had you picked up for impeding the investigation. I hoped it might persuade you to stop snooping."

I couldn't decide if I ought to snatch my hand free and insist he leave, or come around the counter and fling myself into his arms like a lovestruck teenager. I finally opted to do neither. "Well, I have—but not because of anything you've done. I'm still grappling with this upcoming birthday. I've made more resolutions than I made over the last thirty-nine New Year's Eves combined. One of them is to swear off apologies, so I'm not going to say I'm sorry you got chewed out by the captain because of me. Another is to stop telling Caron she'll be sent to a boarding school in Greenland, although I have not completely discarded the possibility. I will no longer feel guilty about my failure to join an aerobics class, my fondness for scotch, my aversion to dogs, and my ineptitude in matters of technology. I shall become as crotchety and miserly as the MacMert sisters. I have no intention of mellowing in my old age, and I cannot imagine why anyone would desire a permanent relationship with the new Claire Malloy."

"Nor can I," Peter said as he tightened his grip and gave me what I presumed was intended to be a seductive smile, "but for some inexplicable reason, I'm willing to give it a try."

The new Claire Malloy was not impervious to his charm. "I just don't know what I want," I said, sighing. "I've told you before that I'm afraid to give up my independence, and the thought of a significant commitment makes me uncomfortable. What would happen if I woke up six months from now and realized I wanted out? I don't want to be responsible for anyone's emotional carnage—yours, mine, or Caron's."

"Marriage can wait if you're adamant."

"I'm not *adamant*. I'm confused."

"We could start in a small way and see what evolves. Sublet your apartment. We'll find a house with a separate wing for Caron, and two bathrooms

off the master bedroom so you won't have to divide
the cabinet space. If you prefer, we'll each have our
own bedroom and we won't trespass without an explicit invitation. I'll handle all of the living expenses,
as well as the jaunts to Tahiti and Europe."

I tried for a flippant tone to cover my panic. "That
doesn't seem equitable in this day and age. Shouldn't
we merge the accounts, meticulously split the bills, and
mow our respective halves of the yard?"

"I want you to have the resources to leave if and
when you choose to do it. You can continue to run
the store and keep the profits in an account under
your own name."

My mouth was faster than my mind, and it's possible
I was subconsciously desperate to change the subject
before I found myself co-signing a lease. "Did you
know that Ruthanne Gorgias had accounts under her
maiden name?"

"No, I didn't know that," Peter said, his voice calm
but his eyes glazing with a light frost. "Why do you
know that?"

Earlier I'd had the urge to crawl under the counter.
Now the idea was positively mesmerizing, but I swallowed and said, "Harry sort of let me in her hotel
room, and I found some letters in her briefcase. She
had at least one bank account as Ruthanne Adair.
There may be more, including ones in Switzerland and
the Grand Cayman Islands. I think she may have been
stealing money from Zeno."

He resolved my dilemma by jamming his hands in
his pockets and stalking out of sight behind the science
fiction rack. I didn't know exactly what he was doing,
but curses were audible above the traffic outside the
store.

"That adds to his motive," I said loudly. "He had
yet another reason to be angry with Ruthanne. Maybe
she said something when they were inside the house

Friday evening that made him suspicious. She'd just learned they were going to be audited, and she could have let something slip. Jasmine told me the two had a screaming match Saturday afternoon. It could have come out then." The response I received was irrelevant, not to mention vulgar. "All this does is strengthen your case, Peter. I'm only trying to help, you know. If Zeno's guilty, he deserves to be locked up for a long while."

"Does this mean you have no interest in a house with three bedrooms, three baths, and a formal dining room?" he asked from the region of the travel guides.

"Why would I want a formal dining room?" I replied evasively. "You know I don't cook."

"One is allowed to eat pizza by candlelight."

I was trying to come up with an adequate rebuttal when Miss Parchester came into the store.

"Good morning," she said. "I wanted to drop by and thank you for all you did for me last night, Claire. I don't know what I would have done without your help. Even if I'd had my car, I couldn't have carried dear Nora. Dr. Hassard called to say she's doing well and is ready to come home. I'm on my way to pick her up now." She gave me a vague frown. "There's a reason I came here rather than calling you with the good news. I can't seem to recall what it is, though."

I glanced at the rack, then smiled brightly at Miss Parchester and did my best to steer the conversation in a more circumspect direction. "I'm delighted that Nora has recovered. May I assume your car has recovered as well?"

"Yes, a man delivered it to me this morning and even accepted my invitation for a cup of tea and a poppy seed muffin. He proved to be quite interesting. His first two wives were sisters; one of them attacked the other with a barbell and spent a year in prison. He and his third wife live in a trailer just past the airport. She's an aspiring country singer and has performed several times at a club in some little town."

"Oh, really? Maybe we should go listen to her sometime. Do you know the name of the club?"

"No, but if you truly want me to, I can call Birdie at his garage and ask him."

"That's a splendid idea." I came around the corner, took her arm, and tried to propel her toward the door. "Let me know what you find out and when this woman will be performing in the future. You and I can put on our cowboy boots and have ourselves a night on the town, Miss Parchester. Maybe I can persuade Luanne to join us."

Miss Parchester's orthopedic shoes seemed to be glued to the floor. She held her purse aloft and said triumphantly, "I've finally remembered the purpose of my visit. It's right here in my handbag."

"Good for you," I said. "Now you'd better run along and fetch Nora. I'm sure she'll be thrilled to see you and Nick after a lonely night in a cage. Thanks for dropping by, Miss Parchester. Drive safely—and give my regards to Dr. Hassard."

"But don't you want the list, Claire? I began working assiduously on it as soon as Birdie left. There may be some omissions, naturally. My memory's not as good as it used to be when I was a young girl. I used to memorize poems to recite at our Sunday afternoon tea parties. I was particularly fond of Emily Dickinson. 'We never know how high we are/Till we are called to rise . . .' Oh, dear, how does the next line go?"

I literally dragged her out the door to the sidewalk. Ignoring her obvious bewilderment, I whispered, "I'll take the list now."

As soon as I'd tucked it in my back pocket, I tersely thanked her and aimed her in the direction of her car. I would have preferred to accompany her to the vet's office—or anyplace else she was going, including a fruit stand at the far edge of the county—but such a pusillanimous act would only heighten Peter's suspicion that I had not retired from the case.

I went back inside and was easing onto the stool as he came out from wherever he'd been lurking (and eavesdropping).

"It's good to know the dog recovered," he said, flashing his perfect white teeth.

"Isn't it?"

"And so thoughtful of her to come all the way to the Book Depot to deliver a list."

"Isn't it?"

"While the two of you were outside, I tried to guess what this mysterious list contains, but I couldn't come up with a single conjecture. It wouldn't have anything to do with the homicides on Willow Street, would it?"

"Is that your best shot, Wimsey? I'm disappointed in you. If you must know, it isn't a list at all. It's Mama's recipe for rhubarb pie. It won honorable mention in a contest."

"Did it? Why don't you let me make a copy to send to my mother. She's back at home now and is forever complaining about her cook's uninspired desserts. If this recipe is good enough to win honorable mention . . ." He flashed even more teeth at me.

"You must be terribly busy with the investigation, especially now that the captain is breathing down your collar. I'll make you a copy and give it to you later."

"Later? Does that mean we have plans?"

"I thought you wanted to go house hunting. If you've changed your mind, you'd better say so. Otherwise, I'll close the store promptly at five o'clock, and we'll have a couple of hours of daylight to drive around and look at neighborhoods. Once we've found ones we particularly like, we can work with a real-estate agency."

Peter's stunned expression indicated that he had not

been prepared for this. "No, I haven't changed my mind. Do you want me to pick you up here or at home?"

"Here will be just fine," I said sweetly. I managed not to giggle until he had walked out the door, and then I promptly fell apart as I replayed the scene. This led to the discovery that I'd pulled muscles in the vicinity of my rib cage, but the pain was not enough to curtail my mirth.

The arrival of a customer finally obliged me to regain a semblance of propriety, even though it was only my aged-hippie science fiction fan. I doubted he knew his fashion statement (baggy, torn, stained) was back in style. He would have found it deeply depressing.

"Having a good day, huh?" he asked before he wandered out of view behind the rack.

"I guess I am," I said as I watched his head bobble above the top row of paperbacks. Once he'd bought a book and left, I took out the pages Miss Parchester had given me and smoothed them out. Her spidery handwriting in lavender ink was familiar; when she'd coerced me into dog sitting, I'd been presented with six pages of directions, including an admonishment to converse daily with her African violets.

Rather than a succinct list of times, I was treated to a rambling narrative replete with psychological analysis and acerbic remarks about the violation of the spirit of the First Amendment. Ten minutes later I'd deciphered the final word and had a reasonably clear idea of the moments when the dogs were agitated.

Nick and Nora had been barking sporadically since the day Zeno moved into Uncle Stenopolis's house, but, according to Miss Parchester, they'd become inured to the point of rarely bothering to do more than growl if Zeno or Melanie came too near the fence. The son et lumière on Saturday evening had provoked

them into an extended outburst even before it began.
Miss Parchester had been "most terribly discouraged"
when they began to bark shortly before Joshua
Dwain had appeared with a gun. After a paragraph
debating the possibility that they possessed some
sort of psychic ability, she concluded that they were
still nervous about the earlier confusion. And about
the bears.

Her explanation may have satisfied her, but I wasn't
convinced. I took out my diagram and added a column
for the dogs. Their bouts of barking almost—but not
precisely—coincided with what logically should have
been the provocation. I don't know what Sherlock
Holmes would have deduced from dogs that did bark
in the night.

I made a mental note to ask Miss Parchester if she
was certain about the times, then glumly studied the
other columns for inspiration. I myself was most terribly discouraged when Caron and Inez came into the
store.

"What are your plans for today?" I said politely.
"You should make the most of the next two weeks.
After that, the public school system will seriously in-
terfere with your idyllic freedom."

Caron snorted. "Gee, Inez, should we go to my
house and watch boring old movies, or go to your
house and write a hagiography featuring Rhonda?
We've only got two more weeks to have all this fun."

"What's a hagiography?" I asked her.

"I Don't Do Vocabulary drills in the summer,
Mother. Bookstores carry dictionaries, don't they?"

"I suppose we could play tennis," said Inez.

"It's only a hundred and twenty degrees outside,"
Caron said, her sarcasm verging on savagery. "We'd
fall over dead after one set. Let me write out my will
before we go put on our perky little white dresses and
get our rackets. I think I'll leave everything under my

bed to Rhonda. She's got dust balls for brains—maybe some more will make her smart enough to figure out how a straw works. You'd think she'd be an expert at it. After all, she certainly sucks."

"It was just an idea," Inez protested with rare spirit.

"Yes, it was—and a Very Stupid one, if I may say so. We might as well go lie in the middle of the tracks and wait for a train."

Inez yanked off her glasses and rubbed them on her shirttail so vigorously they squeaked. "If you want to do that, I'll sit in the shade and keep you company. How does that silly poem go? Something about a peanut sitting on the railroad tracks, his heart aflutter—and splat! He's peanut butter."

"I'll splat you!"

"Try it!"

I intervened before the tension escalated to the point of fisticuffs. "Trains don't come through Farberville anymore. Why don't you go to the pool at the city park and swim? There was an article in the paper this morning about how high the attendance has been this month."

My daughter stared at me as if I'd suggested they spend the afternoon giving each other lobotomies. "Grungy little unwashed children swim in that pool. Many of them are too lazy to go into the locker room when they need to urinate. Do you honestly expect me to swim in yellow water?"

"Then why don't you buy a box of Choco-Bones and visit Nora? She ate some drugged meat last night, and I had to rush her to the vet's office. This morning Miss Parchester was allowed to take her home."

"Choco-Bones?" Caron said incredulously. "How utterly disgusting."

"Or T-bones, if you have enough of your allowance left," I said. A fragment of a previous conversation tumbled into my mind. I pulled out my diagram and tried to recall when I'd seen Nick and Nora with steak bones. Sunday afternoon, I decided, right after Melanie had hopped over the fence and disappeared behind Miss Parchester's garage. The steaks could not have been laced with barbiturates; Nick and Nora had been serenading the neighborhood when Miss Parchester had hitched a ride home after her car broke down.

Caron was not intrigued by my perplexed expression. "I am not spending a dime on something called Choco-Bones. If I actually had a dime, I'd make a down payment on a Maxima. It's a Really Hot car."

"That's nice," I said, trying to think of a reason why someone would give expensive steaks to the dogs. As far as I knew, there was no philanthropic foundation dedicated to such a noble cause. A neighbor who was unable to put up with the barking would be more likely to speak to Miss Parchester or call the animal-control office and make an official complaint.

"Let's go," Caron ordered Inez. "We can sit on the wall at the corner of the campus and count the number of times the stoplight changes in an hour. It'll distract us from thinking about what a bitch Rhonda is."

"Only temporarily," Inez said as she loyally fell into step behind her intrepid leader.

"Only temporarily," I echoed under my breath. Someone had tried to distract Nick and Nora, but only temporarily. When that had failed, he or she had taken a more drastic (although less costly) step with the hamburger meat. Had someone been determined to break into Miss Parchester's house through the back door?

I bent over my chart. The owner herself had been absent all day Sunday. Why not break a window on the side of the house, where the bushes would provide adequate cover? The next day, Miss Parchester had been at home. Was this prowler willing to risk her hearing a noise at the back door and calling the police?

And what was the purpose of this unauthorized entry? There were a few good antiques, but most of the clutter was worthless. The mismatched china was chipped. The silverware was plate. The clock on the mantle had ticked its final tock years ago; the hands were rusted and the glass cover cracked. Miss Parchester was more than willing to share her family history over tea and muffins, and she was not picky about her companions. No one would leave with the erroneous notion that she had thousands of dollars under her mattress and jewelry in the canisters.

I considered the possibility that someone was trying to harm her. She would not have kept back potentially damning evidence in order to blackmail a murderer. Could she have seen something without realizing its significance?

"What?" I asked myself irritably as I ran my finger down her column, searching for a clue. When I failed to uncover even a microscopic one, I gave up and dialed Miss Parchester's telephone number. She did not answer, although she'd left the Book Depot more than an hour earlier. But she could have taken a detour to buy a box of Choco-Bones, or dallied to chat with Dr. Hassard about becoming his assistant.

There was nothing I could do except keep trying. Peter would not be impressed with my reasoning—at least not impressed enough to put out an APB and assign an officer to act as her bodyguard. Calling him with such demands might put a damper on our cozy plans for later in the afternoon. I'd agreed to house hunt to throw him off balance, which it most noticeably had. But was I really going through with it?

I looked at my watch. I had less than four hours to make a decision that was going to have a significant effect on my future, no matter what I chose to do. Earlier the hippie had asked me if I was having a good day, and I'd said I was.

But I wasn't.

FIFTEEN

When the bell above the door jangled, I was sitting on the stool—and doing nothing productive. I wasn't sorting out the whereabouts of the suspects. I wasn't reorganizing the diagram to reflect more accurately the times when Nick and Nora had barked. I wasn't wondering how many times the stoplight by the campus changed every hour. Most importantly, I wasn't examining my emotions in order to figure out what to do at five o'clock when Peter came into the store. Even Miss Marple takes a break for a cup of tea now and then. In my case, it was iced tea and a chicken-salad sandwich. Chicken salad is one of my comfort foods—and I needed all the comfort I could get.

"How're you doing?" asked Harry Tillington, loosening his tie as he came across the room. "You look pretty glum. I hope all this business with Zeno and the murders isn't getting to you. He's been charged, and as far as I'm concerned, it's up to a jury to determine if he's guilty or not. He's got a good lawyer who'll put up the best possible defense."

"That's true," I said, "but I can't help feeling as if the police are overlooking something vital."

He made a little noise that meant, I thought after a brief moment of interpretation, he agreed without committing himself. "I stopped by on my way from the airport to the hotel. As soon as I take a shower, I guess I'll go by the police department and try to cheer up Zeno—if they'll let me see him. After that, I was wondering if you might want to go out for an early supper with me?"

"I can't, Harry. A friend is picking me up at five o'clock. We're going to drive around for a couple of hours."

"At least you didn't say you have to wash your hair. That was the most common response I got when I was in school. Some of those girls washed their hair so often it was a miracle it didn't fall out."

I managed a smile for him. "Maybe another time. Zeno's out on bail, by the way. I should think he'll be at the hotel."

"I'm glad he's out and all, but I don't think I'm in the mood for him right now. He's so friggin' exuberant I want to put a paper bag over his head—or a plastic one over mine. A few years back, I asked this bigshot psychiatrist who collects art what he thought about Zeno. He said he didn't think it was manic-depression, but it could be a milder form of bipolar affective syndrome. Whatever it is, it can be hard to stomach at relatively stress-free times. This is definitely not one of them."

I opted not to wander into the realm of bestselling psycho-babble. "What did you learn from Ruthanne's files?"

"Just what I thought I would. The savings account has a couple of thousand dollars in it, and the last time a deposit was made was over two years ago. There's been no activity with the brokerage firm since then, either. She owned a few stocks, but the entire value of the account was less than a thousand dollars."

"Did you find any evidence of accounts in countries with permissive banking regulations?"

He shrugged. "No, and I looked carefully through all the files before I left. Everything appears to be in order, but I'm not an accountant and I sure don't know anything about foreign bank accounts. I could have missed something."

"Probably not, but if Ruthanne was squirreling away money in a secret account, the police will discover it."

"The police? I didn't know they were even aware of those accounts. They searched her stuff the same day"—he stopped and looked away for a moment—"her body was found. They didn't say anything to me."

"At that time, they didn't notice the two different names, but I mentioned it to the lieutenant who's heading the investigation. If he decides to pursue it, he'll ask the Houston police department to have someone knowledgeable check out all of Ruthanne's financial affairs just to make sure she wasn't pulling any scams on Zeno."

Harry wiped his face with a crumpled handkerchief. "Any chance we could have dinner after you finish driving around? I can't deal with Zeno tonight, and I'm not excited at the prospect of room service and the company of Vanna White. Yesterday afternoon when I got to the house, some friend of Ruthanne's who hadn't heard the bad news called. I started brooding and ended up with a sandwich and a beer out by the pool. I sat out there till midnight, watching the moonlight on the water, listening to the phone ring inside, and being devoured by bugs. If you can get free, I promise we won't talk about the case or anything related to it."

"Sorry," I said. "Let me ask you one last thing, Harry. What effect is all this going to have on Zeno's career?"

"I asked myself that all the way to Houston and

back. If Zeno's sent to prison, I doubt they'll put him in a spacious, well-lit studio. His existing work will probably increase in value; people are damn weird. Did you read about the guy who had all those bodies buried in his basement? He was selling his art right up until he got a lethal injection courtesy of the state of Illinois."

"And if Zeno's acquitted and resumes painting?"

"That's harder to predict. The notoriety will linger, that's for sure, and the elite of the art world are proud of their contempt for someone whose face appears in the newspaper anyplace but on the society page. In fact, I called my secretary this morning, and he said the gallery in San Francisco cancelled the show. If Zeno had died in the fire, his work would have sky-rocketed in value. There's nobody the collectors love better than a dead painter, especially one who died tragically and in his prime. The Museum of Modern Art would have hosted a champagne memorial service to kick off the retrospective."

"But there wouldn't be anyone to spend the fortune," I said drily, then paused to consider what I'd said. Greed was a motive I hadn't explored, perhaps because I'd been blinded by all the emotional turmoil. "Did you happen to come across their wills when you were searching the files?"

"Yeah, I did. The bulk goes to the surviving spouse, with a few minor bequests to relatives like Ruthanne's mother and sister, and Zeno's parents back in Brooklyn. It appeared pretty standard to me—but I'm not a lawyer, either." With a soulful look that reminded me of Nick, he left for his date with Vanna.

But Anthony Leach was, and I hadn't given up on him as a suspect. For that matter, I hadn't completely given up on Joshua, but it was getting harder to keep him near the top of the list now that two witnesses had placed him in the hospital at the time the fire broke out.

My diagram had numerous blank spaces in Leach's column. Both nature and I abhor a vacuum (although I have no idea if nature also shares my aversion to a vacuum cleaner). The idea of trying to wheedle alibis out of Leach was distasteful, but I came up with a ploy, gritted my teeth, and dialed the number of his office.

"I'd like to speak to Mr. Leach," I said to the secretary, hoping she wouldn't recognize my voice.

"He's in court all afternoon. May I take a message and have him return your call tomorrow?"

Blessed are the meddlers, for they shall get lucky occasionally. "But I don't understand," I said indignantly. "He was going to show me his house this afternoon. I drove by it several days ago and fell in love with the neighborhood. If the house's interior is as charming as its exterior, I am prepared to meet his price on the spot. But now you're saying that he's unavailable?"

"There must have been a misunderstanding. Mr. Leach will gladly call you this evening to reschedule your appointment for tomorrow. Your name?"

"I'm leaving in the morning for an extended trip. My husband and I are—are going on safari in Kenya for three months. I dearly want to write Mr. Leach a check for the entire amount so I can feel confident the house will be waiting for us, should we return. Safaris can be dangerous, you know. Only last year three Swedish ladies and a native guide were mauled to death by"—I was beginning to regret I hadn't said I was going to Chicago, but the itinerary had been set—"an albino rhinoceros with an attitude. The very next week, an anthropologist was eaten by the very tribe he was studying." I gave her a minute to digest all this before I resumed. "If I can't see the house within the next hour, I'll have to hope it's still on the market—if and when we get back to Farberville."

The secretary, whose accent was sounding more like Kansas than Kent, was bright enough to get the gist of what I'd said. "Mr. Leach should be finished by five o'clock. Perhaps he could show you the house then?"

"I'm getting my malaria shot at five, and after that, I absolutely must start packing my pith helmets. If there's no way I can take a quick look, then so be it."

"Would it be possible for you to see the house on your own? Mr. Leach leaves a key under a flowerpot by the back door, and I'm sure he wouldn't mind if you looked around. He's very eager to sell the house."

"Not as eager as I am to buy it," I said with only a fleeting smile of triumph. I gave her a phony name and address, and we effusively thanked each other several times before ending the conversation.

Ten minutes later I parked in Miss Parchester's driveway (she still had not returned), made sure no patrol cars were cruising up the street, and went inside Leach's house. The decor was unimaginative, dominated by blond maple furniture with plaid upholstery, table lamps with frilly shades, ceramic figurines in a cabinet, and color-coordinated throw pillows. A remarkably neutral decor, best categorized as Early American Yawn.

Leach had let the housekeeping slip in his wife's absence, however. The furniture was dusty, the pillows less than plumped, the morning newspaper scattered on the floor. In the kitchen, dishes had been left in the sink and cabinets were slightly ajar. The plastic trash can overflowed. I curled my lip at the sour odor emanating from it and decided that any evidence concerning Leach's movements before the fire would be found in a more hygienic location.

Upstairs were two bedrooms, one neatly primed for guests, the other with a rumpled bed and clothes on

the floor. Leach's clients would not have been heart-
ened to see such sloppiness in the man who stood
between them and a lengthy prison sentence, or worse.
I had no idea how they would have reacted to the red
satin nightie and the pair of black high heels under
the bed. Not well, probably.

I went downstairs to the room he used as an office.
It was marginally tidier, although books had not been
replaced in the allotted space on the bookshelves and
gum wrappers littered the floor. A small closet was
crowded with cartons, each with a year written on its
top. The wastebasket was full, but with wadded papers
and torn envelopes rather than coffee grounds and
grapefruit rinds.

I began uncrumpling papers and scanning them.
Most of them were of a mundane nature: exhortations
to subscribe to professional journals, announcements
of upcoming conferences, and a letter from a former
client who now resided in a federal penitentiary and
wanted Leach to negotiate a million-dollar book deal.
Toward the bottom of the basket I found a letter concerning his pending divorce. It was written in cryptic
legalese, but I looked carefully at the name of the
lawyer who represented Delphine G. Leach, plaintiff.

I replaced the papers and moved on to the desk.
Lying ever so innocently on the blotter was a calendar
book. I flipped it open to read his schedule for the
day of the fire. That morning Leach had two appointments with what I supposed were clients, a lunch date
with someone named Jack, and an afternoon of unre-
corded activities—one of which I knew had been
searching for a judge to sign the restraining order.
The final notation indicated he'd made eight o'clock
dinner reservations.

On Sunday's page, he'd scrawled a note to meet
Joshua Dwain at the hospital in the middle of the
afternoon. There was no intimation of a trip to the

grocery store to buy steaks for Miss Parchester's dogs nor any indication of his plans for the evening.

I skimmed the routine entries for the previous week, set aside the book, and warily eyed the desk drawers. I'd been invited to enter the house and look around, but I'd accepted under false pretenses. Then again, Peter and I were in the market for a quaint and comfortable love nest—and the red satin nightie might be included in the price.

This ultimate thought did little to erase my apprehension. Biting down on my lip, I eased open the middle drawer. It contained ordinary office paraphernalia, as did the three on the left side and the top two on the right. In the bottom drawer, beneath a folder, was a large and unwieldy gun that looked capable of doing serious injury.

Leach might own a gun for self-protection, I thought as I continued to goggle at it. After all, he was a lawyer, and therefore a member of a perpetually endangered species. Some of his clients could have been displeased about the outcome of their trials. Delphine G. Leach might have been showing up on the doorstep, waving her own gun.

A door opened somewhere in the back of the house. I stood up and started toward the hall, then stopped as I realized I had no desire to explain myself to someone who owned at least one lethal weapon. The furniture offered nothing in the way of potential concealment. I doubted I could open a window, remove the screen, and exit without being heard.

"Hello?" Leach called. "Is anyone here?"

Although I might have been able to brazen my way through a confrontation, I chose instead to panic. I darted into the closet, closed the door, and sat down just as my knees gave way. My heart was thumping so wildly that I was surprised Leach couldn't hear it from another room, and the rush of adrenaline was

enough to create blotches of primary colors in the
dark. I certainly was spending an inordinate amount
of time in confined spaces, I thought as I forced myself
to breathe slowly and deeply. If I'd been claustropho-
bic, I'd have been carted away to a mental ward
days ago.

The floor creaked as Leach came into the office. I
abandoned my efforts to breathe in any manner whatsoever and held my breath. Unlike the rest room at
the Bible Academy, this door had an old-fashioned
keyhole. It provided a limited view of Leach's back
as he sat down at the desk and dialed the telephone.

"There's no one here," he began brusquely. "What
time did the woman say she was coming?" After a
pause, he said, "The back door was unlocked, so she
must have come and gone. I just don't understand
what this is about, Francie. I am quite certain I made
no appointment to show the house to anyone this afternoon. Give me her number so I can call her at
home." He paused again. "A malaria shot? Well, I'll
try this evening, then. I'm going to work here the rest
of the day. My client lost her nerve at the last minute
and agreed to negotiate a property settlement rather
than allow the judge to start dealing out the family
assets. I need to review all the previous proposals and
put a new one together. I'll be at the office at nine
tomorrow."

He stood up long enough to remove his coat and
tie, then took a folder from his briefcase and spread
papers out in front of him. He wiggled around in the
chair, scratched his neck, and settled back with a
wheezy sigh. There was a depressing sense of perma-
nency about the scene.

I tried to make myself comfortable. As long as he
had no need of an old file, he would not open the
closet door. Sooner or later, he might decide to go
upstairs to change into more casual clothing, or de-

velop a craving for Chinese food. In the interim, I was trapped.

Time did not fly. I sat and thought about everything that had happened on Willow Street, from Miss Parchester's tea-party invitation to the disappointing contents of Ruthanne's mysterious accounts. The barking dogs. The paintings that had been destroyed in the fire. Melanie Magruder, who was quite as unique a character as Zeno.

I had dozed off when I heard Leach push back his chair. Hopeful that I might escape, I peered through the keyhole. To my profound regret, he went to the window and pulled back the sheer, stared for a long while, shaking his head and grumbling to himself, and then resumed his seat. I resumed thinking and dozing. The sound of his voice startled me out of an uneasy dream of a house with three bedrooms and a corpse in every closet.

"May I speak to Mrs. Goodall?" Leach said in the voice of an itinerant preacher with a wagon filled with snake oil. "No, I'm sure this is the right telephone number. She came by my house—hello?" What he said as he slammed down the receiver was not at all likely to bring converts into the fold, hymnals in one hand and checkbooks in the other.

A ghastly realization hit. I positioned my watch to catch the small amount of light through the keyhole. It was after six o'clock. More than an hour ago, Peter would have arrived at the Book Depot, found me conspicuously absent, and come to all sorts of conclusions that did not reflect well on my integrity. A three-month safari might be my only chance to salvage any kind of relationship, and for the first time, I allowed myself to consider how important it was. Peter was not the man of my dreams, but I wasn't in a delirium; I didn't want an ephemeral equivalent of a mindless male centerfold, either. Then again, maybe I'd convinced myself I did. What did I want? I exhaled more loudly than I'd intended, but Leach did not grab his gun and throw open the closet door.

An hour later I awakened to the encouraging sounds of drawers opening and closing, papers shuffling, and the most encouraging sound of all—the click of his briefcase. Rather than leaving, however, he made another call.

"Ashley," he murmured, "this is Tony. I'm truly sorry about losing my temper last night. You know I want to help you with your tuition and living expenses—in any case. I was wondering if we might get together tonight? I'll come get you, and on the way back here, we'll pick up steaks, a bottle of wine, and a movie or two. There's a video rental store out by where you're staying that has a fascinating selection in the X-rated room. Can you be ready in twenty minutes?"

Say yes! I pleaded silently.

The reply must have pleased Leach, in that he left the room with the same distinctly predatory look on his face that I'd noticed when he was contemplating a multimillion-dollar lawsuit on behalf of Joshua and Tracy Dwain; reveries of money and sex seemed to affect him in similar fashion.

Even though I heard his footsteps on the stairs, I decided to stay where I was until he left the house. I eased the door open a scant inch to allow some fresh air, readjusted my numb derriere, and speculated on this new development. Leach was having an affair. I wasn't learned in matters of divorce, but it seemed likely that his wife could use it to put pressure on him—especially if Ashley was significantly younger than he. His reputation was already frayed. Rumors of adultery with a juvenile might put it in tatters.

The back door finally closed. I came out of the closet and went into the living room to watch out the

window until his car backed out of the driveway. I'd
gotten myself into an unholy mess, I thought as I let
myself out the back door, conscientiously locking it.
Peter had been stood up more than two hours ago.
Even if he were willing to listen to me, he might not
appreciate my explanation.

I headed for Miss Parchester's house, then veered
into Zeno's side yard and went along the fence to the
expanse of honeysuckle. Nick and Nora began to bark
but quieted down when I hissed at them. From this
vantage point, I could see the dark windows of Jasmine's office on the second floor. Could she have seen
someone in this spot, someone doing something
suspicious?

Just before the son et lumiére had begun, she'd seen
something that puzzled her, although she'd attempted
to dismiss it with an idle remark about the presence
of television cameras encouraging Zeno. The gorillas
had been inside, sweltering in their suits. Melanie had
appeared on the porch almost immediately, and Zeno
had been in the coffin. Miss Parchester had claimed
that the dogs were barking by then. Unfortunately,
this was not an overly cozy mystery novel in which
pets could type out cryptic messages or drag their mis-
guided master to a heretofore unnoticed clue the size
of Mount Rushmore. These two could barely waddle
and wag their tails at the same time.

I sat in the grass and swiveled my head back and
forth until my neck began to ache. Nick and Nora
lost interest and withdrew to the forsythia bushes. The
breeze was redolent with the sweetness of the honeysuckle blossoms. I was about to go home to have a
drink and try to figure out what to say to Peter, when
a theory entered my mind. Not necessarily a brilliant
one, I'm afraid, but one worthy of a brief investigation.

A dedicated sleuth would have leapt over the fence

in a single bound. I went around to the front of Miss Parchester's house and knocked on the door.

"Oh, Claire," she said as she gestured for me to come inside, "I was so worried when I saw your car in my driveway and no sign of you. I was considering if I should call that policeman of yours to report your disappearance. Come have a cup of tea and tell me where you've been all this time."

"Before I do, would you mind if I have a look around your garage?"

"Whatever for?"

"For six very valuable paintings done by your ex-neighbor. I think it's possible the fire was set to cover their theft. Whoever stole them has made several attempts to reenter your yard over the last few days, but Nick and Nora have protected their turf."

"And that's why Nora was given the barbiturates?" Miss Parchester sank down on the sofa and took a tissue from her cuff. "How could someone be so heartless as to endanger her precious life for inanimate paintings?"

"Half a million dollars might have been the motive," I said as I sat beside her and patted her knee.

She sniffled but kept her composure. "We shall have to bring this blackguard to justice, Claire. I will not be satisfied until he's locked behind bars for the remainder of his life. Papa always said, 'He who transgresses in haste will repent in leisure.' "

I did not tell her that Papa had been misquoting William Congreve, who was more concerned with hasty marriages (as was I). "Why don't you put on the teakettle while I go out to the garage?"

"It's really quite dark now, and I don't like the idea of you going out there alone. Let me put on a sweater and I'll accompany you. I believe I'll take one of Mama's brass candlesticks just in case we encounter someone. Would you like one, too? They were a wedding present from a first cousin of President Taft."

"I don't think that's necessary, Miss Parchester. The dogs are quiet, which suggests that there's no one anywhere near your yard. Put on the teakettle and set out the cups and saucers. I'll be back in five minutes."

"I cannot permit it," she said with all the authority of a veteran high-school teacher who'd quelled riots in the classroom for forty years. "Now wait here while I fetch the candlesticks."

I was sitting on the sofa when she returned, wearing a sweater and carrying two hefty candlesticks and a flashlight. If there was to be a solution to the game, would it be: Miss Parchester in the garage with the candlestick? Zeno in the living room with the ouzo bottle? Joshua Dwain on the sidewalk with the gun? Anthony Leach in the bed with a bimbo? Melanie Magruder on the lam with my money? Harry in the hotel with Vanna?

"You have a most peculiar look on your face," Miss Parchester said worriedly. "Shall we have our tea before we sally forth? We could even add a tiny dollop of brandy if you're feeling faint."

Perhaps there'd been less than adequate oxygen in Leach's closet, I told myself as I stood up. "No, I'm fine. Bear in mind this may turn out to be nothing more than an exercise in futility."

She handed me my weapon and started for the door. "Speaking of bears, did I mention that there were two in the backyard several nights ago? Papa would have dealt with them in the same manner as Teddy Roosevelt, but I myself found them ever so fascinating. How do you feel about bears, Claire?"

"I'm very fond of them," I said as I followed her out the front door.

SIXTEEN

We searched the garage with admirable diligence and much explosive sneezing on my part (mold, as always, was the culprit). There were a few dingy paintings in chipped frames, but Miss Parchester explained that they were the work of a great-aunt who'd toyed with a career in art forgery before she left town with a traveling minstrel show (and with Papa's gold pocket watch, not to mention Mama's walnut Ouija board).

I teetered on a ladder to make sure there were no paintings among the pieces of plywood laid across the rafters. I lifted stiff muslin sheets to look under three-legged tables. At Miss Parchester's suggestion, I switched on the headlights of my car and crawled into the dustiest of the dusty corners. And finally acknowledged defeat.

"It does make sense, though," I said as we walked back to the house. I stopped to rub my itchy nose, sneezed anyway, and continued. "Someone decided to take advantage of the preshow hysteria, locked the storeroom door from the outside, and then moved the paintings. Later, he or she came back and started the fire. Harry was telling me earlier that the value of Zeno's work would shoot up if he were dead."

"That's dreadful!" Miss Parchester said, shaking the

candlestick as if it were a bejeweled scepter and she were the Queen of Hearts. "Absolutely dreadful! In my day and age, people killed each other for much nobler motives than money. Even bank robbers tried to be chivalrous. If a witness was shot, it was in the excitement of the moment rather than out of pure bloodlust. What is the world coming to, Claire? Perhaps I should reconsider retreating under the back porch with Nick and—"

"The porch," I interrupted. "There's a lot of space under the back porch, isn't there?"

"It's quite damp, which is why Nick and Nora find it a pleasant haven on hot afternoons. However, I don't honestly believe you'd be comfortable, Claire. It's better suited to—"

"Let's have a look." I guided her through the house and onto the porch. The dogs trotted forward enthusiastically, their ears brushing the ground and their faces greedy with great expectations.

"Can you keep them at a distance?" I asked Miss Parchester as I peered dubiously at the black hole. For all I knew, a colony of skunks had taken up residence along with spiders, centipedes, scorpions, snakes, bats, and who knows what else. I was not a coward, but I wasn't a jabbering idiot, either.

"Good luck," she said firmly, grasping a collar in each hand and watching me with a reverent expression. Columbus couldn't have had a better send-off as he set sail for the edge of the world.

I switched on the flashlight, took a deep breath, and crawled into the pit. The mud had the consistency of overcooked oatmeal and made sucking noises as I shifted my knees. The flashlight kept spurting from my hand like a slippery silver missile.

Eventually the beam illuminated a misshapen bundle that was approximately four feet square. I lifted a corner of the plastic tarp and saw an edge of canvas stapled on a frame. I counted five more frames, tucked the tarp back, and crawled into the fresh air.

"Did you find them?" asked Miss Parchester.

"Just as I'd theorized," I said modestly as I wiped my muddy hands on the grass, then found a much-gnawed steak bone and scraped what I could off my knees. Nick and Nora approached, perhaps willing to assist me with their slobbery tongues, but I glared at them until they retreated.

Miss Parchester handed me a towel. "What does this mean?"

"It confirms my theory that someone stole the paintings and then set fire to the house. The problem is that I'm not sure who it was." I tossed the towel to the dogs, who began fighting over it as if it were the Golden Fleece instead of a souvenir from a defunct motel. "Caron and Inez changed into their costumes in the storage room and went to the front room to watch out the window. Right after Tracy's accident, they discovered the door was locked. It seems logical to assume the paintings were removed during this ten-to-fifteen-minute period, when the guilty party could reasonably expect everyone's attention to be focused on the front yard."

"Who?"

"I don't know," I admitted. "Could I have that cup of tea now?"

Once we were settled with tea and cookies, Miss Parchester said, "We shall assume the paintings were stolen during the time you suggested. Melanie could have done it before she went out onto the porch. Am I correct?" Without waiting for a response, she whipped out a notepad and a pencil, wrote the name, and made a checkmark. "Zeno appeared from within the coffin, but we don't know how long he'd been there. His motive for stealing his own paintings is less clear, but he could have been up to No Good."

I was so amazed she, like Caron Malloy, could speak in capital letters that all I could do was goggle. Finally, I managed to swallow a mouthful of tea and say, "Zeno wasn't in the coffin when the girls arrived. They had a conversation with him about their roles."

Miss Parchester made a notation. "What about Joshua Dwain? Do you know where he was before the show?"

"I was a little bit surprised they weren't among the picketers, but I didn't see Tracy or Joshua until after she was hit by the motorcycle."

"So we don't know where they were during the significant time," she said with another slash of her pencil. "And Anthony Leach?"

"I saw him after the accident and then much later when the fire trucks arrived. I have no idea where he was during the three hours . . ." I halted as I thought about his calendar book. "He told the police he was at his office, but his calendar book indicated he had dinner reservations. Odd, isn't it?"

"Oh, Claire," she said, giggling, "your naïveté is so refreshing."

"My what?" I said in a voice that was hardly refreshing.

"Never mind, dear. What about Jasmine Hadley?"

"She joined me a minute or two before the son et lumière began. I didn't notice which direction she came from."

Miss Parchester added Jasmine's name to her list. "All in all, those known to have been in the neighborhood and could have stolen the paintings are Zeno, Melanie, Anthony, Joshua, Tracy, Jasmine, you, and I. Do you concur?"

"Zeno did say something about no one else knowing the paintings were in the storage room." I put down my teacup and sighed. "I'd better call Peter and tell him where the paintings are now."

"Let's not be hasty," she said as she absently refilled my cup, took a sip, and then handed it to me. She picked up her list and poised her pencil. "I think we must ask ourselves why the paintings were concealed under my porch. In Zeno's case, he would not have had enough time to take them out of the immediate area. Melanie had the same problem. As for the others, they may have been worried that the theft would be discovered and their houses searched. They also may have believed that their presence at the son et lumière would give them an alibi of sorts."

I remembered another bit of dialogue. "Shortly after Tracy's accident, Caron and Inez saw a car out in the alley behind your house. But if the driver had stolen the paintings, why didn't he put them in the car and take them someplace where they'd be more accessible—and less likely to be found?"

Miss Parchester pinched her lips together as she considered this. "I don't know," she said at last.

"Nor do I," I said as I took my cup and saucer into the kitchen, then dutifully went to the telephone. I called Peter's house, but there was no answer. I was even more reluctant to call the station; they would beep him wherever he was, and I didn't want to disturb him if he was in the act of proposing to some punctual, dependable woman whose taste in literature ran to romances and wallpaper books.

However, I dialed the number, gave my name, and asked to speak to Lieutenant Rosen.

"He's out on an investigation," said the desk sergeant. "He and Jorgeson left about half an hour ago. Do you want to leave a message?"

"When he checks in, ask him to call me at Miss Parchester's house." I related the telephone number, then added, "It's important."

"Okay, but it's liable to be several hours. A kid in a trailer park shot himself during some kind of bizarre

sexual thing. The neighbor who found him called the
media right after he called us. According to officers
on the scene, it's a real zoo out there and getting
worse. Oh, I almost forgot—Lieutenant Rosen left
a message for you, Mrs. Malloy. He said that if
you called, to tell you that this one is not your cup
of tea."

"No, I don't suppose it is," I said politely, then
repeated my request and went back to the living room,
where Miss Parchester was studying her list as if it
were the definitive formula for longevity. It looked as
though what she was sipping was no longer her cup
of tea, either. "I gave the desk sergeant this number,
so I suppose I'd better wait here," I said as I went to
the window and looked at Leach's house across the
street. If he and his girlfriend had returned, they'd not
bothered to turn on any lights before retiring to
the bedroom. Jasmine's apartment was dark. At the
Dwains' house, a light shone from a room on the
second floor, but the blinds were closed; if Joshua
was sacrificing a fatted calf, he was doing so
discreetly.

Just another peaceful evening on Willow Street, I
concluded as I went back to the kitchen and looked
out the window above the sink to make sure Nick
and Nora weren't mauling Styrofoam cups. Nick was
prowling along the fence while Nora watched him
from the porch. Both appeared to be no more languid
than usual.

"So when do you think he'll try again?" Miss Parchester asked as I returned to the living room and sat
down. "He must be frantic to retrieve the paintings
before they're inadvertently found."

I suddenly wished I'd demanded that the desk sergeant contact Peter immediately. All the suspects were
at large, including one who had reverted to her status
as a fugitive—and taken refuge in the very house in

which I was sitting. "Melanie Magruder escaped from the city jail this morning," I said casually.

"Yes, I know," Miss Parchester said with a hiccup. "She told me she pretended to have an attack of appendicitis, then ran out the door while the paramedics unloaded a gurney. She is very resourceful for her age, don't you think?"

This time I goggled as if she'd spoken in Mandarin Chinese. "She told you about her escape? When did she do this?"

"I think it's rather obvious that, if she escaped only this morning, she must have told me sometime today. Let me try to recall the precise moment ... It could have been when I was driving her to the bus station."

"The bus station?" I tightened my grip on the arms of the chair to keep myself from leaping out of the chair. "You took her to the bus station?"

Miss Parchester nodded benignly as she finished whatever was in her cup. "She could have walked there, but she was concerned that she might be spotted on the sidewalk and taken back into custody."

"Did she show up on your doorstep to ask for a ride?"

"I found her in the backseat of my car when I came out of the Book Depot. After we went to Dr. Hassard's office to collect Nora, I drove to the bus station at her request. A police car was parked at the edge of the lot, so we did not stop."

"Where is she now?"

"I couldn't say," Miss Parchester murmured as she took her cup into the kitchen. She barely avoided a collision with a floor lamp as she came back into the room, but she'd had plenty of practice over the years. "We had a leisurely lunch at that little tearoom near the square and then drove out to the fruit stand to purchase peaches. When we arrived back in town, she asked me to drop her off at the library. That would have been about five o'clock."

I wondered if Melanie was at the Drakestone Hotel, industriously making beds while she tried to figure out how to sneak into Zeno's room. Her chances weren't good; Peter had said earlier that the hotel was under surveillance.

She was more likely to be in my garage, I decided. It occurred to me that I hadn't told Peter or Jorgeson my theory that she'd slept there Sunday night. Were sins of omission as condemnatory as sins of commission? I was about to pose the question to Miss Parchester when the telephone rang.

I snatched up the receiver. "Peter?"

"This is Harry, Claire. I called your house and your daughter said you might be there. I'm sorry if I'm interrupting, but I need to ask you something."

I tried to keep the disappointment out of my voice. "What is it?"

"Have you talked to Zeno since he made bail this morning?"

"No, I haven't. Why are you asking me this?"

"Well, when I got back here, there was a DO NOT DISTURB sign on his door. I figured he was taking a nap, and like I told you at the bookstore, I wasn't much in the mood to deal with him anyway. I took a shower, made some calls, ordered room service—that kind of thing. Finally, though, I started feeling guilty, so I went across the hall and knocked on his door. When he didn't answer, I called his room every five minutes for half an hour. A few minutes ago, I convinced the manager to unlock his door in case Zeno had done something to himself. The only thing he did was leave. I was kind of hoping he called you before he took off."

"He might have had a phone call from Melanie," I said, frowning at one of Miss Parchester's African violets. "She escaped from the jail this morning and was last seen in this neighborhood at five o'clock."

"It was mentioned on the news," Harry said. "She's still the prime suspect in that Hadley woman's murder. You'd better warn your friend to keep her doors locked until Melanie's recaptured."

I did not mention who had so graciously expedited Melanie's escape by driving her around town and treating her to lunch at a tearoom. "I'll do that, Harry, although I think it's more probable that Melanie and Zeno are at some shabby motel, interacting."

"Maybe," he said skeptically. "I'll let you know if I hear from Zeno."

I replaced the receiver and went back to the living room. Miss Parchester's head had drooped and she was snoring, her cup cradled in her limp hands. I set the cup on the table, covered her with an afghan, and then searched the house to make sure Melanie wasn't under the bed or folded neatly in a wardrobe alongside cardigan sweaters and hatboxes.

It had been more than an hour since I'd called the police station. Surely Peter would be getting my message any minute, I told myself as I continued to wander uneasily through the house. Perhaps my message had not sounded urgent enough—or perhaps he was so angry that he was intentionally ignoring it.

Leaving the kitchen door open so I could hear the telephone, I went out to the porch and stood over what I knew to be more than half a million dollars' worth of art. The soles of my feet did not tingle. Miss Parchester had included me among the list of suspects, but I would have no idea how to even begin to convert the canvases to cold cash. If I chanced upon an autographed first edition of an Agatha Christie novel (in my dreams, of course), I would have no problem ascertaining its value and courting bids from collectors. But the art world that Harry kept referring to with varying amounts of derision was an alien culture. I'd read enough fiction to know there existed a flourishing black market for stolen art. However, I doubted I could find the applicable telephone number in the Yellow Pages.

A distinctly hostile bark interrupted an intriguing thought. I edged toward the door, prepared to dart inside if it seemed imperative. The bark was not repeated. I finally decided one of the dogs had been spooked by a bird, but I also decided I made a splendid target beneath the porch light. On that disquieting note, I went inside and locked the door.

The temptation to call the police department was so compelling that I had to bite my knuckles as I walked past the telephone. Miss Parchester had not moved. A light was now on in Anthony Leach's house, ruling out any wild ideas I may have had about borrowing his gun from his desk drawer. Farther up the street, the light in the Dwains' house had been extinguished. A car drove by and continued around the corner to Washington Avenue. Another pulled into a driveway; the couple who emerged were nuzzling each other as they went inside their house.

My eyes drifted back to Jasmine's upstairs apartment. She had observed a lot from her window, I thought as I envisioned her standing there, her mouth twisted and her fists clenched as she listened to the clangorous wind chimes and watched the sprouting visual clutter. If she had seen someone stealing the paintings, she might have felt only grim, quasi-sadistic satisfaction in Zeno's loss. Or a prick of cupidity at the prospect of blackmailing the thief.

I took a step back, then stopped and looked more closely at the window in Jasmine's office. I'd assumed the black stripe across the bottom was a shadow cast by the eaves, but now I could see the window was open several inches. The crime squad would have closed and locked it when they sealed the apartment. Someone had opened it.

A really, really good theory came to mind.

I made sure Miss Parchester was covered by the afghan, turned out all the interior lights except a single lamp, and went out the front door, intent on my mission to regain a position in Peter's good graces by returning a fugitive to his clutches. I walked briskly across the street, then switched gears and crept cautiously up the stairs.

The seals on the door had been torn, as I'd anticipated. I eased open the door and said softly, "Melanie? I know you're here, so there's no point in pretending you're not. Just don't attack me, okay? I'm too old for any more physical assaults this week."

"Then come on in the kitchen and have a drink," she drawled. "This place is so damn hot that I went ahead and helped myself to a glass of wine. It's cheap stuff, but not all that bad."

I followed her voice around the corner and into a dim room, where I could make out her form in a chair. A fan on a table whirred steadily; a stout bottle of wine rested nearby. "How'd you get inside?" I asked curiously.

Her teeth glinted in the diffused glow from a streetlight. "I guess I must have picked up a key when I was here earlier. I wasn't expecting any company tonight, but I don't mind if you want to sit and visit for a few minutes, as long as you don't start in on how I should turn myself in to the law. That is getting to be one stale theme, honey."

"Zeno was released on bail. Have you talked to him?"

"I thought about calling him, but then I changed my mind," she said wearily. "I'm real close to thinking he killed his wife. She was a cold-blooded bitch, but we're all sisters in the long run. Besides, if he killed her, he could do the same to me if he had a mind to. He didn't have any reservations about killing the woman who lived here."

"I don't believe he killed anyone," I said as I sank down in a chair across from her and propped my elbows on the table. After a long period in which I had more than a few revelations, I said, "Once upon a time, I was musing about my inability to lie. I did not consider it a disability. Obviously, you have a degree of talent in such matters, but you're not the only one who's been regaling me with story after story."

Melanie snorted in the darkness. "I may have embellished explanations on rare occasions—"

"Someone has lied—not once or twice, but consistently. And I fell for it all. It's a good thing this person wasn't selling me beachfront property in Wyoming. I'd own so much acreage I could walk for a week without trespassing." I flinched as I heard a noise somewhere below us. "Is there a back door?"

"Not that I saw. What's bothering you?" Melanie demanded, gulping down her drink and beginning to rise. "Did you call the police already? If you did, you should have told me when you got here. That would have been the polite thing to do."

"We would have been in a much better position if I had told the police," I said. "I had this very grandiloquent idea that I would convince you to turn yourself in by confronting you with irrefutable logic and a goodly dose of maternal concern. I wish now that I had proceeded without wasting time. We would be at Miss Parchester's house, sipping tea and awaiting the patrol car. As it is, I'm afraid we're in danger."

"So why are we sitting here?"

"We can't go down the stairs, and you said there was no back exit." Rejecting decorum, I picked up the wine bottle, took a deep drink, and wiped my mouth on the back of my hand. "And I led the way here like a perky tour guide with a flag. That's the most annoying thing of all."

I swiveled around as I heard footsteps behind me. "Nice of you to join us," I said with a great deal of insincerity. "Would you like a glass of wine?"

SEVENTEEN

hat are you doing here, Claire?"

"I came here to convince Melanie to turn herself in. What are you doing here?"

Harry Tillington took his sweet time before he replied, "I guess I'm just still trying to protect Zeno from his baser instincts. I suspected that Melanie would be here and that he might be with her. As maddening as he can be, he's my friend as well as my primary source of income. I wanted to get him out of here before she tried again to kill him."

"Tried again?" Melanie said indignantly. "Is your brain a couple of quarts low on Pennzoil? I am not gonna sit here and take this!" She stood up and cocked her fists. "Why don't we step outside and discuss it, you bald-faced sum-bitch!"

His hand slid into his coat pocket and reappeared with a gun. It was preciously petite, as if designed to be carried in an evening bag, but it nonetheless looked sufficiently lethal. He pointed it at her but spoke to me as if we were alone. "Jealousy is a malignant emotion. Maybe Zeno said something that led her to believe he was going to attempt a reconciliation. She called the hotel and lured Ruthanne to the house, killed her, and then set the fire to kill Zeno, too. Jasmine Hadley must have seen her at the door."

Melanie looked at the gun, then sank back and helped herself to the rapidly dwindling wine. "You're a damn liar. I didn't kill anybody."

"The police believe otherwise," he countered.

"Oh, yeah?"

"Yeah."

"Please," I said, "let's not sink to the level of kindergarten pugnacity. I think you're right, Harry. After all, I'm the one who caught her with a smoking gun in her hand. Why don't we go across the street and use Miss Parchester's telephone to call the police?"

"Wait just a minute!" the accused said as she banged down the bottle hard enough to splatter the tabletop with dark droplets that unfortunately resembled blood. "Whose side are you on here? Why don't you ask him what he was doing in Zeno's backyard Sunday night? He didn't seem any more inclined than I was to hang around after a patrol car pulled up. He went over the fence like it was a hurdle."

I was rather sorry she'd brought up the subject. "Is that when you followed him back to the Drakestone Hotel?"

She nodded. "The hotel's only a couple of blocks from here. I guessed that's where he was going, and I was in the lobby by the time he parked in the garage and came inside. I couldn't exactly ride in the elevator with him, but I saw how it stopped on the fourth floor."

"So what?" said Harry. "I walked around Zeno's yard to see if anything survived the fire. The only place I saw any patrol cars was at the police department, when I went back later to find out if Zeno was going to be released."

"I believe you," I said, smiling so earnestly my ears probably wiggled. "Lieutenant Rosen will, too. Shall we call him so he can have her picked up before she disappears again?"

Melanie stuck out her chin and growled, "You have developed a real bad attitude. Don't ever think about inviting me to lunch in the future, 'cause I wouldn't be caught dead with the likes of you." She looked at the gun. "Or you, either," she said with less conviction.

I pushed back the chair and stood up, although I had to cling to the edge of the table. "Let me go first so you can cover her, Harry."

The gun wavered indecisively between Melanie and me, making it obvious that neither of us had any chance whatsoever of leaving the kitchen without Harry's consent. "Do you truly believe me, Claire?" he asked in a childish voice.

Oh, to have Melanie's (or Caron's) talent, I thought as I forced myself to cross the room and pat his arm. "Of course, I do. You were never on my list of suspects, since you were at the hospital when the fire started. Joshua Dwain told the police he saw you there. You've got a great alibi." I realized I'd gone one tiny step too far in my attempt to reassure him, and hastily added, "I think he did, anyway, but—"

"Shut up!" he said, knocking away my hand. "Just get over there by the window and let me think. I want both of you to keep your mouths closed."

Melanie waggled her finger at him. "Did you tell a little white lie to the police, honey? They're not going to like that one bit. You should have seen the expression on that lieutenant's face when—"

Harry shot her.

"What have you done?" I shrieked as I hurried around the table and caught her before she slipped off the chair. I steadied her and examined the wound. Blood seeped onto her shoulder in an irregular circle, but her breathing seemed steady. I knelt next to the chair. "Melanie? Can you hear me?"

Her eyelids fluttered, but before she could answer, Harry said, "Get up, Claire. You're coming with me."

"What's the point?" I said without looking at him. "The police have already been told about the paintings. They'll go back to the hospital and question people until they confirm that no one actually saw you in the lobby between nine-thirty and ten o'clock. You shouldn't have told me you recognized Joshua Dwain in the hospital parking lot. He wasn't around when you and Ruthanne first arrived at Zeno's house or when the two of you returned after the accident. The only time you could have seen him was while he was waving the gun—and you were inside the house, waiting for Ruthanne."

"How could I have known she was coming?" he said coldly.

I stood up and stepped in front of Melanie. I wasn't particularly pleased to offer myself as a human shield, but the last thing I wanted her to do was further incense him with another wisecrack. "On Saturday at six-thirty, you left Ruthanne at the hotel and parked in the alley behind Zeno's house. You went into the storage room, took the paintings, and hid them under Miss Parchester's porch."

"Why would I do something stupid like that?"

"It wasn't at all stupid to steal them. You yourself told me they were worth more than half a million dollars. But you had to put them someplace, didn't you? You couldn't take them back to the hotel, where Ruthanne might find them. You couldn't leave them in the car for the same reason. What was stupid, I suppose, was doing something to the dogs that earned you their steadfast animosity. Did you kick one of them?"

"They were jumping all over me." He pointed the gun at my face. "I'm getting tired of this conversation. Let's go."

I glanced back at Melanie, who gave me a sly wink before groaning piteously and slithering off the chair like a silk robe. Disconcerted, I turned and said, "Where are we going, Harry?"

He gestured with the gun, which was answer enough for me. I went down the stairs, exceedingly conscious of my vulnerable back (which, unlike the soles of my feet, was tingling madly), and out into the yard. A sharp jab between my shoulder blades motivated me to continue walking until we'd arrived at the fence in Miss Parchester's side yard.

Nick and Nora came galloping toward me, then clumsily braked as they spotted Harry and began to bark. It should have been enough to rouse Miss Parchester (and everyone else within a six-block radius), but no light came on in the kitchen.

"Make 'em shut up," commanded Harry.

"I am not a canine drill sergeant," I said. "Furthermore, not even Miss Parchester can make them do anything they don't want to do. I'd have better luck making them recite poetry or—"

"I'll shoot them if I have to."

"You can't shoot everybody and everything that gets in your way, Harry. At some point, you'll run out of bullets. Your best chance is to get in your Cadillac and drive as fast and as far as you can. Go to the airport in Dallas and try for a flight to South America. You don't need these paintings. Surely after transferring all of the money Ruthanne had stolen to your own account in Switzerland or wherever, you can get by without a paltry extra half a million."

"Aren't you clever?" he sneered.

"It has been mentioned in the past," I said, edging away from him as I noticed a familiar car pull up to the curb. Whether or not the occupants of the car noticed us was another issue.

Harry was much too distraught to notice much of

anything. "Let's find out if you're athletic as well. Climb over the fence and hang on to those damn dogs. And remember—you won't be nearly so clever with a bullet between your eyes."

I wish I could say I effortlessly scaled the fence and arrived on the other side to thunderous applause and high marks from the judges. Instead, I grunted and cursed as my toes became entangled in the honeysuckle vine, and managed to land on my derriere hard enough to bring tears to my eyes.

Once I'd grabbed the dogs' collars and pleaded with them to be quiet, Harry joined me. "Over there," he said, pointing at the porch. "As soon as you've gotten the paintings and put them in my car, you can go call your pretty lieutenant and tell him how badly you were treated. Maybe he'll come lick your wounds."

"I doubt it," I said as I started for the porch, now praying Miss Parchester had not been roused and was not toddling toward the back of the house to gently admonish Nick and Nora for disturbing the neighborhood.

Just as we reached the edge of the porch, my worst fear was realized (or so I thought). The light in the kitchen went on. The door flew open, banging into the side of the house, and Zeno came out onto the porch. "Claire!" he said, waving enthusiastically. "I've been looking for you! Have you seen Melanie? Harry, good to see you! When did you get back from Houston? This afternoon I drove out into the country and found an old summer camp that will make a perfect retreat for young—"

Harry shot him.

Or tried to, anyway. The lightbulb inches above his head exploded, raining down splinters of glass.

Zeno stared for a paralytic moment, then said, "I'll tell you about it later, okay?" He ducked into the house and slammed the door. No more than a second later, the kitchen light went out.

"Hurry up," Harry said shrilly.

"What do you want me to do with Nick and Nora? Shall I let go of their collars—or take them along with me and drag the paintings out with my teeth? I had a lot of expensive dental work done last fall. If I—"

"Shut up!"

I waited patiently while he pondered the problem. If I released the dogs, they would attack him. If I didn't, I would have an insurmountable problem achieving his goal. I decided to see if I could ease him into a more repentant disposition—then kick him in his most susceptible zone, grab the gun, and run like the devil. It may not have been an overwhelmingly clever plan, but it was preferable to being shot and left to bleed to death. As Melanie had been. I had to get help for her.

"You know what this is about, don't you, Harry?" I said as softly as I could over the growling of the dogs. "You're jealous of Zeno. He gets the attention, he gets the money, and he gets the women. You get the schedule to arrange and the excuses to concoct. It's not nearly as much fun, is it? I don't think anyone would blame you for . . ."

He pressed the barrel of the gun against my neck. "Blame me for what, Claire? For killing Ruthanne and setting the fire in hopes it would kill Zeno? For killing that woman across the street when she threatened to tell the police who she saw stealing the paintings?"

It wasn't going well, frankly. If Peter and Jorgeson were sneaking up on us, they were doing it so stealthily that I couldn't discern their movement. "Why did you kill Ruthanne?" I asked in a strangled voice.

"Why do you think I did?"

"Well, the IRS audit might have exposed irregularities that would motivate them to do a more thorough audit." I gulped as I caught a glimpse of a figure in Zeno's yard. "Were you juggling the books before Ruthanne took over?"

"Very good," Harry murmured, although without appreciable admiration. "I transferred as much as I could back to his accounts, but I'd spent some of it. The IRS auditors would have caught the discrepancy. Zeno might have laughed it off. Ruthanne would have hounded me to the gates of hell and escorted me inside."

"Really?" I said, determined not to allow my gaze to waver from his eyes.

He increased the pressure on my throat. "You don't sound at all clever now, Claire, but I'll give you one last chance to redeem yourself."

"Only God can offer redemption," Joshua Dwain said from the far side of the honeysuckle. "The Bible states, 'He shall redeem their soul from deceit and violence; and precious shall be their blood in his sight.' "

Harry swung around. "Precious shall be *your* blood in *my* sight," he said as he aimed the gun at Joshua.

" 'Yea, though I walk through the valley of the shadow of death, I will fear no evil,' " Joshua responded promptly, but with a squeak in his voice that contradicted his testimonial.

It was not a bolt of lightning, but it was probably as close to a manifestation of divine intervention as we were going to get. I released the dogs, stepped back, and kicked Harry between his legs. From the way he doubled up and fell to the ground, I deduced I'd used adequate force. Deduced cleverly, that is.

Even Joshua would have been obliged to acknowledge that all hell broke loose. Howling happily, Nick and Nora flung themselves on Harry and did their best to rip off his clothes. Peter and Jorgeson came stumbling out onto the porch and down the steps with the nimbleness of a pair of Keystone Kops. I told them about Melanie. Jorgeson took his radio and called for an ambulance. Peter tried to fend off the dogs while he handcuffed Harry. The dogs obligingly turned their attention to Harry's trouser cuffs. He found his voice and began to curse. Miss Parchester stayed in the doorway, shrieking at the dogs to remember their manners. Zeno peered at us from behind her.

I went over to the fence. "Thanks for distracting him. He was out of control, and I have no doubts he was reserving the last bullet for me."

Joshua shrugged. "Miss Parchester always has been very kind to Tracy and me. When I heard a shot that sounded as if it originated from here, I came over to investigate."

"How's Tracy doing?"

"She was transferred out of intensive care this morning. She's going to stay with her parents until I graduate in December. We've been posted to a clinic in El Salvador."

"Good luck," I said lamely.

"We won't need luck to do God's work, Mrs. Malloy, but we can always use your prayers."

I reminded myself that he'd approached the fence and spoken to Harry at a time when many others might have crept away. "I'll give it my best effort," I said with a beatific smile.

EIGHTEEN

Then," Caron said, pausing to make sure we were all adequately engrossed in the melodrama of her narrative, "I rushed right at Rhonda, thumping on my chest and growling. She jumped backward, which was not a wise move on her part since she was standing at the edge of the pool. Carrie and Kathryn started screaming, which brought Mrs. Maguire out to the patio. She took one look at us and joined Rhonda. Emily and Merissa ran inside the house, both of them bleating like terrified sheep. Meanwhile, three of the boys scrambled up on the roof of the garage and kept on going. The other two climbed the magnolia tree. It was Too Funny."

Inez blinked at us. "Until Mr. Maguire came to the door with a rifle."

"It was more like a bazooka," Caron corrected her. "However, we decided not to stick around any longer, since we weren't invited to begin with. I bet Rhonda will think twice before she makes up her next guest list."

Miss Parchester gazed disapprovingly at them over the rim of her teacup. "Wasn't it rude on your part to disrupt the party? It seems to me you were infring-ing on this girl's inalienable right to entertain whom she chooses. But there was the time Papa was not invited to go duck hunting with several local lawyers. He called the game warden and arranged to have them arrested for public drunkenness when they drove home. I suspected it was an abuse of his office, but of course I said nothing."

"Just a minute," I said as I felt a knot forming in my stomach. "Rhonda didn't know who you were, did she? If her parents call the police, you're going to find yourselves swinging through the trees at some penal colony off the coast of South America."

Caron took a ladylike nibble from the corner of a cucumber sandwich, but her hand was trembling. "There's no way Rhonda could have figured out who we were."

"If she had," Inez volunteered solemnly, "I think we'd be locked in a cage at the animal shelter—and this time we wouldn't have any money to bribe the officer."

"You bribed that woman?" I said, choking on a mouthful of tea.

Caron gazed contemptuously at me. "Would you have preferred that our arrest made the front page of the newspaper? You're the one who was So Worried about your precious reputation, you know. I wasn't the least bit delighted to fork over my hard-earned fifty bucks."

Miss Parchester smiled at her. "It's comforting to learn that some members of your generation are capable of such sacrifices. I'm sure your mother must be feeling very proud of you at the moment."

I was certainly feeling something, but I decided it could be discussed later.

Caron accepted the compliment with a majestic nod, then lapsed into a smirk and said, "According to Carrie, Rhonda was so furious she broke out in hives. In fact, she was still so furious the next morning that she had a big fight with Louis and told him he could never swim in her pool again."

There are moments when my maternal acumen fails me. "Why was she angry at Louis?" I asked.

"Because he didn't jump in the pool to rescue her. I don't know why she made such a big deal about it— it's not like she can't swim. I can't count the number of times she's mentioned that she's the captain of the swim team and has won All These Trophies. What did she expect—Sir Galahad?"

Miss Parchester sighed. "But it wasn't very gallant on his part not to make an effort to protect her, even in this day and age. Our so-called heroes are sorely lacking in selflessness these days. Perhaps it's society's fault for choosing them from among athletes and celebrities."

I glanced at Caron, who appeared to be pondering the last remark with more seriousness than I would have expected. "Speaking of celebrities," I said to Miss Parchester, "what have you heard about Zeno?"

"He called yesterday to say good-bye. He's going back to Houston to deal with financial matters, then on to Greece for a three-month vacation. He was not at all sure of his plans after that, but I had the impression he would not be returning to Farberville."

"He's given up his idea of a retreat for needy young artists?"

She took the teapot to refill our cups, then insisted we divide the remaining sandwiches. "He didn't mention it. He did say that the value of his artwork has increased dramatically due to the lurid publicity regarding Harry Tillington's arrest. He's planning to buy some terribly expensive car and possibly a château in the south of France. He implied he was doing all this to escape painful memories ... but I was not convinced of the purity of his motives."

I was not surprised. "Did he ask about Melanie?"

"Not once," she said with another sigh. "I was going to tell him that she was recuperating nicely, but I could hardly get in a word. I believe I'll go by the hospital in the morning and give her a jar of peach compote. This batch came out so very well, don't you think?"

Not for the first time, I spooned some on a slice of pound cake. "It certainly did. I dropped by to visit her yesterday. I'm probably making a terrible mistake, but I told her she could work at the Book Depot during the fall rush. I'll find the money to pay her a salary—if she doesn't take it directly from the cash register. She's going to sleep on our sofa until she finds a modest apartment."

Miss Parchester gave Caron a piercing look. "That, young lady, is an example of selflessness."

"And another reason why I won't get a car," Caron said, unimpressed. "Come on, Inez. We can walk All The Way to the square so I can look for something marginally decent to wear when school starts. If I can't find anything, we can walk All The Way to the thrift store out by the bus station. Grunge is still in, isn't it? I can be the most fashionable sixteen-year-old in the junior class. Maybe the cheerleaders will let me wash their cars. All Of Them have cars, don't they?"

I waited until they were gone and then said, "I saw a sign across the street advertising an apartment for rent. I never did find out what it was that Jasmine Hadley wrote. I've checked every resource available at the library, but her name doesn't appear."

"You should have asked me," Miss Parchester said as she went into the kitchen and returned with a brimming teacup. "She was a ghostwriter. Now, I suppose she's merely a ghost. I do hope she's in a special corner of heaven set aside for mystery writers, where she's enjoying the company of Edgar Allan Poe and Sir Arthur Conan Doyle."

"A ghostwriter?"

"She told me all about it one evening while we were playing pinochle. She's done the actual writing for books attributed to well-known political figures, as well as a few Hollywood stars."

I gaped as Miss Parchester reeled off the names. "I never suspected they didn't write the books themselves," I said when I recovered. "Some of those authors make the bestseller list with every book."

"That, I imagine, was the root of Jasmine's bitterness, even though she was quick to admit that the finished products weren't very good. Some of her clients insisted on adding their input."

I was going to ask more questions when I heard a muted honk outside. I put down my teacup and said, "Thank you for tea and a lovely afternoon. Peter is picking me up here. We're ..." I struggled valiantly, but I couldn't get out the fateful phrase and finally said, "We're going for a drive."

"Oh," Miss Parchester said as she took my arm and toddled alongside me to the front door. "How disappointing. I was hoping you and your young man might be inclined to go on a double date this evening."

"A double date?" I said blankly.

"Yes, Patrick and I are going to the Dew Drop Inn to listen to Birdie's wife perform. You did say you were interested in listening to her."

Now I was the recipient of the disapproving look. Resisting the urge to squirm, I said, "Who's Patrick?"

"Dr. Hassard, of course. You met him the night—"

"I remember," I said as I opened the door. "I'll ask Peter if he might want to go another night. At the moment, he's obsessed with the idea of looking at houses."

"And you?"

"There's nothing wrong with looking," I said weakly, then kissed her cheek, went out to Peter's car, and climbed into the passenger's seat. "I saw in the paper this morning that Anthony Leach was arraigned for murder," I said, just to get the conversation started on a low note.

"The captain thanks you for the tip. We knew the young man had been doing yard work locally, and it was a matter of time before we bumbled across his employer's name. Leach saved the taxpayers a lot of money by confessing."

"Please assure the captain I was gratified at the opportunity to assist the authorities," I said demurely. "When I heard Leach say the name on the telephone, I assumed he was speaking to a woman. I suppose there are a few die-hard Southerners who insist on naming their children after ancestors—or characters from *Gone with the Wind*."

Peter sat back and regarded me with a bemused expression. "Are you ready to do some serious house hunting, Claire? Don't feel as though you have to indulge me. Your car's right there in Miss Parchester's driveway. All you have to do is go get in it and drive home."

"If we wait two years, we won't need three bedrooms. Caron will be away at college."

"If we wait forty years, we won't need two bedrooms," he said drily. "We'll be more interested in denture cream than in the distance between twin beds. Or maybe we should just wait indefinitely and make an offer on adjoining cemetery plots?"

"You've made your point," I said. "So, why are we just sitting here, Sherlock? Shouldn't we be hot on the trail of three bedrooms and two baths?"

I was going to offer another smart remark when he leaned across the seat and made known the reason we were sitting at the curb of Willow Street. Despite the suffocatingly hot sunshine, the cheerful voices of residents arriving home from offices and classes, the barking of a dog, the slamming of car doors, I felt as if I'd been transported to the bumpy lot of a drive-in movie theater on a balmy midsummer's eve. I was no longer approaching forty years old; I was seventeen and loving every minute of it.

As I may have said, Peter is a man of many talents.

Chapter One

Solitude can be a wonderful thing. It allows one to ponder the perplexities of the universe, to examine one's strengths and imperfections (no matter how infinitesimal), or even to invite a billow of whimsical ideas into one's mind. On the other hand, solitude is not a condition to be treasured when one relies on retail sales to pay the rent, and one's accountant is forever harping about quarterly tax estimates and other dreary things of that nature.

I'd dusted every rack in the Book Depot, my charmingly drafty store beside the abandoned railroad tracks. It's situated on the main drag of Farberville, the home of thirty thousand or so good-natured souls and several thousand industrious college students. After lunch, I'd arranged an artful display of cookbooks and culinary mysteries in the front window, then stood out on the sidewalk under the portico to admire my effort as pedestrians streamed by, seemingly unimpressed. By mid-afternoon, I'd worked the crossword puzzle and was reduced to trying to decipher the personal ads ("SWCF seeks BMD with IRA") when my solitude was interrupted. With a vengeance, I might add.

"Mother," Caron began as she stomped across the room, her face ablaze with the degree of indignation that only a sixteen-year-old can produce, "before you say anything, I just want you to know It Wasn't My Fault."

Her best friend and co-conspirator, Inez Thornton, soulfully shook her head. "It really wasn't, Mrs. Malloy."

I folded the newspaper and put it aside. Caron was maintaining a belligerent posture, but I could see apprehension lurking in her eyes. For the record, she and I share red hair, green eyes, and a complexion prone to random freckles. Without this physical evidence, I might have believed—or at least suspected—that she'd been swapped in the nursery, and somewhere out there was a child who spoke only in lower case and had never stolen frozen frogs from the high school biology department or had been taken to the animal shelter in a gorilla suit. Caron has an impressively eclectic rap sheet for her age.

Inez does, too, although as an accomplice rather than a master criminal. She's soft-spoken, when she can get in a word, and she tends to observe Caron with the solemnity of a barn owl. Then again, hawks and owls are perceived differently, but that matters very little to a mouse caught in the moonlight.

"What's not your fault?" I asked reluctantly, assuming we were not about to discuss volcanic eruptions, EuroDisney, or the federal deficit.

Caron sighed. "All I was doing was trying to see who was in Rhonda's car with her. Louis has basketball practice until five, so it couldn't have been him. If she's so going steady with him like she claims, then why would she have another guy in her car?"

"It was like in a movie," volunteered Inez. "We stayed back so she wouldn't notice us in the rearview mirror. But then—"

"Then a moving van got in the way," Caron cut in, deftly regaining center stage. She gave me a moment to ponder the enormity of this outrage, then continued. "When we got to the corner of Willow and Thurber, Rhonda's car had vanished. I explained it to the cop."

Maternal perspicacity failed me. "Explained what?" I asked her.

"That I had to catch up with Rhonda. If the stupid moving van hadn't pulled out right in front of me, we could have found out who was in her car when they got to wherever they were going. If anyone deserved a ticket, it was the guy driving the van. I practically had to slam on the brakes not to crash into him and end up in traction at the hospital. Or paralyzed for the rest of my life."

I swooped in on the key word, which she'd tried to cloak in the torrent of verbiage. "You got a ticket, right?"

"It wasn't my fault," she said as she drifted behind the science fiction rack. "I may not have come to a complete stop when I turned onto Willow, but it wasn't like I barreled around the corner at fifty miles an hour and ran over some little kid on a bicycle."

I looked at Inez, who had her lower lip frmly clamped beneath her teeth. She aspires to achieve Caron's level of disregard for the facts, but she's not yet a proficient liar. "The ticket was for running a stop sign?"

"He wasn't very nice about it, especially after Caron pointed out that he'd ruined any chance we had of finding Rhonda."

I tried not to imagine that conversation. "How much does the ticket cost, Caron?"

"Seventy-five dollars," she said, peering at me over the rack to appraise my reaction. "But there's good news, too. If I take some idiotic defensive driving class, then the violation doesn't go on my record and your insurance won't go up too much. The class only cost twenty-five dollars."

"So playing private eye is going to cost you a hundred dollars," I said. "How much do you have in your piggy bank these days?"

"Nowhere near that much. I was thinking you could pay for everything, and then Inez and I can work it off here next month. You're always saying how busy you are in December, and gawd knows you could use some help with the window display. What's there now is pathetic."

"Thank you," I said.

The conversation from this point on did not take on any overtones of jocularity. Once we'd established that I was more perturbed by the cost of the crime rather than its nature, we discussed various financial strategies. The more lucrative possibilities at the mall were summarily dismissed, in that their totalitarian demands might interfere with Christmas shopping. Babysitting was much too tedious, and housework was compared to slavery in the salt mines of Siberia.

I finally gestured at the door. "Your driving privileges are suspended until this is resolved. We'll talk about it tonight."

Caron's lower lip shot out. "But it's Friday night and there's a football game. How are we supposed to get there?"

"Don't go," I said without sympathy. "If I remember correctly, a year ago you decided football was, and I quote, 'nothing more than a philistine ritual in which the players' IQs are displayed on their jerseys.'"

"That was last year," she said, then shrugged and started for the door. "By the way, some woman called last night while you were at the movie with Peter. She said she'd try again. Come on, Inez, let's take the railroad tracks to the bridge and go up the path. If we're lucky, no one will see us and we won't be the laughing stock of the high school Monday morning."

"Who called?" I asked.

Caron paused only long enough to say, "I think her name was Veronica Landonwood."

Seconds later the bell above the door jangled and they were gone. And I was staring at the door, my jaw dangling and my heart beating entirely too quickly. The store was drafty, but the sudden chill that raised goosebumps on my arms came from within me.

Even though I put on a sweater and kicked the rebellious boiler into a semblance of cooperation, I was still shivering when Lieutenant Peter Rosen on the Farberville CID arrived later that afternoon. He was dressed as usual in an exquisitely tailored suit and Italian shoes, courtesy of a family trust fund; he looked as if he would be more at home in a high-powered law firm than in a squad room. Even in baggy gym shorts and a sweatshirt, he's handsome enough to merit a page in a calendar. Curly brown hair, molasses-colored eyes, an aristocratic nose, and a cute derriere constitute eligibility.

"I brought cappuccinos and chocolate chip cookies," announced my candidate for Mr. November. His smile faded as he looked more closely at me. "What's wrong, Claire? Are you coming down with the flu?"

"You probably should say that I look as though I'd seen a ghost," I said with an unconvincing laugh, "because in a way, I have."

"Has Mr. Grimaldi arisen from eternal rest to demand you stop contaminating his precious bookstore with romance novels, study guides, and sorority stationery?"

"Come into the office and I'll tell you," I said, allowing him to put his arm around me and give me a quick kiss. Peter and I have been working at a relationship for several years, and I regret to say that despite our ages, we tend to approach it with what might be described as adolescent ineptitude. We'd come perilously close to sharing bed and board to determine if we had any hope of long-range compatibility, but he'd been drawn into a sleazy drug case and the issue had been shelved. For the moment, anyway.

I sat down behind the desk and accepted a Styrofoam cup. "According to Caron, I had a call last night from Veronica Landonwood."

"Should I recognize that name?"

"I had a cousin with that name, although everyone called her Ronnie. She was seven years older than I, so we weren't particularly close. She was always very nice to me, though, and I was in awe of her because she lived in Hollywood. Well, technically in Brentwood, but it was close to Hollywood."

Peter took a sip of cappuccino, his eyes narrowed as he watched me above the rim. "And she called last night?"

"Somebody called last night, but if it was Ronnie, I'm going to have to rethink my views on the possibility of afterlife. She died thirty years ago, Peter. I was ten at the time, and I was devastated. My only experience with death had been the loss of a nasty yellow tomcat named Colonel Mustard."

"How did she die?"

"She and her parents were in Mexico for a vacation, and their car went off a mountain road. I'd received a postcard from her only a few days before I was told about the wreck. I still have that postcard packed away somewhere."

Peter came behind me and began to massage my shoulders as I blinked back tears. "Then this is just a grotesque coincidence," he said, "or Caron wasn't paying attention and got the name wrong."

"Maybe," I said. Despite my efforts, my hand was

shaking so violently I could barely raise the cup to my mouth. A wake-up call from the grave can do that.

I lingered at the bookstore well past closing time, trying to convince myself that trivial chores were, in reality, consequential. By seven o'clock, however, all my pencils were perfectly aligned and the plastic paperclips were sorted by size *and* color. I locked the store and drove home to the duplex across from the Farber College campus. In winter I have a view of the condemned landmark that had once housed the English faculty (one of whom had been my deceased husband, Carlton, who'd had an unfortunate encounter with a chicken truck; our turbulent marriage was responsible for my current reluctance to make a commitment to Peter). The downstairs tenants moved in and out on an irregular basis. The current one was a bewildered retiree whose wife had kicked him out of their house and taken up with her aromatherapist. Neither of us was sure what this implied.

Caron had left a note indicating that despite my hard-hearted scheme to destroy her life, she'd found a ride to the football game and would be spending the night at Inez's. I suppose I might have saved it for reference when I got around to writing my memoirs, but I tossed it in the trash and made myself a drink.

Shortly thereafter, I was in my robe and curled up on the sofa with a mystery novel. The faint sounds of a Brahms concerto from the first floor mingled with the rustling of leaves outside the window and an occasional car. I was so engrossed in the wily amateur sleuth's exploration of the darkened conservatory that I let out an undignified yelp when the telephone rang.

I finally persuaded myself to pick up the receiver. "Hello?" I said with such timidity I wasn't sure the word had been audible.

"Claire, this is Ronnie—Ronnie Landonwood."

"If this is some kind of prank, it isn't the least bit

amusing. I don't know who you are or why you're doing this, but I can have a trace put on my—"

"On your seventh birthday, I sent you a tutu that I'd worn in a dance recital. You wrote me a stiff thank-you note saying you planned to be a detective when you grew up and would prefer a magnifying glass on your next birthday. When you were nine, you fell out of a tree and broke your arm. Later that summer you sent me a poem that vilified Joyce Kilmer. Shall I continue?"

"Hold on a minute, please," I said, then put down the receiver and went into the kitchen to splash some cold water on my face and some scotch in a glass. I sat back down on the sofa, and after a couple of sips, wiped my decidedly damp palms on my robe and picked up the receiver. "I'm still not sure what's going on. Would you care to explain?"

The woman exhaled as if she'd been holding her breath all the time I'd been trying to regain my composure. "It's a complicated story. My parents and I went to Acapulco in December of nineteen-sixty-five. My father, who was a second-rate screenwriter, was hoping to cozy up to Oliver Pickett. Oliver was one of the most influential directors in the business, and was scouting locations in that area for his next film. He'd won an Oscar that year for a much acclaimed medieval epic."

"I'm familiar with his name," I said.

"Perhaps I shouldn't burden you with this. I chose to disappear all these years, and I have no right to pop up out of the blue and ask for your help. I'm sure you have a busy enough life with your bookstore and your daughter. I was just hoping that your admirable accomplishments in matters of crime—"

"How do you know all that?"

"I hired a private investigator. He didn't delve into

your personal affairs, but he found a few articles in the newspaper morgue."

"You hired someone to spy on me?" I said.

"Only to find you," she said in a reproving voice. "I need someone I can trust. Everything I fought for and attained is in danger. If you'll allow me to finish my story, I think you'll understand the gravity of my situation."

Not at all flattered to have been the subject of a PI's report, I glanced over my shoulder to make sure the deadbolt was engaged, then said, "I'll listen to your story, but that's all I'm promising to do."

"My father borrowed enough money so that we could stay at Hotel Las Floritas, where Oliver Pickett was staying. I expected to be utterly miserable all three weeks. My parents were at ease with the Hollywood types, but I was shy and gawky and sadly deficient in social skills. At seventeen, I'd never had a close girl friend, much less a date. Like many tall girls, I slouched and wore drab clothes to blend into the background. My mother kept enrolling me in cotillions and etiquette classes, but none of them helped."

"I always thought you were glamorous. You knew all the current slang and told risqué jokes." I did not add that I'd never understood them, even though I'd laughed uproariously.

"Younger cousins didn't intimidate me," she said. "But to return to the story, the day we arrived, Oliver Pickett's daughter came to our bungalow and introduced herself. Fran was a year younger than I, but much more sophisticated. She had streaky blond hair and large hazel eyes, and was built like a model. My parents urged me to accept her invitation to go to the beach. From that moment until—until the tragedy, she and I whizzed around Acapulco in her father's limousine, shopping and hanging out at the beach clubs. At night while the adults were partying in hotel bars and private homes, we'd have Jorge drive us to seedy bars in the *Sona Roja* where we drank margaritas until we had to go outside and throw up in front of the prostitutes."

"Your parents allowed this?"

"My parents did whatever Oliver said. If he'd told them to dive off the cliff at La Quebrada, they would have put on their bathing suits and started climbing. Oliver had divorced Fran's mother years earlier, and was accompanied by his so-called secretary, an aspiring actress named Debbie D'Avril. She was quite the party animal, as was Chad Warmeyer, Oliver's assistant. The five of them would start celebrating at sunset and stagger back to Los Flamingos at sunrise to sleep until noon. Fran and I had virtually no supervision. Occasionally, we were deprived of the limousine when Chad was sent out to photograph a house or beach, but then we took taxis."

I grimaced as I imagined Caron and Inez in a similar situation. The potentially serious consequences of their actions was rarely a factor. "You mentioned a tragedy," I murmured.

"On New Year's Eve, the adults went to a party. A few days before, Fran had decided that we should have our own party in her bungalow. She'd invited a dozen kids from the beach, and by midnight, there were three times that many. I drank too much and smoked pot, and eventually passed out in the master bedroom. When I awoke, everybody was gone. My hand and shirt were smeared with blood, and I was holding a knife. Oliver Pickett's body was on the balcony. Two days later I was arrested. Shortly after that, my parents decided to rent a car and drive to Mexico City to get help at the American embassy. I was informed the next day that they'd been in a fatal car accident. A matron smuggled in a newspaper for me;

I couldn't read Spanish, but I could tell that I was presumed to have been in the car with them."

I was too shocked to attempt a response for a long while. The story seemed ludicrous, more suitable for low-budget movies and exploitative true crime novels. My cousin the killer? My cousin the convict? "I don't know what to say," I said inanely.

"Very few people do. I was convicted and sentenced to twelve years in prison. After serving eight, I was released, ordered to leave the country, and given enough money to take a bus to the border. I was too ashamed to make contact with any of the family, so I stayed in San Diego and worked as a waitress and maid until I'd completed my GED and put myself through college. My grades were good enough to get me into medical school. Between moonlighting and student loans, I earned a degree, did graduate work, and went into research."

"But how could you allow us to believe you were dead? Didn't you feel any obligation to the people who cared about you? Couldn't you have written from prison, or at least after you were released and were back in the country?"

"I killed a man, Claire. I stabbed him in the throat, then tried to escape retribution by throwing his body off a cliff in hopes the police would believe he'd fallen to his death and cut his throat on a sharp rock. I spent eight years wishing I'd died with my parents. When I got out, I wanted nothing more than a new identity and a fresh start. A judge heard me out and allowed me to legally adopt my mother's maiden name."

I licked my lips. "Why did you kill him?"

"He came back unexpectedly—I think he'd fallen in a swimming pool and wanted to change clothes—and busted up the party. Fran managed to slip away. Oliver discovered me in his bed, and was attempting to rape me when I grabbed the knife and stabbed him.

I kept stabbing him until he collapsed. I still have nightmares in which I'm screaming silently as my arm goes up and down and blood splatters my face."

"Earlier you said that his body was on the balcony. If he assaulted you in the bedroom, how did you get a knife?"

"The knife was on the bar in the living room. I fought my way out of the bedroom, but he came after me and I grabbed it. I was taller than he, and probably weighed more. Afterwards, I went back to the bedroom and passed out again, I suppose this time from the shock of realizing what I'd done. Fran's scream wakened me. She started worrying about leaving me behind, and had Jorge bring her back to the hotel. She was clear-headed enough to point out that I had no scratches or bruises to back up my accusation of rape. I'd been in his bed, and I would have had a problem persuading the police I hadn't been there with the intent to seduce him when he returned."

"But surely the police would have believed you. You were only seventeen, and as you said, shy and unsophisticated. He had to have been at least twenty years older. He'd been drinking, and he was angry about the party. It seems reasonable to assume he might have turned this anger on you, since you were vulnerable."

"And very frightened," she said in a low voice. "Fran convinced me that my only hope was for his body to be discovered at the base of the cliff. Once we'd done that, I wiped up the blood while she disposed of my clothes and the evidence of the party. Then she gave me a pill, and I went back to my room and went to bed."

"But the police arrested you?"

"The body was found the next morning, and at first it was assumed that he'd fallen. My parents, Debbie D'Avril, and Chad Warmeyer all admitted they'd been drinking steadily at various parties, and that Oliver could barely walk. The owner of the hotel was desperate to hush it up, and something my parents said led me to believe bribes had been offered. Fran went into shock. Her mother arrived that day and arranged for her to be sedated and kept in bed. Then my bloodied shirt was found in a garbage can behind the hotel restaurant. Details came out about the party, and Fran was forced to admit I remained there when everyone else left. The police searched my room and found my diary. It was filled with accounts of sexual encounters, but the police refused to believe they were only the fantasies of an unhappy teenaged girl. I finally broke down and confessed. After that, everything was a hideous blur of interrogation rooms, a filthy cell, hearings held in Spanish with no interpreters, and a mockery of a trial in front of a disapproving judge. I was not allowed to testify, and I don't know if my lawyer believed me, either. I'm not even sure my parents did after they were shown my diary, but at that point I was too depressed to care."

"Where was Fran during all this?" I asked.

"I wasn't allowed to see her until the trial, when we were both found guilty. She was glassy-eyed and unwilling to speak to me, and I never saw her again after we were transported to the prison. I tried without success to find out what happened to her. She could have been transferred, released, or buried in the paupers' cemetery just outside the prison wall. Dysentery and tuberculosis were rampant. I had pneumonia numerous times because my cell was so damp. Someone sent me packages of food and medicine every month; without them, I would have starved."

Ronnie's recitation had been unemotional and devoid of details, but it evoked such repugnant images that I felt nauseous. At seventeen, I'd not been obsessed with creature comforts or expensive toys. I wasn't at all sure, however, that I could have survived for eight years in a cell in a foreign country, with no one on the outside to fight for my freedom. Caron wouldn't have lasted eight hours.

"You were very brave," I said. "I don't know if I could have gone through it."

"I didn't call you to start a fan club," she said drily. "What I did in Acapulco was unforgivable. Not a day goes by that I don't say a prayer for Oliver Pickett. I never married or took a vacation, and I work eighteen-hour stints at the lab. Now, when I'm close to something that will have major significance in the field of drug-resistant viruses, someone's trying to snatch it all away from me by exposing me. I'll lose my position, my grants, and my credibility in the medical community."

"You're being blackmailed?" I said.

"A week ago I found a message on my answering machine. The voice had been distorted electronically, so I wasn't sure if it was male or female. The message was intelligible, though. If I don't deposit half a million dollars in a shielded bank account in Grand Cayman within the next thirty days, copies of the court transcript will be sent to my colleagues, along with a photograph of my passport and other proof of my previous identity." For the first time, she sounded as though she were in pain. "I can't let that happen."

Surely the private detective had reported on my financial status, I told myself. "I don't see how I can, help," I said. "I barely earn enough at the bookstore—"

"I'm not asking for a loan, Claire. I could borrow the money in a matter of days, but I know it won't stop there. I'll never be sure that this person won't send the evidence out of spite, or make further demands. I can't live with that kind of tension pervading my every thought. I want you to find this person and reason with him—or her. Make some kind of deal in exchange for the money."

"Wait a minute," I said, trying not to gurgle, "I'm a bookseller in a small college town. I have no idea how to deal with something of this magnitude. I may have assisted the police on occasion, but this is way out of my league. Why don't you talk to the private detective? He has the training and resources to track down people. I wouldn't know where to start."

"Acapulco, I should think."

I went ahead and gurgled like a coffee pot. "Call the private detective. He undoubtedly has cohorts in Mexico who can determine who got hold of the court transcripts."

"I don't trust him," she countered, clearly having assembled her arguments in advance. "He knows I'm wealthy. How can I be sure he won't decide to blackmail me, too? You're the only person I can trust, Claire, and as far as I'm concerned, my only relative. I sent that magnifying glass on your eighth birthday; now I'm begging you to dust it off and use it."